Out of the Dungeon

Lisa Bell

DEDICATION

To my HeartQuest sisters, who know what it means to fight for freedom.
Keep standing firm.

ACKNOWLEDGMENTS

I give thanks to Jesus Christ, the true Haniel in my life. Without Him I would not know freedom. To Richard and Paige Henderson, thank you for following in obedience and remaining faithful to the ministry of Fellowship of the Sword. Through HeartQuest, Father God broke many chains of my past.

To my daughters, family and friends who stood by me while I spent time writing this book and always encouraged me. Melinda in particular who constantly asked for the next chapter, spurring me forward to completion. Without you, I might still be writing chapter four. To all my critique partners and writing buddies, the countless hours of your input and feedback moved this story from mediocre to good. John, Leigh Ann, Jan and Scott, you all drove me deeper and challenged my writing to go beyond a good book. Some nights frustrated me, but always improved my writing. You helped me create a compelling novel with strong characters and conflict along the way. I'm a better writer because of you.

To Frank, Linda and all of my North Texas Christian Writer friends, thank you for encouragement, challenge and believing in me as a professional writer. I do not take lightly the blessing of having an incredible organization behind me.

Chapter 1

"Someone help. My buddy's been shot."

Charissa's head snapped up from a patient's chart.

A man staggered through the doorway under the weight of his friend, who looked more like a dead body than someone in need of the ER. The chart in her hands clattered against the floor. Memories of long nights in Dallas flashed as comprehension of the scene before her unfolded. This couldn't be real – not in her safe little hometown.

The man's eyes drilled into her. Pain streamed over his face, teeth clenched and struggling to speak. "Help…me."

Charissa stood, her legs moving as if immersed in molasses. Then with a blink and shake of the head, her mind shifted into crisis mode.

She grabbed a gurney and propelled herself toward the two men yelling, "GSW! Code Blue!"

After nursing school, she spent five years in Parkland's ER. They treated more gunshots in a single night than most hospitals saw in a year. But the child…

Not now. I can't think about that right now.

Procedures for a gunshot wound raced through her mind as she reached the patient. She slipped an arm around him, moving the limp body onto the gurney. A camouflage jacket covered a blood soaked t-shirt. She pushed aside the jacket and cut away cloth. Warm ooze from his abdomen mingled with cold clamminess of skin.

So much blood.

The stench hit her nostrils catapulting her stomach into a double somersault. The nausea caught her off guard. It wasn't her first time to smell blood gushing from a hole in someone, but this time was unexpected. She still hated the tang of senseless death hanging over someone.

As Charissa bent down to check for breathing, hands gripped her shirt. She pulled back, filled with apprehension, but the grip tightened.

"Don't let me die." The man's chest rattled with rapid, yet labored breaths, as if he sucked through a straw covered with water. "I can't die...you have to save me."

Compassion pushed down every ounce of dread. She covered the man's hands, forcing calmness into her voice. "You're not going to die. We'll do all we can for you. Stay with me and don't worry. We'll take care of you."

His eyes pleaded for mercy. "Please." His voice shook. "I need...to see my wife. Don't let me die."

Double steel doors banged against the wall as her supervisor, Ann, ran into the reception area with another nurse at her heels. Fresh out of nursing school, Kim's eyes widened. The area around her lips turned pale.

Ann fired questions at the victim's friend. "What's his name? How long ago was he shot?"

"I only know him as Bubba. An hour ago, maybe longer. We were out hunting; took a while to get back to the truck."

"Any drug allergies?"

The man shrugged his shoulders.

God help them if they saved him from the gunshot and then killed the man because of a drug allergy.

Ann's irritation slipped through in her tone. "Great. We know nothing about this man. Don't suppose you have any idea about his blood type?"

"No. Sorry."

The supervisor turned her attention to the nurses. "Let's get him into a room and start an IV. Cross and type match. He'll need blood."

Kim froze.

Ann bellowed orders. "Kim, wake up. Move it. He's in shock. Be sure to warm both the IV and blood. Dr. Stone is on his way from the cafeteria."

Charissa grabbed Kim's sleeve and thrust her toward the doorway as she shoved the gurney through and down the hall.

Inside the trauma room, Charissa grabbed warm blankets and covered the man, noting the distension of his abdomen and bluish tint of his fingers. She suspected a liver wound – not good, especially if it happened more than an hour ago. Her only gunshot victim since coming home, and the situation looked bleak. Kim's hands shook and fumbled with an IV kit. Charissa snatched it from her and tore open the wrapper.

Calm down. You can handle this.

Taking a deep breath, she prayed for steady hands and a good vein. She found none. "Ann, I'm going for the subclavian vein. Kim, we need vitals stat."

Ann shook her head. "You better know what you're doing."

"I've done it before. Don't worry."

Ann drew a small amount of blood and thrust it into the hands of a waiting tech. "Cross and type match, priority."

Kim fumbled with wires and connections. Charissa threw a pulse oximeter on a finger and slapped a blood pressure cuff around one arm. With connections to a monitor, the steady bleep representing heartbeats filled the room with a welcome sound. Dr. Stone rushed in and demanded stats.

Charissa responded. "BP 50 over 30. Pulse—irregular, weak, about 175. Oxygen—70 and dropping, respiration—50."

"Heart rate's too high, and I don't like any of those levels. He's in hemorrhagic shock." The doctor did a quick exam. "Without a scan, I can't be sure, but it appears the shot hit the liver. Has he been typed and cross-matched?"

"The tech just left."

"Fine. Get O negative going until we get results. Ann, do you have a surgeon on the way?"

"Yes, but he's about thirty minutes out."

Sweat popped out on Dr. Stone's forehead. "Great. I haven't seen too many gunshots."

Charissa whispered. "I have – far too many. Move him to OR. We'll have him prepped by the time the surgeon gets here."

Dr. Stone shook his head. "We should stabilize him first."

She whispered. "He's not getting more stable."

"You're right. Let's move."

Bubba's eyes shot open and he touched Charissa's arm. His pale face took on a grey pallor, deepening with every breath. He whispered, "Tell my wife…I love her…and I'm sorry…for everything."

She looked into his eyes. A small sliver of green surrounded his dilated pupils. Not even a hint of a sparkle appeared, but the glassy appearance against his grey skin spoke volumes. They needed to move fast.

Emotion squeezed her throat until it ached. "Just hang on. We're taking you to surgery."

"Just…tell her." His voice dropped. "Promise."

She managed a weak, "Okay."

He drew in a deep breath filled with a pronounced rattle. She knew that sound. The monitor changed to an unbroken whine, alarms sounding loud and long.

"No. Don't you dare die on me."

She looked at Kim. "Get an ambu bag on him. Now."

Chapter 2

Kim didn't move. Charissa grabbed an ambu bag and slapped it on his face, then jumped onto the bed, hit his chest and started CPR compressions. She kept working—willing the man to live. Sweat and tears combined and ran down her cheeks as she alternated chest compressions and pumping the bag.

A flurry of activity filled the room, but she didn't care. She glanced at Dr. Stone and Ann who both wore panic as a facemask. Neither of them ever worked in a city hospital. She wondered if either saw a gunshot before.

Charissa yelled, "Do something."

The doctor and supervisor moved beside the gurney and sprang into action. Charissa paid little attention to what they said or did other than a vague awareness of someone packing his injury. Her primary concern was keeping this man alive. She had to trust their knowledge, even without experience.

Please, don't die.

Faces swarmed through her mind. Men and women wearing the same gray color, covered in blood. She'd seen far too much death. But the last one—a little boy—was too much. She moved home after he died. No more.

She willed away the faces and kept pushing on Bubba's chest, hoping for another breath—even a rattled one.

After a few minutes, Dr. Stone rested his hand on her shoulder. "Charissa, stop. We can't do anything now. Let it go."

"No. He can't die—not from a gunshot wound. I'm not giving up." She reached for the man's chest again. Kim stepped beside her and took over the ambu bag pumps.

Dr. Stone said, "We got him too late."

"No. We have to get his heart going again and get him to surgery."

"The surgeon's still at least ten minutes out."

"Then you do the surgery."

"I'm an ER doctor, barely out of residency from a small community hospital, not a surgeon. I can't handle this kind of wound. You know that."

"You can try."

"And lose my license? Let it go." He pulled her arm. "Kim, what's the time?"

"No. I won't give up. I won't let him die." Charissa shrugged away his hand and yelled at the patient. "Can you hear me, mister? You hold on—for your wife. Don't you dare give up."

Dr. Stone surrounded her with strong arms and pulled her from the patient. She fought and almost broke loose before he hauled her off the bed. "You've done enough. I'm calling it."

Charissa wilted. "Why? This isn't some big city. Llano is a little town with good people. How could this happen?"

Dr. Stone shook his head. "Hunting accident maybe. People get careless."

"I grew up in this town and heard of hunting accidents, but not this bad. It's just wrong."

"I know." He caressed her shoulder. "It seems so senseless, but accidents happen."

He nodded to the other nurse. "Time?"

"Eight seventeen, doctor."

"Note the time of death. I'll go tell his family."

Charissa glared at him. "And what will you tell them?"

"The truth—the same thing I'm telling you. We did everything we could, but he lost too much blood before we got him."

Turning to go, he paused and then glanced back over his shoulder. "Don't beat yourself up over this, Charissa. You gave it your best shot. More than most would have done."

Dark emptiness settled over her mind. *My best still wasn't good enough, was it?* The lifeless face blurred behind tears as she stared down.

She'd returned home to avoid this kind of trauma. Sniffles, broken limbs, maybe an elderly person with a heart attack, but nothing prepared her for this. Her hometown; secure without big city crime or gangs, where eagles nested nearby, and seasoned hunters went out prepared for anything. It was supposed to be a refuge from senseless deaths.

Too many experiences with brutality suffocated and drove her home. An innocent boy died in her arms the day she resigned from Parkland. She ran like a frightened child back to safety. As she looked at Bubba, reality bit her as terrifying as a copperhead. Violence again, and all of her efforts made no difference. The years of training meant nothing. She didn't even know his real name. The still body taunted her. Sorrow washed down, pushed her to the brink of despair. The blank stare condemned.

"I tried," she whispered and bolted from the room.

She ran through the hall into the staff restroom, a thin door providing shelter from reality. Locked inside, she slid down the door. Faces flitted from her subconscious mind to the surface. Memories of wounds, unnecessary yet fatal, sickened her. And the little boy's face came again with eyes pleading for help. Tiny eyes, so similar to Bubba's, wanting to survive, yet a life cut short by a bullet not intended for him. In both instances, nothing she did mattered. It didn't help whether she wanted desperately to save them, or kept trying after everyone else quit. In the end, both still died. Waves of grief shook her entire body, engulfed by sobs. Fear that someone might hear suppressed the idea of banging her head against the door.

Why? This is too much watching a man die from a gunshot again in the middle of my secure world. So fast and all alone.

The sobs subsided as she wrapped arms around herself and rocked back and forth. The cold, hardness of the tile floor merged with a growing numbness inside.

The little space isolated her from feeling, alone and trying to make sense of the situation. Asking why seldom brought answers, but she wanted to ask. Minutes clicked by.

Enough.

She pushed herself off the floor and washed her face. The man left a message for his wife. How could she comfort a young widow with so much grief pouring over her heart?

Blast this stupid job. It isn't what I want for my life.

She longed for a pair of tiny arms from a Honduran orphan around her neck at that moment. She never witnessed any of them die, and at least she could take care of those little ones. Food and love came easy. But no arms, tiny or otherwise, comforted the pain.

She looked up, alone in the stark bathroom. Dim light bounced off the mirror. She didn't look, knowing its inability to hide red-rimmed eyes laced with anguish peering back. She forced a slight smile, splashed cold water over her face and patted it dry. Get over it. You have a job to do. Self-pity swallowed, stale air filled her lungs.

She pulled a lab coat from the shelf, put it on and buttoned it over red stains.

Outside of the restroom, Haniel McCrae leaned against the wall. She knew this man well, although never quite understood why he spent so much time in this God-forsaken place. Still, she thanked God for his presence. His towering, muscular frame looked intimidating, but those chocolate eyes twinkled as he looked down at her. The peace that exuded from him held her attention, comforted her.

"Charissa, are you okay?"

She nodded, not trusting herself to speak.

Haniel raised his eyebrows. "Are you sure?"

"I'm a little shaken. We treated a gunshot victim tonight, but he didn't make it." Hot tears stung again. "I tried, but it wasn't enough."

"I heard. I'm sure you did all you could. Don't blame yourself for his death. People die sometimes. It's part of life."

"He was young. People around here die from old age, not gunshot wounds. It isn't as though we have gangs or drive by shootings. I came home, sick of that kind of death. I saw too much of it, and never expected it here."

Haniel touched her shoulder. "I know. I'm sorry."

Charissa inched closer and melted into Haniel's hug. "I have to work through this. I'll be okay when I get home and process everything."

"I'm here if you need to talk."

"I know. Thank you, Haniel. You're a good friend."

His smile strengthened her spirit and renewed peace. She gave her best. No one asked for more, but defeat and weariness hung over her head, a dark storm cloud ready to burst with a deluge of hopelessness. She stepped back and forced a smile for him.

"I need to go find this man's wife and deliver a message. Thank you for caring. Really, I'm fine."

He didn't look convinced. She headed to the nurse's station.

Ann sat in the swivel chair. The victim's friend leaned against the desk. His broad shoulders blocked her view of the waiting room, and his relaxed stance made her wonder if something delayed Dr. Stone. Surely, he'd already delivered the bad news.

At the desk area, Ann's giggles revolted her. The other woman's eyes drooped as she placed a hand on the man's arm. Unbelievable. This man just lost his friend. How could she flirt with him at a time like this? The huskiness in his voice left the impression he didn't mind.

Disgusted with the whole scene, Charissa pushed past the man and glanced over the waiting room. Empty seats lined the walls.

She turned to Ann. "I'm sorry to interrupt. Has Dr. Stone talked to the family?"

Ann rolled her eyes. "No family. Only Drake here and yes, he's been notified of his hunting buddy's death."

She faced the man. "I'm sorry for your loss, sir. He spoke of his wife. Have you been able to reach her?"

He held out a hand. "Hi. I'm Drake Hannibal. Bubba's wife left him years ago. I never met her—but from what he told me, she's no big loss. He never got over her—always seemed depressed. Maybe he's better off dead."

Charissa gasped and gawked into the man's eyes. Dark brown ice peered back. She shuddered.

Drake said, "Sorry. I guess that seemed rather heartless. I barely knew the man. We hunted together sometimes. He always said maybe he'd get shot. I think he hoped for it – didn't have the guts for suicide but wanted to die. You know what I mean?"

He moved nearer and put a hand on her shoulder. The tone of his voice mesmerized her – smooth as honey. Musk, pine and earth all comingled and drifted from his body. She grabbed onto the desk and steadied herself.

Ann interrupted the downward spiral. "I'm sure you can make it your mission to find the widow and offer her some comfort. Such an easy task for a sweet little Christian like you."

Charissa bristled and pulled away from Drake's touch. *I'm about to show you a sweet Christian.* She hesitated, used every ounce of strength to control the mounting flame, sighed and spoke through clenched teeth. "She deserves to know."

Drake agreed. "Yes, she does. I think there might be a kid too. Maybe I can find out something for you."

"That would help. Thank you."

Charissa's mind reeled as she looked at the supervisor. She caught a flicker of emotion in Ann's smoldering eyes.

Am I detecting a little jealousy? You shouldn't even be talking to this guy. What would your husband think if he knew the way you flirt around here?

A thought reared up inside her. She'd seek forgiveness later, but she didn't try to resist such an appealing temptation.

Reaching deep and grabbing her best Southern belle voice, she said, "By the way, Ann, your husband left a message for you earlier. It's there on the desk."

Daggers flashed in Ann's eyes, but Charissa didn't care. Picking up a chart, she rushed down the hall without looking back. Lord help her if Drake found out anything. She never wanted to see or talk to him again.

Chapter 3

Charissa pushed open a trauma room door. Tan skin contrasted against the white sheet, big brown eyes peeping from beneath long lashes. Two streaks ran the length of the little girl's face, leaving a rivulet of clean skin between the outside corners of her eyes and the bottom of her chin. She held one arm against her body. Varying colors of purple and blue along with the swollen size touted a break or at the very least a bad sprain.

Charissa spoke gently. "Hi, sweetheart. What's your name?"

The little girl blinked. "Sheila."

"How old are you?"

Sheila sat up a little straighter. "I'm nine years, nine months and nine days today."

"Wow. You must be looking forward to double digits." She looked seven.

The little girl beamed. "Yes, ma'am. I'm having a party at the rock climbing gym." She glanced over at her mother and lowered her voice. "Mom doesn't think I'm big enough."

The mother brushed bangs away from Sheila's brow. "And the fact we're here might just prove that point, young lady." Her feigned strictness melted into concern lining her eyes and forehead.

Charissa patted her hand. "Well, your vital signs all look good. What happened to your arm?"

"I was practicing rock climbing…"

Her mother interrupted. "In a big oak tree without a harness."

Sheila shrugged her shoulders. "I would've been fine if the stupid limb didn't break."

Dr. Stone entered the room. "What've we got here?"

Charissa answered, "Apparently, a tree got perturbed with my new friend, Sheila, climbing it and threw her down on one arm."

"Ooh. Mean tree. How bad does it hurt?"

Sheila scrunched up her nose. "Not as much as before. At least not until I move it."

He gingerly took the thin arm in his hands and examined it, then scratched his chin. "It might just be a sprain, but we better get some x-rays. How are the vitals, Charissa?"

"They're good." She turned the computer screen with the numbers displayed.

"Good." He jotted down some notes. "Please set it up." Touching her arm, his eyes searched hers. "Okay?"

Charissa nodded. "Sure. Setting up x-rays is my specialty."

Dr. Stone cocked his head to one side and raised his eyebrows. His fingers lingered, a ray of sunshine on a cold day, while his after-shave weakened her knees. "I'll be in my office if you need anything, or when the x-rays come back."

"I'll let you know."

Confusion skipped around her as she used the computer to input orders. Dr. Stone showed more compassion than any doctor in the hospital, but he usually targeted patients. Why did she suddenly think he worried about her? Her emotions must be on edge after the episode with Bubba. What a crazy idea. Dr. Stone only knew she existed when he needed something.

She finished the orders and turned to her patient, whispering silent thanks for the distraction. She rose and wet a washcloth with warm water. Moving to Sheila's bedside she softly wiped her face.

"We don't want the orderly to see those tear streaks when he comes to get you. No point making him think you're a sissy, is there?"

Sheila shook her head with the fierceness of a determined little warrior. "I'm not a sissy at all. The tears sneaked out when I wasn't lookin'."

"I know. That's why I'm wiping away all the evidence of them."

Sheila's mother smiled and mouthed, "Thank you."

Finished, Charissa patted her shoulder. "I've got some other work to do, but no worries. They'll get your x-rays and we'll have you out of here soon. Either way, you might have to stay out of trees for a little while so you'll be ready for your birthday party. Deal?"

"Deal." Sheila surprised her with a hug. "Thank you for taking care of me."

"My pleasure. If they don't finish before I get off work, you be careful. As much as I adore you, I do not want to see you in my ER again." Charissa smoothed stray hairs away from the tiny face.

"Yes ma'am."

Charissa smiled to herself as she exited the room. Helping patients feel better made being a nurse rewarding. Sheila's mom cared about her, so it wasn't exactly like taking care of orphans, but the interaction left a toasty spot in the middle of her being.

Looking up, she lost all desire to smile.

Drake stood against the wall, arms folded over his chest. He had taken off his jacket. Bulging biceps pressed against his shirt so tightly she thought the sleeves might rip. Perspiration ran down her back in spite of the cold air around them.

Dark brown eyes drilled into her, and perfectly layered hair with a hint of stubble surrounded by an olive complexion gave him a rugged look. Attractive, but not someone who turned heads. She glanced down the hall. Haniel waved, watching over her as usual, flashing reassurance with a smile.

"Charissa. Beautiful name," Drake said, pushing off the wall.

"How…"

He gestured with his head. "Your name badge."

"Oh." She fought against running away. "Can I help you with something?"

"I thought maybe you'd allow me to get you out of this dreary place…maybe grab a bite?"

She sighed. "That's very nice, but I'm not off for hours. I appreciate the offer, but I'll have to pass." Relief flooded over her. This man enticed yet left her unnerved.

"Too bad. Maybe when I have information about Bubba's wife?"

"Maybe." She hunted for an escape. "I really have to get back to work so I don't get fired." She turned from the empty glare of his eyes.

"I'll see you soon, Charissa."

His voice rubbed against her senses and left cold chills in the wake.

Chapter 4

Drake exited through the ER doors. This night went better than planned. Ann waited as a nice prize for later, but he wanted Charissa. The sweet goodness of her soul intrigued him. He sensed her breaking point lingered moments beyond the next crisis, and he fully intended to benefit when she fell from her pedestal of purity. He wiped spittle from the corner of his mouth. She was worth drooling over.

Haniel appeared next to him. "You can't have her."

Drake laughed. "I wondered how long you'd wait before you came after me. You're worried aren't you? You're shaking like an earthquake; afraid she'll choose me over you."

"Not at all. She's faithful. Go ahead and try, but know I will go to battle for her. You will not destroy Charissa Imani. You will not do to her what you did with Zoe."

"I'm not scared of you, Haniel. I will steal her right out from under you." He laughed and walked away, breathing arrogance until his chest swelled. He must be on the right track. Why else would his long time enemy confront him?

Faithful? Yeah right. Like a pet cobra. She'll be mine in no time at all.

The night air hung thick around him. Anticipation mingled with the plot forming in his mind. He turned the corner absorbed in plans filled with darkness. A form stepped from the alley. Smitty, his associate, stood before him dressed in black jeans and t-shirt with a black leather jacket. He ran a hand through his long jet-black hair. The goatee and mustache completed a look teetering between frightful and enticing. No wonder women enjoyed this man.

Drake merely tolerated him. "Well?"

"The stage is set, Boss. Everything is ready."

"Excellent. Now we put the players in place and see how the game unfolds. Miss Charissa will fall soon. And she will fall hard."

Chapter 5

Charissa woke early the next morning. The comforter on her bed hung halfway to the floor with the sheets no longer tucked tightly under the mattress. An insistent recurrence of Bubba's face throughout the night slammed against her skull. The blank stare haunted her, even tucked away in her private haven.

A familiar cold, wet nose nudged her foot, eliciting an unintentional jump. Her faithful companion pounced onto the bed and pushed against her. A leash between his teeth coupled with big brown eyes begged for his morning walk.

"Okay, Rusty, okay. I'm up. Gee, you aren't a lap dog you know."

She buried her face into the soft, golden fur of the Labrador. At 75 pounds, he never quite recovered from being treated as a small dog when she first got him. Just a puppy then, he fit perfectly in her lap. At three, he covered most of her body. His tail beat against her legs as he nuzzled against his mistress.

"How about a hike in the woods today? Huh, boy? Would you love a little time outdoors? Maybe we'll throw in the tent and sleeping bag so we can stay a few days."

Rusty's tail wagged harder combined with a firm bark of agreement. Why not? Some time surrounded by nature, away from reality, sounded perfect—a distraction from thoughts running in circles. For a moment, she wondered if she dreamed all of yesterday. She stumbled out of bed, and shuffled to the bathroom, dodging bloody scrubs on the bedroom floor. Truth crashed as every detail of the previous night rushed over her again. She closed her eyes, but the pounding continued.

I have to get out of here or I'll go crazy.

She picked up the scrubs and threw them in the trash.

∞∞∞∞∞∞∞∞∞∞∞∞

Hair whipped across her face as Charissa drove her jeep along the highway. Rusty rotated between sitting beside her in the front seat with the wind rushing into his face, and happily bouncing to the back. She cranked up the stereo and sang along with a worship CD. Maybe Ann was right. Her faith seemed worthless sometimes, but then nothing made sense after last night. If she let go of faith, she had no lifeline at all. She clung to the only hope she could muster. Besides, these songs felt like an old friend, and singing kept unbidden internal words at bay. The CD ended, and she swapped it for oldies.

One last turn onto a dirt road took her the final miles into Colorado Bend State Park. She wanted seclusion. Not many people camped at this park during this time of the year. No electricity, hot showers or nice bathrooms kept the weekend RV campers away, which left the area for true nature enthusiasts or those seeking solitude. She hoped for one of the sites on the river. The jeep bounced along the rough road for the last thirty minutes to her destination. She put Rusty on a leash and entered the park headquarters.

A ranger greeted her. "Hey, Charissa. It's been a long time."

"Too long. Please tell me you saved a river front site for me."

"You're in luck. Good time of the year, and a week day – it's all yours. Which one you want?"

"Give me number seven. I need a little peace and quiet for a few days."

"You got it."

The camp came together in record time, and she headed into the woods with Rusty by her side. Short hike today followed by a trek to the waterfall starting early tomorrow morning – perfect way to clear cobwebs of confusion.

The pain in her head subsided as fresh air with the scent of leaves and dirt flowed through her body. The river peeked between trees lining one side of the trail. Tall rock cliffs lined the other side. In spite of the beauty and serenity of her surroundings, yesterday's events stuck in her brain. Bubba's eyes still stared, and the haunting memory troubled her. Then a multitude of other faces joined, including the saddest little boy, begging for mercy. She willed the images away.

Last night stirred too much emotion and left a devastating wake of doubt. What did she really want? She felt good about her job – loved helping people. After all, she pursued nursing because... Why did she pursue this career? She hated the paperwork and bureaucracy. Most of the doctors – arrogant fools with egotistical god-complexes – made her angry. And Ann... Better not to dwell on the supervisor who enjoyed finding every fault and constantly chiding her faith.

Yet, the words of patients rang in her ears – praises for having such a gentle, sweet spirit. Something about a gentle and quiet spirit tugged at her. She pondered the phrase. Something about a gentle and quiet spirit being precious in the sight of God. People apparently saw it in her mannerisms, but inside a storm raged.

There must be more to life than this. She thought again about the orphans in other countries. Those trips to Brazil and Honduras during high school left her happier and more fulfilled than any day in the emergency room. As crazy as it sounded, her heart wanted that life. Who in their right mind would move to some foreign country to take care of children without parents? Conversations with her family drifted across her memory. They made a point to tell her how insane the idea sounded—everyone except Aunt Victoria. She understood.

Charissa remembered the last time she saw her Aunt. Victoria's eyes danced while she told stories about the children. Charissa never tired of the stories after one of those mission trips, and neither did Victoria. She, in fact, paid for most of them. It all happened years ago and now existed only in the deep recesses of her mind. The dream died when Aunt Victoria passed into eternity. She wiped away tears.

Movement at the top of a cliff interrupted her reflections. A dark figure ducked behind a tree. She scanned the rocks for more movement or a person, but saw nothing. What an imagination. Without rock climbing gear and a trustworthy partner, no one dared climb those cliffs. Without a trail across the top, the idea of a person there was ludicrous. Still, nerves gnawed at her stomach. Probably some animal, but maybe she'd take the cave tour tomorrow instead of hiking alone. Then later she'd drive to the falls.

Her anxiety level reached higher than the cliff. Another hiker never scared her before, especially in this park. But at such an easy pace, the heart palpitations didn't come from exertion. The back of her neck tingled. She stopped and looked up. Still nothing—except a feeling of eyes drilling into her.

Rusty whimpered and then emitted a low growl. That did it.

"C'mon boy. Let's head back to camp and get a fire going."

She turned and quickened her steps back up the trail.

Chapter 6

Charissa zipped her tent door and sunk into the sleeping bag. She preferred the open tent roof with a sky full of stars hanging above. The night air made her shiver, though, and the faint scent of rain drifted up her nostrils. She settled for a small patch of sky visible through the clear plastic triangle of the rain fly. The glimpse of stars partially hidden by clouds still looked amazing.

Rusty curled up close and settled for the night.

Weariness seeped into her bones, but sleep eluded her. Logic and desire wrestled in her mind. She sighed and prayed out-loud. "Lord, what should I do? I'm lost and can't hear Your voice."

Only wind brushing against the trees responded.

Fresh tears coursed down her temples and trickled into her ears. She let them flow.

Nothing will change. I'm stuck and don't know the way out. My life isn't so bad – really. Maybe it's time to grow up and accept the way things turned out – forget about some senseless dream from my teen years.

The silent tears grew into sobs as she curled into a tight ball. Gradually, they dwindled as she drifted into a restless sleep.

Strange sights and sounds filled her dreams while she ran frantically, trying to escape…from what she didn't know. The zip of a tent interrupted her dream and a low growl escaped from Rusty's throat. She willed herself to wake up, but her eyes refused to cooperate. She struggled against a heaviness that weighed down and crushed her chest producing difficult breathing. Something held her. She desperately wanted to face this opponent—fight him off, but she couldn't move. Her throat constricted. Words hung in her mind, but stopped short of finding her voice. The tent walls moved in the night. If she could only wake up… Why couldn't she move? *Lord, help me.*

Suddenly, the heaviness left. She sat up. Rusty growled and barked.

"What is it boy?" She listened. An eerie silence settled over the tent. A strong current of air floated through and chilled her sweaty forehead. Eyes straining against the darkness, she groped for a flashlight. Her hand shook against the cold metal as she switched on the light and swung it around the tent. Nothing.

A shadow beside the tent? No…it's nothing. Get a grip.

As her light beam played along the tent walls and moved to the door, her breath caught. The tent door flapped as wind swept over her, and chills ran the length of her body. The dog's growl intensified.

"Is there an animal out there, Rusty? You know deer come into camp sometimes."

She soothed him in spite of a heart beating against her ribcage. Something unzipped her tent, and it wasn't a deer. Suggesting a harmless creature calmed some of the terror.

She felt under her pillow. Soft leather sheathed a ten-inch hunting knife, wonderfully smooth and comforting. Trees creaked in the distance as the river cascaded over rocks. Normally those sounds soothed her, but not at the moment.

She strained her ears for any other sound. Still nothing, but something felt out of place. While Rusty's growls decreased, his ears remained tensed; the muscles in his sleek body twitched and his hair bristled directly above his tail.

"I will not be afraid. This is ridiculous." She thought back to her childhood and how her mother always came in and prayed with her when she felt scared. "Jesus, please protect me."

From outside of the tent a guttural groan filled the quietness.

A tree groaning in the wind?

Charissa shivered; Rusty sprang to his feet and darted through the tent door.

"Rusty. Come back here."

A short, sharp hiss made the hair on her arms pop to attention. She unsheathed her knife.

"Rusty. C'mon boy."

A yelp propelled her to the tent door, where Rusty collided with her face. She dragged him in and pulled his quivering body close. She zipped the tent and swung the light around, looking for any sign of shadows, but saw none. She listened. Only the splash of the river made a sound.

Rusty wagged his tail and licked her hands. She buried her face against the dog and breathed a sigh of relief. He returned her affection only for a moment, then curled up beside her and licked his paws. She sensed peace from her dog and the gnawing fear vanished.

"What was it Rusty? Huh? He's gone anyway. We're okay. Everything is okay. Come what may, we'll be all right."

She switched off her light and curled up next to the dog, convinced Rusty acted as a faithful protector, less certain about the rightness of her world. She sighed loudly.

So many things still confused her, but a gentle rain pelted the tent offering comfort and peace. Rusty relaxed and soon snored softly. She yawned. The emotions and physical exertion from the day overwhelmed her mind and body. The river sang a soft lullaby as Charissa drifted off to a dreamless sleep.

Chapter 7

Drake savored the lobster tail on his plate. Not the best he ever tasted, but passable for a quaint restaurant in Alabama.

Smitty sat across from him. The imbecile seldom did anything right, but he had an uncanny knack for charming women. He specialized in luring the most faithful of women into deep depravity. His valuable advice served a purpose in winning Charissa, so Drake tolerated the tales of conquest through dinner.

As the meal wound down, the incessant blubbering droned, pricking his mind with a thousand tiny needles. Each word jabbed various nerves, sending a tick down his neck. As his temper mounted, he cut Smitty off in the middle of a sentence.

His jaw tightened. "Just give me some suggestions already. She'll see past deceit so I need an alternative plan."

Smitty pursed his lips. "She's compassionate — like most good nurses — but she has a weakness, doesn't she?"

Drake considered the facts he knew about the woman from his research. "Her father abandoned her. She keeps men as far away as China — not very trusting. She excels at driving men away, so she remains alone which works to my advantage. Except, I need her trust, and I'm a man. Her work isn't satisfying. I saw frustration in her eyes."

"Then you'll have to come across compassionate. You messed up when Bubba died, left too much heart calluses showing. I sure miss tormenting him about his old lady."

Drake grew more impatient. "Perhaps I should send you where he is then."

"Someone's a little testy tonight. Where is your compassion, huh?" He snickered. "This one will be tough for you. Promise her security and love. Give her lots of attention and romance. Calls, flowers, definitely lots of time."

"I'd be fine with that, but she sparkles all the time. She needs a little depression in her life. Of course, the circumstances with Bubba definitely poked a hole in her little bubble world, but still — too much peace on her face. She's far too happy and sweet. Can anyone really be so nice all the time and it be real?"

"Well, Haniel..."

Drake clamped his hand onto Smitty's arm. "Don't say that name. I hate him. Why do you think I want to take Charissa?"

"Sorry, Boss. You asked."

"It was a rhetorical question, you idiot. I did not need your answer. She knows Haniel well, and he affects her deeply. But not when I'm finished with her."

"Of course." Smitty downed his drink, and then continued. "I have someone in mind who might help with your plot."

"Really?" Drake released his associate's arm and sipped his wine, slightly intrigued, yet skeptical.

Smitty rubbed his arm. "Yes. A woman I met in New York. Her name is Edna Broderick. Her lust for power and wealth amazed me, and her influence over others is incredible. Get her involved in your circle, and she'll bring your little pet Charissa around in no time. She'll relish the opportunity to learn from you. Controlling Charissa – nice extra prize. Throw out the bait, and she'll come after it without a single thought."

"We'll see how it goes. You might just have done something right for a change, but don't get cocky. You screw up far more than you please me."

"You sent me to find the right women for you." He ran his tongue over his lips. "There's nothing I enjoy more than tempting women."

Drake took another gulp of wine and refilled his glass. The effects dulled his senses as he pictured this fool with any woman.

He smiled to himself with thoughts of his conquests over the years. His approach wasn't always as pleasant as Smitty's ways. The imbecile relied on lust, which worked well for him. But Drake preferred a more straightforward, sometimes harsh, method.

Nevertheless, Smitty knew women well. If he approached Charissa aggressively, she'd run. He could overcome her loneliness and desperation for love with some well placed caresses and kisses. Melt away her lack of trust for men. Then sit back and gloat as the woman fell far away from all she ever believed.

Raised voices at the next table caught Drake's attention and brought his mind back into the restaurant.

"Valorie, c'mon, baby. I'll only be gone a few days."

"Mitch, you know Mom and Dad are taking the kids. I hate being at home alone."

"Honey, you have triple locks and double security all over the house. Why are you so afraid all the time?"

"I'm not afraid." Her voice quivered.

Drake ignored Smitty's continued rambling. The woman's fear excited him – pulled him into a deeper plot. A thought hit him like a lightning strike. He seethed with anticipation of Valorie's deep fears feeding Charissa's lesser fears. He'd bring the two women together; use this woman's fear against

Charissa. Shivers ran through his veins as pictures of using Valorie to break his target cascaded from his brain.

The need for behaving with compassion turned into disgust and perhaps anger. The possibilities reeled endlessly before him. He closed his eyes and imagined the games for this new pawn. Perfect. Fear permeated every bit of her soul— it emanated from her, tripping over the floor and falling at his feet. The pleasure at her angst welled up inside with an intoxicating effect.

The young husband spoke softly to his wife. Sickening.

"Val, baby, it'll be okay. I promise – two days at the most. You'll have time to relax and then when I get back, we'll still have two or three days before the kids come home. I'll take you some place special. I'll even call my brother and have him check on you."

"Don't. He'll think I'm a sissy." She drew in a deep breath. "I'm okay now."

She appeared calm except for the slight tremor in her hand as she picked up her glass of water. Tight, thin lips forced a smile and convinced Drake she felt anything but calm. He shushed his companion in order to hear her now soft voice.

"It's the nightmare I have, where someone comes in and grabs me from my bed. In my dream, he takes me away from everything I know and love. No matter how hard I try, I can't get back. It haunts me when you aren't at home. With the kids gone the dream gets worse—everything disappears, and I can't get it back." Her eyes misted but she held back tears.

Mitch reached over and embraced her. She blushed at his open display of affection.

"Mitch. People are watching."

He smiled and parked a passionate kiss on her lips. "Now they have something to watch. Let's get out of here."

The couple left the restaurant with arms wrapped around each other. Obvious, deep love thickened the tiny space between the two. Nausea engulfed Drake as he downed more wine. Perhaps he might destroy their happy marriage as a bonus. Wedding vows meant so little. No one kept them, and Mitch certainly never hit her. Still, these two appeared truly happy, and the thought didn't sit well with him.

Not for long.

Brilliant idea with double return. Such a nice little twist to his game.

He leaned close to his associate. "Find out all you can about that couple. Have one of our associates follow the husband when he leaves town. I want him detained – whatever it takes. I'm about to give Valorie a true life nightmare."

Smitty flashed a wicked smile. "Sure, Boss. I can only imagine what your brilliant mind is plotting right now."

"Oh, you will savor every bit. Now go."

Drake leaned back against his chair and finished his wine. Smug contentment overcame him as he contemplated his next steps.

Chapter 8

From the passenger side of the white cargo van, Drake considered the waste of the tourist area. Along the beach area of Gulf Shores, hopes and dreams of entrepreneurs hung on the stilted houses. Convinced by real estate developers of the potential for becoming filthy rich, they bought into the scheme. Instead, empty houses waited for an elusive renter willing to pay a high price for time near the beach.

What drew people here anyway? An airborne volleyball caught his attention. He watched young men with their rippled abs and muscular arms dive into the sand, while tanned girls in their string bikinis jumped high for the ball. The scene explained some of the allure.

Valorie maneuvered the tan Volvo carefully along the beach-front road, never exceeding the speed limit. Past the condominiums and hotels, beach houses dotted both sides of the road. Whether painted hot pink, bright blue or pale yellow, all of the homes stood at least one flight of stairs above sea level. Some appeared abandoned, left in disrepair after the last hurricane. The majority of houses sported signs advertising a local management company. Most yards grew wild and natural, but some of the houses looked more like homes with manicured lawns and signs of constant occupancy.

The Volvo turned off the main road, and soon pulled into the driveway of the most elaborate yard on the block. Smitty passed the house and pulled into the driveway next door. Drake slumped down in the seat and watched Valorie unload two kids from the car as her parents came out to greet them. The wind carried a tinkling of chimes mixed with their voices through his open window.

Rather than send some incompetent flunky, he and Smitty followed Valorie and Mitch to the airport. Nothing eventful happened—the same over abundance of affection on a larger scale. He hoped the affection wasted on Mitch left her devoid of emotion over leaving the kids, but as the family gathered on the porch, he steeled himself against the inevitable.

They sat in big rocking chairs and enjoyed large glasses of lemonade. He looked away when the hugs and kisses began. He pushed aside memories of his childhood, always lying at the surface ready to pounce on his emotions. Happy homes disgusted him, although he never knew how one really looked.

Most of the time, people played at happiness for show anyway. From the outside, everything looked beautiful while war raged inside on a daily basis. No one outside of a house imagined the horrors within the walls. While the hidden truth pleased him, he preferred the stark revelation of such ugliness. In this family though, he sensed genuine love. His stomach churned as he spat onto the driveway.

He muttered under his breath, "Just hurry up and get it over with."

He looked back at the family. Valorie glanced in his direction, but preoccupied with the children, her gaze lasted only a few seconds. Still, Drake pulled out a map to avoid suspicion. Besides this family, no one in the area spent the afternoon outside. He looked down the block. Oblivious to each other or anything around them, the neighbors stayed tucked inside. How quaint and picturesque this neighborhood appeared.

Posers.

The gentle breeze carried Valorie's voice as it morphed into a nagging whine. "Be sure you wear sunscreen. Stay together and don't go too far out in the ocean. Be careful so you don't get swept away."

Grandpa shook his head. "They'll be fine."

"Just please don't give them so much junk food like you did last time. They aren't used to it. And if you don't watch what you eat, Dad… I don't want to think about what could happen."

"Baby, you worry way too much."

"I can't help it. I'm afraid something bad will happen. No one else seems too worried about anything."

Her mother hugged her. "Val, you have to let go sometimes and trust. Why should we worry anyway? You worry enough for all of us." She laughed and patted her daughter's shoulder. "Now go on home and enjoy some time to yourself. The kids will be fine."

Drake clenched his teeth. Annoyance from the delay fueled sadistic thoughts. He closed his eyes against the chattering and laughter coming from the porch and pictured Valorie a few hours from now. Alone in her bed and locked tight in her house, the false sense of security giving him an edge. He pictured the horror on her face when realization hit. Salivary glands worked overtime as he let his imagination run, a hungry lion intent on devouring this woman and her unsuspecting family. The idea tasted like a fine rare steak. He wiped the corner of his mouth with the back of his hand.

Finally, Valorie made her way back to the car. He opened his eyes, as she looked straight into the van. He picked up the map but changed his mind. Why not mess with her head a little?

He looked straight at the woman and dashed his tongue over the top lip. Her eyes grew wide. Score. He smelled terror. She locked the car door and rolled up the window before backing out of the driveway.

Drake sat up straight. "Let's go, Smitty. Don't lose her. And make it obvious we're following her."

Valorie kept glancing back at them as she drove down the street. At a red light, Smitty maneuvered the van so Drake was next to her side of the car. She kept her eyes fixed straight ahead and refused to look at him. When the light changed, she sped off. Through several turns, Smitty stayed right behind her.

Usually, the extreme colors of a sunset over the ocean annoyed Drake, but with this game of cat and mouse, he barely noticed. He envisioned sweat pouring off the woman's forehead. She veered into oncoming traffic at one point while looking back at the van.

Far too soon, they arrived at her house and stopped the van across the street. In the growing dusk, she parked the car in the driveway and ran toward safety. At the door, she glanced over her shoulder straight into the cargo van. The wildness in her eyes fueled his hunger. He blew a kiss. Let her wonder as darkness filled the house with shadows.

He laughed and watched through the window as she placed a stool in front of the door and then drew the curtains. Not too bright. She should have drawn the curtains first. Now the real game began with this woman. If she peeked out, and he felt certain she would, he waited right there in plain sight.

Drake flipped on the police band radio. Within thirty seconds, the dispatcher's voice crackled over the air. Smitty cocked an eyebrow as she gave the street address. He grinned.

Drake laughed. "Guess we better get into the hidden cargo space. The cops will be here soon." He expected as much from this woman, but not quite so fast.

The two men climbed into the back of the van and lifted an opening. From the top, it appeared as any empty van, but underneath the floor, a cutout spot large enough for two people provided a perfect hiding place for a kidnap victim.

Since she called the police, though, they might as well use it for themselves. Ten minutes passed. Sweat trickled down Drake's back, but his breathing remained steady. Smitty fell asleep. The van door handle rattled.

A muffled voice came through the top of the space. "I don't see a thing. I'm sure the driver just wanted to mess with her a little. There's nothing here besides an empty van."

A second voice responded, "Nothing on the van either – not stolen; everything looks fine. She seemed a little paranoid to me. Let's go tell her there's nothing to worry about."

Drake waited another ten minutes, straining to hear better and finally heard a car's engine drive by. He slowly opened the trap door. Cool air rushed in as he glanced out the van's window.

He popped Smitty on top of the head. "Wake up you fool."

Smitty sat up and rubbed his eyes. "All clear?"

"Not that you would know, imbecile. Yeah. We're all clear. Cops are gone, but I don't want any surprises. Besides, let's intensify her fear a little. Go cut the phone line. A dead phone is always a nice touch--a scene from a horror movie. She probably never watches them, but we'll introduce the nightmare personally."

Smitty flashed a malicious smile. "Okay, boss. This should be fun." He slipped out the back door of the van.

As darkness fell, Drake chuckled. One by one, lights came on in every room of the house. He knew her exact position. He stayed in the back, keeping a clear line of sight to the house. Let her see an empty van and wonder.

Chapter 9

Drake grinned. Hours had passed before only one light in Valorie's living room remained lit...her security no doubt. One by one, windows darkened as she moved through the house, indicating her bedroom's location. As if to confirm his guess, a small sliver of light escaped when she pulled back the drapes enough to peek out. Her small face appeared for a moment before she yanked the curtains shut.

Just a little longer.

Anticipatory hunger coursed through his veins, but a little patience meant a much more fulfilling experience.

Not too soon. Let her fall asleep first.

More terror if he surprised her out of slumber. He let the plan run through his mind and succumbed to imagination. A deep groan escaped from his throat as he felt heat rise within his body. His heart raced in anticipation until he thought it might burst.

Unable to contain himself any longer, he stepped from the back of the van and approached the house.

He quickly located and cut wires to the security alarm. *A second rate system.* He considered cutting power to the house, but he longed for the terrorized look on her face.

He pulled a small tool kit from his jacket pocket, and thirty seconds later, the first lock clicked. The bottom deadbolt required a little more finesse, but within two minutes, the pins clicked one-by-one until the lock opened. The top deadbolt challenged him a little, but with the skill of a master locksmith, the final bolt slid back. So much for triple locks and security alarms.

He entered the front door, sidestepped the stool and turned off the lamp.

Foolish woman, all snug in your bed. I'm coming and you don't even know it.

Drake moved quietly along the hallway to the master bedroom. Light snoring. Good. He stood in the doorway. Illuminated by a nightlight, she lay on her back concealed under layers of linens. A bottle of Melatonin and half glass of water sat on the nightstand alongside a wine glass. Sleeping aid and wine? Not too bright.

So many options. He stroked his beard for a minute. The hours of waiting and all the accompanying anticipation rushed over him.

He flipped on the overhead light, closed the distance to the bed and pulled back the covers. Her eyes struggled against a drugged induced sleep. She moaned.

How could she sleep in a gown covering every body part completely?

The lust in his heart had nothing to do with sex; he wanted fear in her eyes. He straddled her limp figure. She moved slightly as small slits appeared in her eyes. He ran his hands beneath the thick fabric and touched her bare skin. Valorie's eyes shot open. Fear beamed from them. Drake laughed.

"You only thought you were safe. You're mine, and I can do with you as I please."

Screams bounced off his eardrums and filled the house.

Drake threw back his head and howled like a wolf. "No one can hear you in your tight little house. And even if they did, no one would come to your rescue."

He bent down and placed his lips close to her ear. He uttered a low growl and licked her cheek. He bit her ear lightly and breathed heavier. Sobs vibrated her body.

"Come on. Aren't you going to fight me?"

"Please," she whimpered. "Don't hurt me."

"Oh, poor little thing, you're scared aren't you? Wondering what this animal will do to you next? Or maybe you are simply waiting in anticipation for what you hope I'll do."

He howled again as he pulled a rope from his belt loop and tied her hands. He ripped a piece of her gown with his teeth and used it as a gag. Her eyes widened. Intense satisfaction filled his senses as terror mounted in her eyes and spread across her entire face.

"Don't worry. I'll give you more pleasure than you can stand later. But I wouldn't want anyone to interrupt our little rendezvous."

He stood and lifted her off the bed. For the first time, she struggled. He tightened his grip and threw her over his shoulder. She beat against his back with her tied hands and kicked her feet. Such futile attempts. Fear snaked through her body creating tension in every muscle and oozing out against him as he carried her to the van. He dumped her into the back, and climbed inside. Avoiding potential problems and unwilling to take unnecessary chances, he pulled out a syringe. Muffled shrieks behind the gag should concern him, but he merely laughed. She kicked wildly and scooted away from him in a feeble attempt at freedom.

Drake nodded at his associate who promptly grabbed the woman and held her arm still. Seconds after the needle entered her vein, she relaxed. Still awake but incoherent, she whimpered again.

"I'm impressed, Val. You have more fight in you than I expected. You'll make a nice addition for our little game. I'll see you soon."

He exited the van and closed the door. He threw his head back, emitting an evil laugh while the van disappeared into the night.

Chapter 10

Drake descended the winding staircase. His subordinates outdid themselves on the design. Musty smells floated up, and he caught a hint of urine in the air as well. Nice touch. Darkness filled the entire room. The single torch he carried kept him from falling down the stairs, but he wanted Valorie in utter darkness.

A grown woman who slept with a nightlight –pitiful.

Disgusted and yet thrilled fear held such a strong grip over her, he smiled to himself. A few more elements and by the end of the week she'd beg for mercy – do anything he wanted for a moment out of this dungeon.

He approached Valorie and nudged her with his foot. "Wake up, sleepyhead."

Valorie stirred. A chain clanked against the stones as she moved her shackle-bound hands and feet and sat up. She hit her head against the top of the small chamber tucked neatly within the cave walls. The natural cutout fitted with rings for the chains created a perfect cell. A thin mattress tossed carelessly into the opening served as a bed.

She whimpered. "W-w-who are you? What do you want with me?"

Drake answered without emotion. "You are part of my little game, but don't worry, Val. I will hurt you. Count on it. You'll have company soon, so you can worry about the other women too. I know how much you worry about every little thing."

He stepped toward her; she cowered away from him. "Please don't hurt me."

He stared down at her. Fear creased her forehead. crept down her cheeks and trembled down her body. A hiss came from behind her. She jerked her head around and backed up in his direction. Drake laughed. Would she choose him or the viper? He lowered the light for her benefit.

Valorie released a high-pitched scream when the snake grew visible in the dim light. He coiled as she scuttled to the opposite side of her chamber and encountered massive spider webs. She batted the sticky strands. Her screams grew louder and drowned out Drake's laughter. He moved the torch so the spiders on the webs came into view. She swung wildly at the webs and hit at the spiders. Sobs mingled with her screams.

"Help me. I'll do whatever you want. Please. Get the snake and spiders away from me."

Drake stopped laughing. Too easy. He preferred a challenge. Valorie provided none, but after all, she was merely a pawn in his game with Charissa, a mere afterthought. He used the torch on the spider webs. The snake slithered to him as if on command. He pinched behind its head, threw it to the ground and squashed it beneath his boot.

"That's only a taste. Many more live here, and you can depend on their appearance when you least expect it."

Sometimes fear-filled imagination worked better than the real thing. Valorie's lack of sleep while worrying about the spiders and snakes returning would push her to the edge. By the time Charissa arrived, she'd find a half-crazed woman in this hole. Perfect for interjecting a little doubt into a mind filled with faith.

Scratching along the wall caught his attention. He swept the torch low again and revealed several big rats sending Valorie into hysterics. *Well, well.* Smitty created the stage for his game quite well. He'd never admit such a fact to anyone. Each detail heightened his senses, set his mind on edge and quickened his pulse. Few things frightened him, but for someone terrified of everything, the dungeon reeked of dread.

He looked at the small woman with her feet tucked as close to her body as possible. He climbed up to the edge of the chamber and sat beside her. The stench of urine on the mattress reached his nostrils. Smitty probably added the touch personally with great pleasure in the process. He winced at what other substances the bedding contained.

Time for a little fun. He put on a tone filled with mockery and disdain.

"That's such a disgusting smell. You didn't wet your pants did you, Val?"

Valorie shook her head and scooted away from Drake.

"What a pity. At least the bacteria would have been your own. Who knows what diseases the last person who used this bed had? Tsk, tsk."

He laughed again, caught the chain attached to a manacle around her neck and pulled her closer. Valorie tensed. Her slim body shook against him as he pressed hard into her. She strained to move back. The muscles in her arms tightened as she pushed him away. She did have some fight in her small mass after all. Nevertheless, he overpowered her easily, flexing his biceps in a show of physical strength over her. Panic flashed through her eyes. She thrashed back with stronger intensity.

"C'mon Val. You can fight harder can't you? Struggle against me – let me feel your fear, baby." He mocked the men in her life and watched with mounting excitement as her face contorted.

She kicked at him, ignoring the short chains which kept her from inflicting much damage. He ripped her nightgown open, exposing flesh. As he touched her body, she screamed, twisted and jerked, bringing her knees up in an effort to move him away. Her nails became claws, tearing at his arms.

"That's more like it, baby. You want it rough, huh?"

He pinned her down with his body. Her blue eyes flashed for a moment before they turned cloudy. She quit fighting and went limp.

"What the…" Drake fumed.

Where did the terror go? He slapped her, but she remained in a shocked state. Her eyes glazed over to a smoldering gray color, an abyss deeper than what he inflicted. He'd struck a memory no doubt.

So I found her greatest fear – reliving something she experienced long ago.

The fear of the dark and being alone made sense. Some man caused it all. Her sudden shock gave him the ammunition to heighten her fear.

He released his grip on her and scooted backwards out of the chamber, moving back into the shadows. Several minutes passed, the dungeon silent and menacing.

She curled into a fetal position and sobbed. The power of this knowledge surged through every corpuscle. He took the stairs two at a time and called several of his men.

"I have business elsewhere. Torment the woman. Touch her, whisper in her ears. Fill her mind with fear. You can come as close as you want without actually raping her for now. I want her beyond the point where she goes comatose when I touch her. She's mine first. She will feel and remember every second when I'm finished with her, and then you can do as you please with whatever's left."

"Yes, boss," they chorused.

Drake sulked off to his office. This might not be quite as easy as he first believed. His servants obeyed his will though, so he fully expected a different reaction the next time.

Chapter 11

Drake brooded in his study. He detested interruptions to his plans. He poured a glass of bourbon and downed it. The golden liquid burned his throat and belly with a smooth fire. He refilled the glass as Charissa flashed through his mind. He envisioned her initial compassion for Valorie. Acid churned in his stomach, before a refreshing notion eased the discomfort.

Charissa had a different side – the dark part which took a verbal stab at Ann wanted to get even with others. She had fears, and no matter how much she wanted to help Valorie, Charissa would fold.

She didn't belong to him yet, but he'd win. He remembered Smitty's suggestions. The prospect of hearing the sweet, peaceful voice revolted him. He drank the bourbon and steeled himself for the unavoidable. Clearing his throat, he practiced his most syrupy voice before dialing the number.

Charissa's voice grated his nerves in spite of an anesthetic effect of alcohol. He recovered a honey tone, hiding the feelings. "Hello, my lovely Charissa. This is Drake."

"Who?"

"Drake Hannibal. Bubba's friend. An associate of mine is looking for the ex. He assured me he'd have her information soon. I'm going out of town for a few days, but would very much enjoy delivering the message in person—perhaps over dinner."

He poured on the charm as much as possible. He might need Smitty if this didn't work, but the victory of wooing her burned as rich as his favorite liquor.

Charissa hesitated. "I'm not sure that's appropriate, Mr. Hannibal."

"Please, call me Drake. I'm barely older than you are. It's a harmless dinner. We can meet at a restaurant if it makes you feel better. You choose."

Silence.

"Charissa, I understand. You are a beautiful young woman, and I'm sure you don't take chances with strange men."

She spoke softly. The sweetness of her voice soured in his stomach. "It isn't a lack of trust. I don't think you're my type."

"Look, we got off to a bad start. I don't deal well with death, so the man you saw in the hospital wasn't really me. I crack stupid jokes or act calloused to cover up grief. Give me a second chance. Let me show you the real Drake."

She hesitated so long he wondered if she hung up on him. "Charissa?"

"Okay – but just a quick dinner, and I expect you to have information on Bubba's wife. When will you be back in town?"

"End of the week. Let's meet Friday night."

"I'm working. It will have to be Thursday or the following week. I have plans for the weekend."

"Okay. I'll make it back by Thursday at 7:00. Will that work?"

She still sounded guarded, but agreed. "Let's meet at Cooper's Bar-B-Que. I know the owners."

The last statement came across as a warning. He didn't care. "Sounds great. I look forward to seeing you again."

Drake returned to the bar after he hung up. He splashed cold water on his face and filled the glass a third time. The liquid produced the slight buzz he sought. It deadened the memory of her voice. He carried the glass and bottle to his desk and leaned back in the oversized leather chair.

Filling the glass again, he picked up a folder. Edna Broderick. Smitty better have done his homework. He needed all the facts about this woman. He wanted no more surprises spoiling his plans. He sipped his drink while he read the file.

∞∞∞∞∞∞∞∞∞∞∞∞

Charissa hung up the phone. Why had she agreed to this meeting? She pictured the dark smoldering eyes. At some level, Drake scared her.

She really expected him to forget about Bubba. His flirting with Ann and callousness while his friend fought for life disgusted her. Still, people dealt with tragedy in different ways. She saw it often in the ER.

Closing her eyes, she pictured the man.

He looked about thirty, clean-shaven and stood at least six feet tall. All the things she wanted in a man. His dark skin and hair complemented his eyes so well, the epitome of the tall, dark, handsome stranger.

He avoided eye contact, perhaps causing the discomfort. She felt drawn to him, yet something about him seemed wrong. Nothing he said or did gave her a reason to resist him so much, but uneasiness bubbled through her body when she thought about him. Then again, she had a hard time trusting men in general.

She rubbed Rusty's belly. He looked up at her, a deep concern in his eyes. "Don't look at me like that. It's one lousy dinner. Besides, he only thinks he wants me. One dinner and he'll be history. Even if he sticks around for a while, he'll leave eventually. They always do."

She flicked a tear from her cheek. "I'm a defective model, Rusty. I leak." Rusty wagged his tail and licked her face.

"Come what may. It will all work out." She eyed the Bible on her coffee table. "Tomorrow. I'm much too tired tonight." She stretched and turned off the light. "Come. Let's go to sleep."

She snuggled down into her bed, but sleep eluded her. She tossed and turned as loneliness overwhelmed her. She drifted into an imaginary scene spending the day with Drake. She pictured the two of them sailing on the lake. She always wanted to go sailing, and the pretend world provided a guarded place for such an adventure. In her dream, a different Drake existed. He did all the right things, and as the sun set, she imagined his soft kiss on her lips.

I'm so glad the devil can't read my mind. God, please. Can't this be the one? I'm so tired of being alone.

Her musings returned to Drake, and she played out the scene of her perfect day with him until she drifted into an uneasy sleep.

∞∞∞∞∞∞∞∞∞∞∞∞

Drake finished reading the file on Edna. Every detail of her life clung to his mind creating movie frames for memory. Ecstasy mingled with the alcohol in his system as he plotted out the next piece of his plan. He tasted the sweet nectar of deceptive power, and the savor left a deep hunger in his soul. The sooner they met, the better.

He picked up the phone again. "Have my plane ready in an hour."

Drake spun around in his chair and gazed through the window. Security lights blazed against a dark sky, blotting out the stars. He hated stars—so bright and a constant reminder of the Creator. He couldn't deny God, but he certainly didn't have to like Him.

Soon I'll add Edna to my harem. Such an easy prey. She'll aid me well when the time comes. He turned off the desk lamp and walked in darkness to catch his plane for New York.

Chapter 12

The law firm of Wells, Smith and Arnold filled the ten-story building. The structure stood smaller than most of the towering office complexes in the heart of downtown New York, yet the elaborate architecture left no doubt about the power behind the doors.

Drake entered the building at precisely 7:52 a.m. and approached the receptionist. "I'm Drake Hannibal. I have an appointment with Edna Broderick."

"She's expecting you. Please have a seat and she'll be with you in a moment."

Drake selected a soft chair near the window and looked at his image in the reflective pane. The Armani suit accentuated his slim figure, accommodating his broad chest, yet form-fitting at the waist. Perfect. He straightened the blue silk tie, and smoothed his mustache. The touch of gray at his temples aged him nicely, but with the exception of a few lines around his eyes, his tan face looked as smooth as a fine scotch whiskey.

Ummm....you look fine. Very impressive.

While waiting, he fine-tuned his plot. Pique her interest this morning and reel her in over dinner tonight. Simple, effective, quick—the way he preferred things.

He pressed his fingers together and grew impatient. At 8:00 a.m. sharp, Edna's assistant opened the door and called Drake's name. The nerve—sending an assistant. Then again, such an important woman needed an assistant at her bidding. She didn't stoop to menial tasks but commanded others much like himself. He admired those traits.

Edna stood when Drake entered her office. Her suit might have been from any designer, but more likely came from a little boutique, where they provided free alterations. Navy linen contrasted the white silk blouse underneath. Such crispness left an expectation of a crackle at any moment. Her short brown hair wisped across her forehead. Flawless makeup partially hid tiny lines around her eyes. Dark circles hung below her lower lashes, the long hours in the office barely hidden by concealer.

Edna held out a manicured hand and introduced herself. "Mr. Hannibal. I'm Edna Broderick. How can I help you this morning?"

The sun bounced off a large diamond ring surrounded by sapphire and ruby stones. A diamond tennis bracelet flashed spots across her office. He dared not look at the wedding set on her left hand for fear the refracting light might blind him.

Nice. No beating around the bush.

"I need a contract executed, and unfortunately my personal attorney is out of the country attending to other affairs for me."

Edna raised an eyebrow. "There are questions of ethics you know. The bar frowns upon attorneys stealing business."

"No worries. My attorney works exclusively for me, and I pay him extremely well. His current endeavor includes enough rewards he won't mind sharing this small piece of work. After purchasing an island on my behalf, he'll get to build a small mansion at my expense and live there most of the time. Assuming, of course, he can figure out how to keep up with my affairs long-distance." He winked at her. "I'm sitting on an incredible deal worth millions, but they want the contract executed tomorrow. Can you handle the time frame?"

"What type of a deal are we talking about, Mr. Hannibal? And how many millions?"

Drake scanned the office. "I'm very cautious about discussing details. One leak and the whole thing becomes smoldering embers."

"If you don't trust me, why did you come here?"

"Oh I trust you, Ms. Broderick. I've done my homework, but you can't be too careful. If I had my way, I'd send in a team to sweep your office for bugs."

Edna rolled her eyes. "Mr. Hannibal, you seem a little paranoid—makes me uncomfortable. Is this deal above board? I won't risk jail time for you, and my reputation thus far is untarnished. I plan on keeping it that way."

Drake chuckled. "Of course it's all legal. We're talking about millions of dollars—maybe billions. Perhaps I am a little paranoid, but I can't risk any leaks. My hotel room is clean without a doubt. If you come for dinner tonight, I'll make it worth your time regardless of your decision. Perhaps I'll even cut you in on the deal."

Edna studied his face. "How big of a cut?"

"10%."

Her eyes narrowed as she weighed her options. She remained stoic but greed flashed across her face. The best motivator for manipulation, she wouldn't resist. She searched his eyes. He remained silent and kept his appearance unreadable.

She finally spoke. "I want 25."

"You drive a hard bargain, but I'm a desperate man. Let's not play games—20 percent.

She nodded.

"Done. I will see you tonight then."

"You know my assistant will check your credentials before you reach the bottom floor."

"I'd expect no less, Ms. Broderick. Come to the Ritz at 8:00. I'll have dinner prepared and served in my suite."

Edna flinched slightly, but enough. He impressed her. "Assuming all checks out I'll be there. I'll let my husband know I'm working late. He'll wait up for me otherwise."

Drake forced a smile. The fine Dr. Broderick caught an early flight for a San Francisco medical conference. He knew the couple's routine. They checked-in with each other only when necessary at best, and almost never talked when one of them traveled. They led separate lives and joined each other only for social appearances – the embodiment of a perfect couple yet complete frauds. They seldom shared the same bed other than for convenience or desire. The corporate ladder held more interest for her than a husband and family. She planned to run this prestigious law firm within a few years.

Smitty's thorough research of this attorney amazed him. The methods used didn't. Apparently, she grew very talkative and uninhibited under the influence of a few drinks mixed with a vial of cocaine. She talked in her sleep and divulged even more information from her subconscious mind. Drake held all the cards if she balked or caused any problems.

Her eyes flashed as she waited for his response. He literally smelled greed in her expensive perfume. He pressed the hook in a little deeper.

"Of course, we wouldn't want your husband worried, would we?"

He turned to leave then stopped and faced her again. "You know...it isn't the money. I have more than enough money to last the rest of my life now. The power with this deal – I'll own the country. You can't buy that kind of power. If I grow fond of you, I might include part of the pie as a bonus."

Edna's face flushed. She held the edge of her desk.

He added one more little twist, securing the barb. "Of course, you'd have to give me your complete loyalty, but I'm sure you don't want to leave this prestigious law firm and join my payroll, do you? Consider it, and tell your husband you might need to take a business trip for a few days."

Drake turned and relished the shocked silence. Hooked. Exactly as he planned. She'd be at the Ritz well before 8:00 tonight—with luggage in hand.

Chapter 13

The clock in Drake's room struck 8:00 p.m. as a firm knock sounded at the door. Ultimate precision. He expected such from this woman. He nodded at Smitty to open the door. Edna stood at the threshold.

"Edna, I'm so glad you decided to join me."

He motioned at the balcony. A table set with fine china waited for them. A waiter dressed in a tuxedo held the chair for her as they stepped through the doors. She straightened her silverware as the waiter uncovered their dishes and poured wine. Drake dismissed him.

"Do you mind if we get down to business while we eat, Mr. Hannibal? No need to waste time."

"My dear, do you ever enjoy the pleasures of life? We eat first and then talk business." She would not have the upper hand. He wanted her relaxed and under his control, yet fully alert.

She gritted her teeth. "Very well."

They dined initially in relative silence. Small talk meant nothing to this woman. While he admired her drive and ambition, he wondered at her total inability to enjoy any part of life outside of work.

"What do you do for fun?" He asked.

"I win important cases. I'm either in court or in preparation for a case. That's my idea of fun."

Drake kept refilling the wine glasses to no avail. He conceded as they began dessert. He hoped for a more pleasurable evening, but she knew nothing about pleasure. He wondered about Smitty's tryst with this one. Given his options though, he'd take her desire for power and wealth over a need for fun.

As he laid out the details of the imaginary deal, she jotted notes. She alternated between a blank stare, wide eyed-wonder, and flashes of rapture. As he finished weaving the irresistible offer, she ran her tongue over her top teeth, leaned back and downed half her wine.

"Mr. Hannibal, I must admit when you came to my office this morning, I thought you were some lunatic. My assistant assured me of your great wealth and after hearing these details….well, I certainly can see the value of this deal. Count me in."

"Please, my dear, call me Drake. I'm meeting with these partners tomorrow at my home. I've arranged transportation for you. I see you have your laptop and am sure you can work on the contract on the way. I want you present when I meet with them. Assuming of course that's acceptable to you."

"Not a problem. I came prepared; luggage is in the car."

"Excellent. I do love business associates who anticipate my needs. Good start to our relationship. Now, if you can learn to enjoy the finer things of life, and give-in to some temptations once in a while, we shall enjoy a wonderful future together."

She laughed. "There's plenty of time for pleasure later. Business comes first."

"So it seems." He motioned for Smitty. "Call for the limo and get Ms. Broderick's luggage while we finish dessert." He raised his glass to Edna. "Here's to a prosperous and pleasurable future."

The glasses clinked as they toasted their new partnership. Drake accompanied her downstairs. As the limousine pulled away from the curb, he watched the lights fade into darkness.

He spoke into the night. "You power-hungry witch. Even with all her fears, Valorie fought for freedom harder than you ever dared. You're imprisoned and don't even know it."

With all her mighty knowledge, she entered the limo as clueless as a newborn. The expectations of her trip fell so far short of her final destination he couldn't hold back his laughter. He imagined her anger and wished he could be there when she woke up in the dungeon. The mental image of those daggers in her eyes pleased him immeasurably. By the time he got Charissa there, Edna's anger should be at the frenzy state.

He laughed again as he returned to his room for a good night's sleep before heading back to Texas.

Chapter 14

The scent of burning mesquite wood drifted into Charissa's nostrils when she neared Coopers. As she pulled into the parking lot, tantalizing wafts of cooking meat collided with the firewood scent hanging thickly in the air.

She waited in her jeep. No sense appearing anxious to see Drake again. After all, she merely wanted information about Bubba's wife, but never rejected a free dinner – especially at this restaurant. She loved the barbeque, and in a strange way, the rustic atmosphere appealed to her senses. She actually took pleasure in the macho décor other women seemed to merely tolerate.

She checked her watch. Maybe he wouldn't show. As she considered bailing, a red Dodge Ram 3500 pulled up beside her. Drake. The truck, complete with Hemi, fit his personality. He climbed out of the cab and spotted her little Jeep. She rubbed sweaty palms on her jeans before jumping down from her vehicle.

Her daddy used to let her jump into his open arms when they came to eat at Coopers. Funny she remembered him at the height of vulnerability while she waited to meet a stranger.

Here goes nothing – keep your cool girl. You're on home ground and it's a quick dinner. No big deal.

Ugh. She got carried away much too quickly—always overanalyzing things. Not this time. She kept her heart tucked hidden behind a strong wall.

"Charissa. You look incredible – jeans are much more flattering than those baggy scrubs." Drake grinned and held out a dozen yellow roses.

Her face grew hot. Uncertain of whether to accept the flattery or back off from a come on line, she tentatively took the flowers. "Thank you. They're lovely, but you shouldn't have."

"The guy on the side of the road looked so dejected, I couldn't resist. Besides, I figured it would be a nice peace offering. You really saw the worst of me when we first met." He swallowed hard. "The night Bubba died, I didn't handle it well."

Were those tears in his eyes? He seemed more upset now, but she wasn't convinced. Men had a way of playing things to their advantage. She wasn't letting her guard down with this one.

"Unexpected death hits hard sometimes. That night wasn't easy for me either, and I didn't even know the man. I don't think anyone claimed his body yet either. Were you able to find his wife?"

"You don't waste time do you? I left her several messages, but so far, she hasn't returned any calls. I finally handed the information over to the sheriff. Don't hold out too much hope. I don't imagine she'll come around."

"Well, give me her number, and I'll call. Maybe she'll talk to me - you know, woman to woman."

"I can't."

"What do you mean you can't?" Her patience gave way to exasperation.

"I told you…I gave it to the sheriff. I didn't keep a copy of it."

Charissa fumed inside but held back growing fury. She took a deep breath before speaking. "Why not?"

He shrugged. "I thought you just wanted her notified. The sheriff should handle it anyway. Why are you worried about it?"

"I promised Bubba I'd give her a message. His last words were for her."

"I'm sorry, Charissa." He hesitated. "Look, from what I know, she wouldn't care anyway. She didn't ever really love the man. She used him and walked away when his money and luck ran out. I'm sure she'd laugh in your face. Why do you want to put yourself through such pain?"

"Because I promised." Tears stung her eyes. She fought them back. "Maybe you're right, but I don't break promises and…" she hesitated. "I can't imagine a man loving someone so much his dying thought is about her. If it were me, I'd want to know."

The tears slipped out and she brushed them away impatiently. She could blame the smoke, but why bother.

Drake touched her arm gently. "Charissa, I'm sorry. I didn't realize it meant so much to you."

"It's okay. I'll ask the sheriff to have her contact me if he finds her."

Drake wiped a tear from her cheek and moved closer. His touch felt soft and comforting. She steeled herself against the rush of emotions sweeping over her. If he held her at this point…

She turned away from him. "Let's get some food. I'm really hungry."

He dropped his hand. "Sounds good to me. If the food tastes half as good as it smells, I'm in trouble."

They laughed and headed over to the giant pits. The smell of cooking meat released the tension from her shoulders, but the knots in her back lingered. Her nerves still tingled as she sighed in relief their intimate moment ended as quickly as it began. She wasn't up to another broken heart.

None of it mattered. At the moment, she concerned herself with only which kind and piece of meat to claim as her own. Beef, steak, chicken and two inch thick pork chops lined the top of the pits. Her mouth literally watered as she breathed in the scrumptious scent of meat sacrificed to the god of gluttony.

Against her better judgment, she picked the pork chop knowing she'd leave half of it on the tray at the end of the meal – unless Drake ate it of course. She saw many different reactions through the years with this particular test of comfort levels. One guy actually lost it because she ate half her meal. He ranted for thirty minutes about wastefulness. She never answered or returned his calls again.

Charissa relaxed when they entered the restaurant. Hometown advantage. She knew many of the people seated at the long wooden tables. Haniel sat with a large group of people at one of them. He smiled, waved and motioned for her to join them. For a split second, his eyes clouded when he saw Drake behind her, but his smile never faded.

Drake paid for the food and guided her to the opposite end of the room. "Do you mind if we sit outside? It's a beautiful night and too crowded inside."

Charissa's instincts screamed against the suggestion. She'd feel much more comfortable near Haniel. She looked in her friend's direction and shrugged her shoulders.

A couple in front of them headed out to the patio. At least she wouldn't be completely alone with this man. Besides, the noise level inside reverberated against the walls at unbearable decibels of sound. They'd yell at each other instead of talking, unless they went outside. She stepped through the doors without answering Drake or looking back at Haniel.

Dinner passed quickly, the conversation light. He was one smooth character, she gave him that much. Before much time passed, they both shared some of their funniest date catastrophes. They both laughed until each reached for extra paper towels off the table to wipe away tears. At one point, she snorted which only made them laugh harder. She relaxed more as the clock ticked away minutes. With her guard down, she barely noticed a change in his expression as he steered the conversation in the direction of more intimate topics.

"So, what made you become a nurse? I'm not convinced you really enjoy it."

She deliberated about how much she wanted to share. "My mom influenced me. I'm not sure whether she considered it as a good income or the best way to meet and marry a doctor." She expected at least a chuckle, but he wasn't amused.

"So is that what you want?"

"I hope to get married and have kids someday I guess, and I do love taking care of people."

"But?"

"What but? I love taking care of people."

"C'mon, Charissa. I sense a "but" in there."

She sighed. "I'm not sure about the nursing thing. Bubba's death made me re-evaluate if I want to keep nursing. I spent a lot of time at a big city hospital, saw a lot of violent death. When I moved home, I believed it all ended – never expected another gunshot death. But it followed me." She sighed again. "I really love taking care of kids. The happiest times in my life were during my teenage years. I went on some mission trips and the orphans captured my heart, you know?"

Drake nodded, but remained silent. His face never changed, and his eyes remained cold.

"Those kids—so easy to love them. It's really all they wanted—to love and be loved. Most of them cried when I left. I remember one little girl, haunts me sometimes. She clung tight until they pried her arms from around my neck. If I could have fit her in my suitcase, I would've brought her home with me. It's one of the few times in my life I felt so loved without any conditions attached."

What was she thinking? She never intended to open up this much with some man she barely knew. She took a deep breath and regained composure. He'd so deftly opened up a sore spot and now sat in silence with those dark, smoldering eyes seeing into her soul. She waited, fearing she'd said too much.

After several minutes, he spoke in quiet, even tones. "I knew you had a lot of compassion, but never saw so much depth, and who would have guessed it was because of some orphans in another country?"

She couldn't read him at all. Was this a good or bad thing? Was he showing compassion or mocking? Suddenly, she wanted the night to end. She looked through a window for Haniel. He understood about her love for those kids. But the table where he sat earlier now held a loud man with a beer belly and pants that threatened to reveal much more of his backside than she cared to see. She sighed.

Drakes eyes narrowed. "So, you want to go back?"

"Yeah," she said. "It's getting late."

"I meant to the other countries — to the orphans."

"Oh that." She sipped her iced tea. "Yes, more than anything. I dream of them sometimes — still feel the little girl's arms tighten around my neck as the director pulled her away from me. I hear her cries in the night, and it breaks my heart."

She looked up into the sky and fought back tears. He could not see her cry again tonight; she wouldn't allow it.

"Well, maybe someday you can go back."

"If God allows it, I will." She said.

A frown crept across his lips and moved upwards into furrowed eyebrows. A glint flashed in his pupils.

"Maybe you need to make it happen. I seriously doubt God expects you to sit around waiting while he dumps a dream in your lap. After all, doesn't God help those who help themselves?" Sarcasm dripped from his voice at the mention of God. "What are you afraid of, Charissssssa?"

Charissa winced. She didn't particularly care for the tone in his voice or the way he drew out her name like some hissing serpent. She appreciated his insinuation even less.

"Nothing. I'm waiting for the right time."

He had a point. She kept waiting, but nothing happened. Maybe she expected God to do everything when she should pursue her dreams.

She sighed. "Come what may. For tonight, I really should be getting home. I do have to work tomorrow."

"Of course. I've kept you much longer than intended." He stood up from the table. "I enjoyed your company very much."

As they headed for the door he continued, "I have another business trip. I'll be out of the state for a couple of weeks, but perhaps when I come back to town, we can see each other again. Wouldn't you have fun getting away from everything? Maybe take a boat out on the lake, sit back and let the wind brush through your hair?"

He reached up and pushed strands away from her face.

How did he know to suggest exactly what I would love most?

Had she said something? She shook off the foreboding.

For a moment, her mind drifted back to early childhood. She envisioned her dad sitting at the wheel of his boat maneuvering through the waves, purposely hitting them so she bounced out of the seat.

Her daddy took on the appearance of the king of everything when he drove his boat. Her mind floated back to those days. His face lit up while a slight smile played on his lips, the wind pushing back his hair. She loved his strong jaw and tanned face. Such a long time ago – before he left and her world fell apart.

She looked back at Drake. He had those same chiseled features and dark complexion.

She sighed and kept her voice nonchalant in spite of a racing heart. "Perhaps…if I'm not working or something."

She wasn't sure if she really wanted to see this man again. The evening had been pleasant, but she wondered if he would bother calling again. Who would blame him after the shameless display of emotion? She turned into such a basket case anytime someone brought up dreams or orphans. They walked to her Jeep, thick silence in the air between them.

As she started to climb in, Drake grabbed her waist, hugged her and kissed her forehead.

"Goodnight, Charissa. I'll be thinking about you."

He turned and walked away; his voice lingered in the air.

Chapter 15

Drake strolled to his truck. The squeal of tires brought out a smile. Still, he had to look. The Jeep slid around the parking lot exit with no more than a cursory stop. Good. He rattled Charissa enough she scooted away, a frightened mouse running from his trap.

A sudden shove from behind knocked him into the truck. Fear and anger propelled him around, ready to fight, but a strong arm pinned him against the metal. A familiar face came into focus.

"Haniel. What the h…?"

"I warned you. Leave Charissa alone."

"You don't own her. How dare you assault me?"

Haniel's voice remained calm, but his arm pressed down into Drake's chest. "This isn't an assault. It's a friendly discussion."

Drake thrust off the arm. "Get your hands off me. I'm not a little boy you can push around. I learned early in life what assault looks like, and how to defend myself from it."

"You hurt Charissa, and I'll show you a brand new level of assault."

Interesting. Apparently, he struck a nerve with Haniel too. "She's nothing special."

"She is to me."

"Exactly. And that's what makes her so very tempting."

"Why her, Drake? You have more women than you can handle now. You always did."

"But it's so much more fun to take your toys away from you. Especially when you get all protective over one of them."

"She isn't a toy."

"Hmmm…actually, you're right. She's more of a token for an intriguing game."

"What do you have in that evil mind of yours?"

"If I told you, it wouldn't be much of a game would it?" A desire to mock his enemy rose and took over. "You used to be so good at reading my mind. Don't tell me you've lost your ability."

"I know your games, and I'm warning you. Leave her alone. She has nothing to do with the rift between us."

"You love her, and she cares about you. That makes her as much my enemy as you are."

"She hasn't done anything. Keep this between us. I'll fight, even die, to keep her out of your hands."

"Oh, but if she chooses me, there is nothing you can do to stop this game. And she will choose me."

Hostility mounted in Haniel's eyes, challenging Drake. His chin jutted out, begging for a strike. But Drake maintained composure. They'd fight eventually, but not tonight. He'd not give this long-time enemy the satisfaction of a physical battle just yet. He had much deeper plans in mind.

"Tsk, tsk. Haniel, thank you for confirmation. You know she will choose me. Otherwise, you wouldn't be here."

Haniel moved toward him. "If you hurt her, you will pay. That's a promise." He paused. "And I never break my promises."

The audacity, staring him down, waiting, not saying another word. Drake stepped closer. A stalemate of two boys playing Monopoly, but with real people instead of tokens. This time, he fully intended to win no matter what it took or whom he destroyed in the process.

He drove Haniel back and opened the truck door. "Promises. No one ever keeps them. Your father didn't, and neither will your sweet Charissa. By the time she figures out what I'm doing, it will be too late. I promise that."

He slammed the door shut and flicked his fingers at the glass.

Chapter 16

The slight crustiness on the cafeteria pudding turned Charissa's stomach. She wished for the leftover pork chop. Why didn't she take it home instead of watching Drake's reaction when she threw it away? She normally wouldn't waste food, but her test…

He barely noticed. At least she felt relatively sure he wasn't some psychopath who'd fall off the edge of the earth because she wasted food.

She settled for the salad bar. Heading through the checkout, she spotted Haniel at a nearby table. A tinge of guilt coursed through her. He waved at her, and this time she accepted the offer. She adored this man and welcomed a reprieve from thoughts of Drake.

"Hello, Charissa. How was dinner last night?"

So much for forgetting Drake.

"It was okay." She launched into defensive mode. "Drake was supposed to give me some information about the wife of the gunshot victim who died in ER. His last words were intended for her – he wanted her to know he loved her."

"Oh." He raised his eyebrows slightly.

"What?"

"It sounds as if you're defending yourself."

Her jaw tightened. "It's not like last night was a date — just food and information exchange between two strangers."

"So you got the wife's name and number?"

"Not exactly. He gave it to the sheriff, so I'll have to get it from him."

"Well, at least you got a nice dinner out of it, and you can be done with Drake."

His deep brown eyes sliced through her. He knew – somehow he knew. Drake wasn't her type and the constant focus on him troubled her, but what right did Haniel have judging her?

"What's wrong with Drake?"

"You can do what you want of course, but I don't think he's right for you."

"I'm no fool. If that's what you think, then obviously you don't know me at all. I left him at the restaurant, and just because he asked to see me again doesn't mean I'll jump at the chance. And, so what if I do? Maybe I'm tired of being lonely, and I don't see anyone hanging around my door waiting to sweep me off my feet. And don't you dare tell me God is my husband. I'm sick of hearing the trite little phrase."

"Did I say that?"

"You wouldn't be the first. I hear it all the time and maybe there is some truth to it. I've memorized the verses, buddy, but it ain't the same."

Her anger burned, and she had no desire to hide it from him, as if she could. He read her like a major news article, and his ability to do it accurately maddened her. She studied his face. He never flinched, but his eyes spoke volumes of disapproval and disappointment.

Her father's face flashed through her mind. She reverted to a lost little girl, desperate to please Daddy. Only this wasn't Daddy. Still, she slumped in her chair, frustrated and on the verge of tears. Did it matter so much whether she pleased

Haniel? If he really cared about her, a relationship with Drake shouldn't come between them.

Haniel's face softened. "No condemnation, Baby Girl, but I know Drake — very well. Be careful."

She unclenched her teeth. "I'm sorry, Haniel. I didn't get enough sleep last night, so I'm a little edgy."

"I understand your feelings, but don't settle for someone because you're lonely. You really need to stay away from him for your own sake. Trust me on this one."

"Haniel McCrae, if I didn't know better I'd accuse you of being jealous."

A smile played across his lips, spread up his face and then exploded through the twinkle in his eyes. He raised his eyebrows and took another bite of food without a word.

Chapter 17

Drake sipped his coffee and skimmed the headlines. Prayer on the Square, Local Church blah, blah, blah. Based on Smitty's reconnaissance and pictorial report, a genuine headline might read Religiosity Meets Peyton Place. Precisely the kind of place his associate loved, where he stirred up trouble with the slightest effort. A bunch of hypocrites and posers, one of which he deemed ripe for the picking.

Smitty didn't catch Ariana on film, but he included more than enough photos of her unfaithful husband. Drake glanced up as the waitress refilled his cup.

The couple at the next table held more interest than the meaningless news of this small Mississippi town.

She twirled a strand of her long, thick red hair as it cascaded against a royal blue shirt. Her jeans fit her slim figure snugly, but not too tight. The man turned the ring on his left hand. He averted his eyes from the scoop of her shirt, but they flicked between her face and the neckline during their conversation. She bit into an orange wedge and let the juice run over her lips before giving him a bite. She wiped the corner of his mouth with her finger and then licked it. As they talked, she touched his hand frequently. He fidgeted and reached for creamer.

Two women sat behind Drake and spoke in hushed tones.

"I hope they leave before Ariana gets here. If she sees them together, it'll break her heart."

"Oh don't I know it. That shameless hussy goin' after Larry...and he don't seem too resistant now does he?"

"Not a' tall. Do you s'pose he's really cheatin' on her with that woman?"

"Supposedly he's counselin' her after the divorce."

"What counselin'? She's the one who left. I hear her husband was cheatin' on her, but I expect it was the other way around."

"Well, I never seen counselin' like that before."

"Is that what they call it these days? Counselin'?"

The two women snickered. Drake found their gossip amusing but shallow.

The door to the diner swung open and a woman entered. Salt and pepper hair braided and twirled into a loop on the top of her head resembled a halo. Her flowered cotton dress stretched across large hips. The drabness of her face repulsed Drake almost as much as the rolls of fat straining against the fabric at her waist. Still, he bet she made a scrumptious apple pie.

The gasps behind him confirmed his suspicions—this must be Ariana. No wonder poor Larry preferred breakfast with the town's most recent subject of gossip.

She sashayed over to her husband's table. He stood and kissed her cheek.

Her voice dripped with honey and the smile plastered on her lips never faded as she greeted him. "Hello darlin'." She nodded at the woman. "Judith. How are you, sugar? Gettin' some good counsel from my Larry? I guess this is much better than a stuffy ole office."

A glint of hatred crossed Judith's eyes, followed by the flash of an evil smile. "Ariana, it's been such a long time." She placed a hand on Larry's arm. "Yes, Larry is so amazing. I would be lost without him."

Ariana took a step closer to the man. His face turned crimson as he looked down at the floor. He tucked his tail and looked for a hiding place, but found none.

Judith's voice dropped. "Larry, dear, I'll see you soon. Thank you for breakfast. Goodbye, Ariana."

She stood and yanked her purse from the chair back.

"Bye, Judith. You c'mon by the house and have a bite with us sometime soon."

Judith ignored the invitation. Every man in the diner watched her backside as she retreated; Larry's disappointment appeared as his face became pale again.

He turned toward his wife. "I have to get back to the office now. I have a committee meeting tonight, so I'll be late. Don't worry 'bout cookin' for me. We're gonna order pizza for everyone."

Ariana swallowed hard, but the smile stayed painted on her face. "What a shame, honey. I had a big dinner planned. But I do have some sewin' to finish, so it's just as well."

They turned in opposite directions without another word or sign of affection. As she walked passed Drake, he lowered the paper and stared into her eyes. She nodded a greeting and joined her friends.

For the next half hour, he listened as the three women danced around the suspicions hanging in the air. Neither of the friends dared bring up the obvious so they prattled on with meaningless chatter. Finally, one of them couldn't stand the eggshell waltz any longer.

"Oh, Ariana, I'm so sorry you caught Larry and Judith here this mornin'. We've s'pected somethin' for quite a while now."

Ariana brushed it off. "Don't be silly, Mae. He's only counselin' her. Not that I agree with her gettin' a divorce – it ain't right. Those clothes she wears and her painted-up face. Well, I chalk it up to her mama. She spent more time shoppin' than she did goin' to Bible study and never had those kids in Sunday school. Course she worked in some bar and grill, so I guess she was sleepin' in come Sunday mornings. She sure delighted in the liquor. Judith needs to see the error of her ways, and my Larry will show her the truth. She'll be out lookin' for that husband of hers in no time, and they'll patch things up."

"How can you be so naïve? They got somethin' goin' on, and it's plain as a fly on dog poop. And you know it ain't the first time he's done this. Ain't nobody gonna fault you for walkin' away. He's been doin' this kinda thing for years. Open up your eyes, girl."

"Just hush up. I ain't gonna listen to you bad mouth my husband. You oughta be ashamed gossiping 'bout your preacher."

The other woman finally spoke. "Ain't gossip if it's true."

Drake stifled a laugh. He'd have to remember the woman in case he needed someone comparable to her later. Ariana's honey-coated voice broke into his brooding.

"Josephine, shush. I have no doubt Judith wants my Larry. He's a good man and still fine lookin', but he'll be faithful to me, and I'm countin' on it. I know what they say 'bout her. But she's a lost puppy in need of salvation, and that's all I'm sayin'. Now, both of you go on and leave me be. I'm gonna sit here and write notes for our sick church folk."

Mae spoke again. "Fine, Ariana. But you listen up…Larry ain't such a good man. I don't care if he is the preacher. I hear things ya know. When you catch him red-handed with one of these floozies I hope you won't be singin' the same tune."

Mae and Josephine left. Ariana ordered a piece of pie and another cup of coffee. Drake turned the page of his newspaper and feigned interest in the local news.

The scratching of a pen assured him the woman still sat behind him. Occasionally the scrape of the fork or a sniffle broke the monotony of her writing. He let her wallow in silent sorrow.

The diner emptied out, and the staff disappeared to the back. Only then did Drake turn to the woman.

"Ma'am, I didn't mean to eavesdrop on your conversation earlier, but I have to be honest with you."

Ariana looked up from her note writing. Her red-rimmed, puffy eyes contrasted with the painted smile she quickly reapplied before answering.

"It ain't nice to listen to other people's conversations, but I'll let it slide right on by this time."

"Well, it seems to me your friends care a great deal for you. They want to protect you and obviously see something that makes them think..." He hesitated, and she lost no time with an interruption.

"Think what, mister?"

"What I saw between your husband and…" He paused again, this time for effect. "Well, ma'am, I've been around the world and the interaction between them didn't resemble an innocent counseling session. He didn't hide his lust very well. Frankly, the whole thing rather disgusted me. I'm sorry, but that's my honest opinion. Don't you think you should confront him instead of standing up for him?"

Her shoulders slumped as weariness crossed her face. The painted smile stayed in place, but tears welled up and cascaded down rouge-covered cheeks.

Her voice quivered. "He's not a bad man, and what am I s'posed to do? Huh? I'm a Christian woman and don't believe in divorce. Besides, God gave me this man, and I won't walk away based on some rumors. Not to mention my daddy would be so disappointed in me."

"So you buy the late night committee meeting crap?"

"Why shouldn't I? I've never seen any real proof of him cheatin'."

Her shoulders straightened, squared off in a defensive position. This might be more difficult than he first imagined. He needed her as part of his little troupe, so he plunged forward.

"I didn't mean to upset you. It's really none of my business." He started to turn away but stopped. "Don't you think you deserve better than what you've been dealt by your God?"

"What I deserve doesn't matter. I got nothin' without Larry. Mama and Daddy can't take me in and – well Daddy's still a Baptist preacher. He'd never forgive me if I get a divorce. Where 'm I gonna go, mister? I got no money, no job. How 'm I s'posed to live, huh? You know so much for a stranger in our little diner, but you don't know squat."

Drake stood to leave. "Ariana, I don't fancy seeing a woman treated this way. I'm a businessman and can always find a place in my organization for someone in need." He handed her a business card. "If you want out, call me. I'll give you a job and a place to live. I'll even send someone to pick you up with your things. You don't have to stay in this mess. Would a loving God want you miserable with an adulterous husband?"

Doubt crept across Ariana's face as she took the card and dabbed at her eyes with a napkin. "I'll think about it. Thank you, and…forgive me if I came across harsh with you."

"Not at all. This isn't an easy situation, but don't wait too long. Things are bound to get worse."

He turned and dropped a fifty on the table. Without looking, he knew that impressed the woman. She'd call in a matter of time – perhaps before the day ended.

He almost laughed at the vision of Judith in attendance at the committee meeting and afterwards. Her low cut shirt might push Larry over the edge tonight. He counted on it.

Chapter 18

Drake sat across from Smitty as the man droned on about two more women who might fit nicely into their game.

"And exactly how do you see these two particular biddies fitting into the scheme?"

Smitty stammered, "well…I thought…I mean… they seemed like…this one…"

"Oh, shut up. They're fine, and yes, I can see some use for them."

"Why ya gotta do that to me anyway, Boss?"

"Because you don't think above your waist most of the time. I wonder if you really get what I'm into here."

Frankly, he had grown tired of the travel and seeking out more characters for his little plot, yet the thrill of trapping these women spread a tingle across his skin. He flipped through the files on his desk and stroked his beard.

Neither presented much of a challenge, but both held promise for further entrenching the doubt and discouragement he'd already rooted into Charissa's mind. Before long, she'd fall. Of course, all of this depended on his ability to woo her and to use these other women against her.

As if on cue, his phone rang. Ariana's voice no longer held a sweet tone. The mixture of sorrow, anger, pain and shock replaced the syrup in her words and provided instant gratification. He didn't need details, but the sobs in her voice pleasured him nonetheless.

"Mr. Hannibal, I hope you remember me – Ariana Marseilles. We met yesterday." Her voice shook through the earpiece.

"Yes, Ariana, of course I remember you. Please call me Drake. How is your husband?"

"Oh, Mr. Hannibal, you were right. All of you were." Her voice broke.

"I assume you're talking about your husband and his mistress?"

"Yes. I trusted him, but I ran into one of the committee members at the grocery store and heard the meetin' was over. I drove by the church and Larry's car was still in the parkin' lot, but so was Judith's little sports car. I walked in on 'em. Buck naked – both of 'em – in the church office. I stood there with my mouth hangin' to my knees and they didn't even know I was there – they just kept at it."

"So you decided to leave him then?"

"No. I figured she seduced him, and I'd forgive him. That's the Christian thing to do, you know. Besides, I couldn't stand the shame of a divorce. But then I was waitin' for him when he come home. I told him I knew, but I'd forgive him – if he just ended it."

"So you called to tell me I was right?" He waited impatiently while sobs on the other end of the line grew. "Ariana?"

"I'm sorry. No, that's not all of it. He...he...he wants a divorce. He had the nerve to tell me God wants him to divorce me and marry her. Can you believe such a thing? I don't know what else to do. Can you still find a job for me? I can't stay here. I'm so ashamed."

"Hmmmm. Well, yes, I can use your services." He nodded across the desk. "I'll have my associate pick you up. We'll take care of everything."

He jotted down her address, ended the call and handed the paper to Smitty. "Go get Ms. Marseilles. Where did he get the idea of God telling him to divorce the pig and marry the hot toddy?" He snickered. "What a novel idea for someone 'listening to God for direction' and missing it by a canyon. Wish I came up with such a suggestion."

Cockiness rolled across Smitty's face. "I learned from the best. This one was nothing. A little porn here and there – ole Larry sure got off on looking. Easy move into a lust for young, sexy women and with a wife like Ariana…" He trailed off and shuddered. Drake entertained a momentary notion of the plump woman without clothes and trembled with his cohort.

Smitty continued. "So, I threw in the hot little divorcee desperate to reaffirm her self-worth in the arms of any man. The rest fell beautifully into place."

"Rather proud of yourself aren't you? But remember I suggested the affair to Ariana."

Smitty's chest deflated a bit. "True, but the two had hardly flirted with the possibility then. Sheer luck they gave into lust at precisely the right moment. The image of their naked bodies and the accompanying sounds will haunt her forever."

Drake threw back his head and laughed. "I love watching a plan of destruction come together. Yes, the lingering image will serve well in the days to come when all of my players fall into place. But luck had nothing to do with it. I devised the whole plot, and you know it."

He led his assistant out the door, his chest protruding a little more than normal. Not only had he envisioned this trap, he taught his minions well. They seldom crossed him and generally carried out his wishes – sometimes even without direction. They found this lifestyle so much better than simple obedience. However, the pride thing sometimes caused problems. He made a mental note to put Smitty back in his place—soon.

He spoke as much to himself as the assistant. "This should be interesting when we add the little cook to the recipe. I'll head to Tennessee after checking on my other little pets." He glared at the man. "What are you waiting for? Go get her."

"Yes, sir."

Drake opened a hidden panel off his study, stepped through onto a landing, and removed a torch from the wall. Sounds of clanking, mixed with Edna's agitated voice, drifted up the spiral staircase. Familiar smells from the dungeon drifted up the stairs with such potency they singed the hairs in his nose.

"You stupid sniveling woman, why won't you at least try to help? These chains are old and rusty. If we work together we can break them."

Valorie whimpered. "No. They'll catch us and it will be even worse."

"Worse than being in shackles and chains? I'd rather die. If I get my hands on that man, I'll strangle him."

Metal against rock reverberated and bounced off the walls like the echo in a canyon. Drake admired Edna's persistence. Banging the chains against the wall was rather useless, but he admired her spunk. He slipped down the stairs anxious to hear more of the bickering between the two women. Most of the words came from Edna as she alternated between cussing at the chains, Valorie and him. Such agitation. Valorie remained silent except for an intermittent plea for the other woman to stop banging the chains and risk making their captors angry.

He reached the bottom step and held up the torch. Edna's eyes blazed. She strained at the chains and cursed him.

"Tsk, tsk, Edna my dear. So much anger will kill you."

"You sorry son of a…"

"Please. Should a lady use such foul language?"

Edna gritted her teeth, but she still glared at him with hatred. He wasn't sure whether to feel offended or very pleased he evoked such a strong emotion from this feisty little wench.

She spoke in a precise tone. "I'd kill you with my bare hands if they weren't chained to this wall. What do you want with me, you lying ba…?"

"What? You're angry I told a little fib?"

"You are an outright manipulative deceiver. I would have never gotten into the limo if I'd known the truth."

"Of course you wouldn't have." He chuckled. "But then you've never lied, have you? Your lust for power and money brought you to my palace. Isn't that fact what has you so upset? You've manipulated yourself right to the top of your firm haven't you? So who is the deceiver here?"

"I never pretended to be something I'm not. You offered me a job as your attorney and an opportunity to be involved in your business. You said nothing about shackles and chains."

"So I left out a few details. You'd never do such a terrible thing yourself, would you? Especially not in a courtroom. I've given you what you wanted. You put yourself in those chains from your greed. Until I know you won't double-cross me, you'll stay in them."

"I'll get out of here somehow, and you'll be sorry you ever came to me."

"Right." He laughed. "You'll get Valorie over here to help you escape—bang the rusty chains against the wall I suppose." He laughed even louder. "You're so in control of everyone and everything, but you can't even get a sniveling weakling to do your bidding. Of course, I don't blame you really. Poor thing is scared out of her wits. Hmmm, she is afraid of…" he paused and closed his eyes. "Yes. She fears even being afraid. Now that has got to be some sort of incurable phobia."

He hissed at Valorie who jumped back and hit her head against the wall. He lunged at her and she screamed. He laughed again.

"Don't worry my sweet." He caressed her face with his hand. "I'm off to add some more lovelies to our little game, but I will return. You have time to quiver in anticipation. Are you afraid of Edna, too? She does have a fierce little bark, doesn't she? But I think she talks big. Intimidation tactics worked rather well for her until now. You keep resisting her and stay in the comfort zone of your little bed. You might watch out for these though."

He swept the torch down and Valorie froze at the sight of two large spiders on the end of her bed. "Maybe Edna can control them for you. She isn't worth much else, and she knows it."

He turned to Edna. "You poor little girl, has all the wealth changed who you really are? Mommy and Daddy are so proud of you. They aren't ashamed of you, even when you won't acknowledge them as your parents."

Her eyes narrowed while her hands balled into fists, but she remained silent. He winked at her and swooped up the stairs, loving the sound of his laughter against Edna's angry curses and Valorie's whimpers.

Blood rushed through his veins and pounded against his eardrums. Every pulse beat thrummed in his veins as he imagined the real beginning of his game.

Chapter 19

Charissa slammed her tray on the table. "I've had it."

Haniel looked up from a book. "Let me guess, Ann?"

"Who else?" She rolled her eyes. "I swear that woman is out to get me, and I probably gave her the ammunition she needs. I can see the insubordination write up now."

He shook his head. "Baby Girl, if you know her game, why do you let her rile you so much?"

"I don't know. I used to control myself, but she makes me so mad. She finds every little thing I do wrong. Then does she pull me into an office or somewhere private to discuss my mistake? Noovo. She reprimands me in front of everyone — doctors, aides, and even patients and their families. It is so unprofessional."

She sighed. "I don't know if this is a test of my will or maybe God's way of leaving me so dissatisfied I can't stand to be here anymore."

Those eyes of his unsettled her. She knew that look too well. His next words would be something profound. She anticipated the chills from his uncanny ability to read her mind and say the right thing. She hungered for those words to calm her spirit and leave her ready for another battle against

Ann or the world. The silence draped her mind and washed away the anger.

"Charissa, what do you want?"

She cocked her head. "To go away and work with orphans. You know that."

"I know your heart."

"Then why are you asking what I want?"

No answer.

"What? I don't understand."

He repeated the question. "What is it you really want?"

The food on her plate swam as she pressed fingers against her temples. "I'm tired of fighting. I try so hard and can't please anyone. I'm lonely and scared. Okay, I'll admit it. I keep pushing but nothing changes. The only time I ever felt loved and needed was with the orphans. I get how they feel. My dad abandoned me, and my mother poured herself into a boyfriend. I was just there, and now all she ever talks about is my needing a husband. I can't pull one out of thin air. Lord knows I try to be a good woman, but no one wants me. Not even you — at least not that way."

She waited again, but he kept quiet. She finally gave up and raised her head to meet his stare. His eyes drilled into her. Kindness radiated from every pore of this man, and for one moment, sadness flickered across his face. Then he spoke.

"You have such a compassionate heart – especially for children. Perhaps some changes need to happen in you before you go running away to any foreign country. Could it be you really want the love of these children for yourself more than what you give them?"

She bit her lower lip. The words stung in spite of the tenderness in his voice.

"I'm sorry your father left when you were little and your mom hurt you over the years, too. Maybe it's why you have such a hard time trusting — even trusting God."

Charissa clenched her teeth and fought back the impulse to yell. "I don't trust men because they always let me down, but how dare you say I don't trust God?"

"In many ways, yes, you trust him, but do you really? I don't see evidence of faith when you continually talk about helping orphans but do nothing about your dream. Why aren't you pursuing it?"

She rearranged the food on her plate and stabbed at a vegetable. "I keep waiting for doors to open, but they never do. Maybe it's a stupid dream, and I've deceived myself all of these years into believing God placed some special call on my life. Maybe he's forgotten all about me, and what I really need is to get over myself and just do my job."

"Is that what you really think?"

He exasperated her with those perfectly placed questions. "I don't know what to think any more. It seems if I were really supposed to work with orphans like I want, it wouldn't be so hard. Why doesn't God make things happen if my dreams are what he wants for me?"

"Perhaps he's waiting for you to ask." A playful smile crinkled around his eyes.

She glared at him. "I have asked for years."

"Hmmm. And has he answered anything?"

She chewed on a fingernail while the picture of an expired passport flashed across her brain. How far had she gone to pursue even the most simple tasks in preparation for returning to another country? Memories of orphanages within a few hours' drive danced across her forehead, creating an ache. It wasn't what she wanted though. The excitement of traveling to other countries fueled her discouragement.

"Maybe. It doesn't matter right now anyway. If I don't get back upstairs, Ann will make sure I don't have the means to even consider doing anything."

She rose from the table. Haniel stood and moved close. His muscular arms wrapped around her. She resisted at first, annoyed with his uncanny gift of well-worded challenges and baffled by the way he influenced, but made her crazy at the same time. Still, his compassion melted her irritation as she relinquished her weariness to his strength. She almost trusted him completely. The realization cascaded fear and confusion from head to heart.

She pulled away from his grasp. "I really have to go now."

His smile defused the few shreds of aggravation remaining. "Everything will work out. Think through things. You know the truth."

She nodded but wished her heart felt the same confidence. So many questions…so few answers.

Chapter 20

Drake waited with CEO, Peter Massey. Within two days of working for Allied Consultants Corporation, he secured his way into this meeting with the top man.

He had not met his target, Dierdre Cokeley, but everything he heard about her since arriving confirmed Smitty's report. He primed himself to flip her world.

Drake drummed his fingers on the conference table and licked his lips in anticipation of Deirdre's arrival.

He turned to Peter. "Where is everybody? Doesn't this company believe in starting meetings on time?"

Before Massey could answer, two junior associates rushed into the conference room. Drake smiled. Tweedledum and Tweedledummer. Their real names meant nothing to him. As direct reports of his target, they provided endless information, and never knew he wanted it.

Tweedledum, the bolder of the two, said, "Whew. Got caught in traffic this morning. I was scared to death Madagascar beat us."

Peter frowned at him.

Drake asked, "Madagascar?"

Tweedledummer chuckled. "That's where they first discovered a man-eating plant. Peter hates it, but only because he's Dierdre's boss, and she shields her real self from him. The rest of us risk getting eaten alive every day."

Peter turned to Drake. "The men around here seem to think she is a man-eater. I've not found that to be the case. Granted, she can be a little tough and harsh at times."

Tweedledum said, "No disrespect sir, but it fits her precisely. Sorry, but if you weren't at the top, you'd understand. Every time she calls me into her office, I cringe knowing the man-eating plant will leave me with far less butt than I had when I entered. If there were a man haters club of North America, she would be the president – hands down, no competition."

"It's still disrespectful. I'll admit she doesn't seem to respect or trust men much, but not one of you can keep up with her. At least not until now. I think Drake here might give her a run for the money. He's got the degree and ambition to become a vice-president very soon."

Dierdre appeared at the door and Drake knew from the expression on her face she hadn't missed Peter's words, which worked to his advantage. From all accounts, she thrived on competition and the thrill of beating an opponent.

Madagascar.

So Smitty hadn't exaggerated her bitter hatred of all men. The scowl on her face and emptiness in her eyes screamed agony from the depth of an embittered soul. Her muscular body fit nicely into tailored pants as she slid into the seat beside Peter. Her perfectly layered and styled short red hair emphasized the power and control she commanded from the moment of her entrance. Even Peter seemed to shrink beside her.

Drake relished Dierdre. He straightened in his chair, ready for a challenge. This one would be incredibly fun and very purposeful in his little game. The woman's deep anger oozed out and filled the room with its presence. He drank in the stench of her decaying heart, the vile bitterness overpowering his senses.

Even her tone prickled his skin. "Sorry I'm late. The traffic this morning…"

Peter cut her off. "No problem, Dierdre. We all just arrived ourselves. I'd like you to meet Drake Hannibal. He's only been here a few days, but he's proven himself quite remarkable. Either of you will make a great vice-president of marketing, but the two of you together might rule the world."

The scowl on her face spoke volumes. "I do my best work alone, Peter."

"Yes, but you tend to offend people. I think you can learn a lot from Drake in the art of finesse and charm."

"I don't need some man to teach me anything about charm."

The two associates snickered and then cowered like whipped puppies when Dierdre cut her eyes around to them.

Peter said, "Dierdre, you are my best employee. Lord knows we wouldn't have half of our accounts without your tireless effort. With Drake beside you, we'll double our business. Trust me; he's as much of a workaholic as you are. Maybe if you work together, both of you can find a little down time and still be more productive. "

"I can do fine without him, but thanks for the offer."

"It wasn't an offer, Dierdre. It's time for you to learn to play nice. There are too many men in this business and frankly, you don't have a great reputation for showing respect. If you can't treat others with dignity, Drake will be my vice-president, and he might let you stay on as director."

She threw Peter a venomous look. Drake waited for a similar glower directed at him, but instead she shoved back her chair.

"Fine. I hope you know what you're doing because I don't have time to carry some good for nothing man around on my coattails." She stormed from the room.

Peter shook his head, drawing in a deep breath. "Went well, don't you think? Okay, so she has a few sharp corners. Her brilliant ideas work though. It's an amazing sight when she gets in the focused zone. Good luck with her."

Drake laughed. "I love a good challenge. I'll have no problem with her. She just wants control."

And I'm the master of making a woman believe she has control – even though it's seldom true.

"Good." He gestured at the other men. "These two are at your disposal. Anything either you or Dierdre need, let them know. Now let me brief you on the assignment I have for the two of you."

Chapter 21

Over the next week, Drake patiently accepted Dierdre's sarcasm and disrespect. He let her think everything was under her control, but in every moment possible, he manipulated her. He put suggestions into her head, but behind her back, he tweaked the ideas and made them his own. As Peter delighted over their joint efforts, her glares directed at Drake grew in intensity. Neither gave the other much credit but instead interjected their ideas. Fierce competition ensued. Each day raised her level of irritability, but Peter pulled her back into line with repeated instructions to play nice.

As she approached the edge of civility with Drake, he set up a major showdown. Hours after every employee left and no doubt slept in their little beds, Dierdre oscillated between frantic tapping at the keyboard, closing her eyes in deep thought, and searching through files and notes. The light on her desk cast a soft glow in the darkened building. She finally stretched and kicked off her shoes in preparation for more work.

He shook his head, poured liquid from a small vile into a wine glass, and approached her door with glasses and two bottles of wine.

"Truce?"

She eyed him with suspicion. "Why?"

"We can keep fighting or help each other. Peter threw us a curveball with a tight deadline. Maybe he has someone else waiting in the wings and wants us both to fail. He's tired of the bickering."

"Fine. I have some ideas, but my brain hurts. I'll be here for hours before I can finish on my own."

"Exactly. But with both of us, maybe we can finish and surprise everyone."

He kept her glass full while they discussed the current project. They brainstormed well into the wee hours of the morning. She unfolded a brilliant proposal, jotted down a few notes and laid out the entire plan for him in detail before she finally passed out on the sofa in her office.

Amazing how her mind worked. Peter had massively undersold the woman's abilities. She even envisioned the best graphics for the presentation. Passion for this game left him as wired as if he consumed multiple cups of espresso.

Drake returned to his office and spent the remainder of the night in fevered work on the proposal. As the first light broke through the window, he laid it on Peter's desk with a personal note. "Dierdre has excellent brainstorming abilities. She led me to this idea. I hope it meets your expectations. Drake."

He rushed to his nearby hotel, napped, showered and returned in time for the fireworks.

He watched from the break room as Peter burst into Dierdre's office and found her sleeping. "Dierdre?" He saw the empty bottles and only one glass. "What is this?"

She stirred from a very sound sleep and wiped drool from the corner of her mouth with the heel of her hand. "I must have dozed off while we were working last night."

The redness of Peter's neck pleased Drake. This was better than he expected.

"Perhaps a little less wine while you were working would have left you alert enough to actually help Drake with the proposal."

"What?"

She leaped to her feet and grabbed the folder from Peter. Horror inundated her face as she flipped through each page.

"This is my idea. He got me drunk and stole my idea."

She turned and riffled through her desktop in a frantic search for her notes. "Drake. You snake. Get in here now."

He approached the door feigning innocence and fear. He must be careful to hide the smugness welling up inside. "Yes, dear Dierdre?"

"What did you do with my notes? Tell Peter. Tell him I came up with this—all of it. All you did was fill my wine glass and nod in agreement to every detail."

"Oh my dear, wine isn't good on an empty stomach. Don't you remember? We brainstormed, and then you fell asleep. You must have had such a vivid dream; but thank you so much. This was my greatest idea ever, and I owe it to you. Peter, I couldn't have done it without our little brainstorming session."

Smoke rose in her eyes. Her neck veins bulged as her face darkened to match her hair. Drake laughed. When she stomped out of her office, he laughed harder.

She returned and yelled, "Get out of *my* office."

Drake snarled like a mad dog. "Lay off the wine, baby, and get your act together. You can't take power over me with your little manipulations and attitude. I know your game, and Peter can see it too."

Peter retrieved the folder from her desk and shook his head, disgust scowling his face. Drake maintained complete control and followed him from the office. She set herself up better than he hoped.

By noon, the rumors ricocheted between every workstation and office. Various versions of the story reverberated through the halls and in the break room. Drake trembled at the speculation over pending announcements naming the new VP. He didn't want or need the position, but he reveled in the attention. Every single woman, and some of the married ones, flirted with him. Posers. Still, he might as well take advantage of the offers while they all kissed up to him.

He drank in the momentary pleasure of Dierdre's embarrassment and defeat. All through the day, she maneuvered through meetings with her shoulders squared and head erect. Admirable. She kept her distance from him, and as she walked through each presentation or meeting with clients, her eyes darted around the room. Midway through the afternoon, she eased out the nearest exit.

He laced his fingers behind his head and watched as she passed beneath his window. She looked so defenseless from his towering position. Perhaps he pushed a little too hard, but now she knew the truth about her boss's loyalty. There wasn't any. Good ole Peter threw her over for the new man without a question of what actually went down.

If he gave her a couple more days to seethe in bitterness and then threw out the bait, she'd bite like a newborn fish. He considered the possibilities of his world with her and Edna by his side. Such an unstoppable trio, if he could utilize her hatred. Giddiness filled his mind and restlessness overtook him. He left the office intent on a night full of unbridled pleasure in celebration for his day's work.

Chapter 22

By the end of the next day, Drake wearied of the constant murmurs. The whole scene bored him. Patience was a virtue, but no one ever described him as virtuous.

He waited until everyone cleared the office, and poked his head around the doorframe. Dierdre's desk gleamed with order, the chair pushed close and the lamp off. Just as well. Let her stew one more night.

Tomorrow – bait and hook.

The new day arrived, and still he waited until after lunch. He approached Dierdre's office and waved a white handkerchief around the doorframe before poking in his head.

She scowled. "What do you want?"

"Truce." He stepped into the office and closed the door.

"Yeah – that's what you said last time. Of all men, why should I trust you?"

"Because we both know the truth about your status here. Peter doesn't value you or your brilliant mind. He'll never make a woman vice-president – you know I'm right. He thinks a woman belongs in the kitchen, barefoot and pregnant. You've seen his wife and their multitude of little Peters."

She crossed her arms. "He's the same as every man then – an untrustworthy pig. Congratulations. You get to become one of his cookie cutter VPs. What do you want with me?"

"Oh, my dear Dierdre, I didn't come here by accident. I have a proposal for you; but we can't discuss it in the office." He looked over his shoulder. "The walls have ears and they echo long and loud." He lowered his voice. "Let's break out of here early and hit the golf course. We can talk there. Then maybe we'll have an extravagant dinner — on Peter, of course."

She smirked. "I know some of the best places in Nashville for dinner. At least if I go out, it will be after leaving him a fat bill."

"Good. Trust me. What I did was for your good, to reveal the truth."

She raised her eyebrows. "Well forgive me if I don't quite believe you, but I'll at least listen. You tricked me, but I let down my guard. It won't happen again, so don't even try." A glint crossed her irises.

"I know you aren't a fool, and I fully expect you to eat me alive if I cross you again, Madagascar."

The glint morphed into a full-blown carving knife. "People think I don't know the meaning behind their petty nickname, but you're right. You ever cheat me again, I will make you beg for mercy."

Drake laughed. "I love you, Mada. You are my perfect match. We can go far together."

He sauntered out of her office in absolute adoration of the hostility in her soul.

∞∞∞∞∞∞∞∞∞∞∞∞∞∞

Dierdre remained quiet through the entire round of golf and all the way to the restaurant. No matter how hard she tried, he beat her at every hole.

Keep her under my thumb a little longer and preserve the competition. Let her see who's in control.

She waited through dinner as he regaled about all his glorious feats. Finally, curiosity crept up and spilled out.

"So when are you going to share this proposal with me, Drake?"

"Wow. I expected you to ask me at least by the third hole. Your patience is much better than mine."

"Everything about me is better than you. So what's the deal?"

"Can I trust you?" He hesitated. "Well, I suppose I'll have to, won't I?"

"You brought me here. Now either serve it up, or I'm walking away."

"Okay, okay. So much for your virtue of patience. I've neglected sharing a little information about myself with anyone. You see, I own a rather prestigious little firm myself and I'm looking for a marketing VP. My sources tell me you're the best. They didn't lie. You have a brilliant mind, and the fact you hate men actually works in my favor. I keep hiring these wonderfully intelligent women who mutate into dingbats when they swoon over some man, and then they get married, have babies and quit." He paused.

"Keep talking."

"In spite of your feelings about men, you appear quite loyal to this company, and you've worked hard to reach your position. Without me around, you were Peter's obvious choice for VP. He sure wasn't looking in the direction of Tweedledum and Tweedledummer."

"Who?"

"The two juniors."

She closed her eyes and sniffed. "It takes both of their brains to make one."

Drake laughed. "You're his best employee, and for the sake of his company, he might have promoted you. Yet, he brought me onboard as viable competition for the position. I wanted you to see the truth about this man, so I could steal you away from him. I knew it was the only way you'd abscond."

"Well you definitely showed me his true colors, but what's in it for me? What's keeping me from telling him about this offer of yours, backed up with proof of your true identity? He's a snake, but I could take this little tidbit to him, watch security escort you out the door, and still have the job."

"Of course, but you won't. We'll work out the details of your contract, but let's say double your salary, stock options, a very generous expense account, a limousine with the driver at your command, and of course much time with me. How's that for a start?"

"I'll tolerate the time with you. The rest sounds intriguing, but I want it in writing."

He reached across the table and lifted her chin so their eyes met. "I wouldn't expect less. For you, I'll even sign it in blood."

His skin tingled as her eyes took on a deep, black luster.

She swallowed hard and her voice came out in a whisper. "What's the catch?"

"It's now or never. I've been away from my business too long. After dinner, we return to the office, leave our resignations and disappear."

She nodded in agreement. "Let's go then."

They left the restaurant and returned to the office building. Within minutes, she appeared in his doorway with a resignation letter in hand.

"I already had it written after yesterday."

He chuckled, finished his letter and printed it. Together they left the documents on Peter's desk with their office badges and rode the elevator down. A black limo waited at the curb. Dierdre looked at Drake.

"I took the liberty," he said. "Smitty will take you to get whatever you need, and then to my home. He'll take very good care of you. I have one more day of business in the area and then I'll return."

She climbed into the car with a low whistle. "Sweet. I'll see you soon, and you better have a contract prepared for me by then."

"Not a problem." He closed the door behind her. "Take her away, Smitty."

He watched as the car drove into the dark, empty street.

"You can't win against me, Madagascar. You're mine whether you know it or not. I will see you soon, my sweet, and I'll have a contract for you. Let's see if you sign it with *your* blood."

The wind howled around him and swept him up in the moment. He let the night engulf and move him away, closer to his last game piece.

Chapter 23

Charissa brushed her hair and admired herself in the mirror.

Not too bad. Losing ten pounds sure couldn't hurt, though.

Although she didn't expect more than friendship with Haniel, she looked forward to this evening. She reflected on the many times they got together and talked for hours over pizza then watched a movie or played cards. Lately, her work schedule and church activities limited her time with him. At least he cared about her. Maybe deep friendship was better than stupid romantic love that ended at the first quarrel.

Guilt rolled over her, a heavy fog bearing down on her. She wasn't that busy. Many of her nights consisted of little more than mindless television shows. The solitude of the little cave of an apartment comforted her. Maybe a little too much. What happened to her passion for life? What made her prefer the hypnotic state of an electronic box over people? Over anything for that matter?

The doorbell shot through her thoughts. She shook them from her conscious mind and hurried to the door. Rusty barked, but when she opened the door, his tail wagged and he panted until Haniel petted him.

"Hey, boy. It's good to see you again." He looked at Charissa. "You look beautiful tonight. It's been too long."

She gave him a tight hug. "I've missed you too."

The night passed far too quickly. They hit on one subject and then moved on to another. They ate pizza, watched a movie and then talked some more before deciding to play a card game. She relaxed into the familiarity of a comfortable friendship.

Out of nowhere, a notion ripped through her mind.

What would it be like if he kissed me?

A rush of blood pulsed in her ears. The cards in her hand flickered and blurred. Heat rose in her face, while she envisioned a bright redness creeping up from her neck. She peeked at him, hoping he didn't notice. If he saw it, he graciously said nothing, sparing more embarrassment.

He raised eyebrows and smiled. "I really enjoy your friendship, Charissa. I've missed these times with you."

She glanced up from her cards. Her voice caught. She cleared her throat and tried again. "Me too."

She dared not say anything more. Blasted emotions. They always snuck up on her, and if she acted on them, they would ruin everything. Obviously, this man wanted nothing more than a friendship, and she either accepted it, or risked losing him altogether. Maybe the ideal of love meant more to her than actually being in love with him.

She found him attractive, but how well did she really know him? She trusted him, but those old doubts reared their ugly heads and reminded her of all the men she counted on in the past. None of them lasted very long. Yes, she was better off keeping Haniel as a friend and forgetting the whole romance thing.

He broke the silence. "Are you okay?"

"I'm fine. It's just…"

As if to protect her from answering, her cell phone chirped. She glanced at the number—no name. "I should probably take this. It might be someone from work."

She answered the call. "Hello?"

Drake's voice came across louder than expected – enough Haniel heard it.

"Charissa, my love, I've missed you. What are you doing?"

She flinched and regretted her decision to answer. Anything to get out of gut-level honesty, but with Haniel's opinion of Drake, this might not be good. Too late. She considered telling him she'd call him back later and then not admit it was him. Haniel's clouded expression said he knew.

"Hello, Drake. I'm hanging out with a friend. What's up?"

"Oh? You aren't letting some other man move in while I'm out of town are you?"

She quivered. "He's just a friend."

"I'm sure. I'm envious I can't be there, holding you close."

Charissa didn't answer.

"I don't want to keep you from your friend, so I'll make this quick. Are you busy on Saturday?"

"Not really."

"How about a day at the lake? Like we talked about. I'll be back in town Friday night and, more than anything, I want to spend the day with you—maybe the entire weekend if you want."

"I would enjoy a day at the lake." She glanced over at Haniel. "Look, I really need to go."

"Of course. I'll see you around 9:00. We'll start with breakfast and take it from there."

"Okay. Bye."

She bit her bottom lip and waited for Haniel to say something. He stroked his beard as he studied the cards in his hand. Disappointment flooded his eyes. Queasiness flitted through her stomach. She much preferred anger, but the silent dissatisfaction ripped through her gut, producing a tidal wave of anxiety. If he yelled she could retort in anger and defend her actions, accuse him of control issues.

Instead, concentration lines his face, but she doubted his pondering centered on their silly card game. He'd been blatantly honest about his dislike of Drake. If only she hadn't taken the stupid call. Awkwardness hung between them as each waited for the other to speak. She hated being a letdown. He won.

She detested her timidity, as if she owed this man an apology or explanation. "That was Drake."

"I know."

The chasm between them grew. She didn't want to care, but she did. "He's being nice. I said something about going out on the lake."

"Do you really think spending the entire day with him is a good idea?"

Something inside of her snapped. "I don't know why you don't like him. What did he ever do to you, anyway? You told me I should stay away from him, but not why."

"Charissa, you need to trust me on this one. You're playing with fire. Things are not always what they seem."

"Well that's certainly the truth, because I thought you were my friend and might be happy someone might stay in my life for a change. Here's this handsome, apparently wealthy man who enjoys spending time with me, and you're mad about it. I suppose you're gonna tell me not to go with him on Saturday and expect I'll obey you with no good reason."

The brown of his eyes deepened. The flash of light from them stilled her tongue while her heart sunk.

The softness of his voice unnerved her. "He's dangerous. If you go, it won't be good."

"That's your opinion." She swallowed. "I'm not sure it's a good enough reason."

Haniel stood. "I should leave." He walked to the door and looked back at her. "Soon you'll have to choose which of us to trust. Choose wisely."

The door closed behind him without his normal admonition to double lock. The quietness deafened her. Hot tears pushed against eyelids and forced past her resolve. She ran to the door and flung it opened. He was already gone.

She retreated into the apartment, turned both locks, twirled and slid down the door as grief released into bitter weeping.

Chapter 24

Drake drove along Highway 41 to Smyrna. The deep grey of the clouds matched his mood much better than the lush green of the area. Only one more stop and a few hours until his plane landed in Texas where Charissa awaited him. He preferred the hotel breakfast, but Smitty assured him he needed the waitress at some little diner. From his associate's description, she might fit his plan well.

His focus drifted to the ancient Biblical town of Smyrna. He hoped this one in the shadows of the country music capital lacked the faithful attitude of the legendary town. Smitty certainly enjoyed roaming the countryside. Drake failed to see why. Hills lined both sides of the road and the variegated colors in the rocks and trees served only to depress him.

Fortunately, his drive lasted a very short time. He followed directions to the diner and pulled into the parking lot at 9:00 a.m. Still early, but late enough most of the regular customers were long gone, off to their meaningless lives.

He checked his image in the rearview mirror. The random strands of grey throughout his dark hair aged him a little, but not too much. The neatness of his trimmed mustache and deep laugh lines fit perfectly for this scenario. He missed the beard, but looked every bit the part of a concerned father. Satisfied, he pushed open the door and grabbed his newspaper from the front seat before heading inside.

A cute, young waitress greeted him. "Good morning, sir. Sit wherever you want. Coffee?"

"Absolutely." He chose a booth at the back away from the windows, yet with a full view of the parking lot and entire restaurant. He perused the menu. Typical country fare.

As the waitress approached him, he glanced at her nametag. "Shamira. Unique name for an ordinary place."

"Thanks. My mom always preferred being different from the average person."

She set a mug of coffee on the table. Purple bruises contrasted the pale skin of her forearm. "What'll it be this morning?"

Pictures of his mother flashed through his mind. Indignation filled his nostrils along with the aroma of coffee. "Those are some ugly bruises."

She pulled back her arm and tucked it to her side. "I'm such a clutz...always running into things."

He nodded. "Everything on the menu sounds good. Give me the breakfast special – over easy on the eggs."

"Got it. I'll have it right out for you."

Drake opened up his paper but cocked his head to one side. The bruises on Shamira's arms confirmed Smitty's story, but he wanted to gauge how easily he might sway her away from this place. He strained to hear the soft voices as an older woman behind the counter pleaded with her.

"Honey, you have to get away from Doug. He's gonna kill you one of these days. I can't believe he's been hitting you all this time, and you didn't tell us."

"Oh, Selma, I didn't want to get you all mixed up in this mess, and if Alex knew, he'd go after Doug. Anyway, I'm almost there—been hiding money for months. I can't go off with nothing."

"You can always come stay with us." She looked back at the cook. "Alex doesn't have to know the whole story, 'though he ain't blind. He's been seeing things for a long time, you know. I told him he was crazy--you would have told me if something like that was happening. You should have told me."

"I couldn't. I don't want you or Alex getting hurt because of me, and admit it, Alex isn't getting any younger. Doug could hurt him bad."

"The way he does you?"

The infamous Alex interrupted their conversation. "Breakfast special up."

Shamira grabbed the plate and coffee pot. "It'll be fine, Selma. Things will change soon. You gotta have faith. That's what you always tell me."

The older woman shook her head. "Yeah, well sometimes you gotta put a little walking to your faith, and I think you're walking time has arrived."

She grabbed a cloth and scrubbed the counter with such force Drake wondered if she might tangle with the abuser. She might win.

Shamira placed the food in front of Drake and refilled his mug. He closed his hand over her forearm. The bruises fell in an almost perfect pattern beneath his fingers and thumb.

"The only thing you bumped into was some man's hand." He reached up with his other hand and gently turned her head. Makeup covered a large bruise at her hairline, but the darkness peeked through. "And apparently you bumped into his other hand there."

She pulled away from him. "It's none of your business."

"I'm sorry. I didn't mean to pry, but your boss over there seems worried about you. I didn't mean to eavesdrop, but I caught a little of your conversation." He paused. She kept her face expressionless. "I have several businesses and a very secure home. If you want to get away from this man, I can help."

"Really? And what's in it for you?"

"Nothing. I used to watch my father pummel my mother. Besides, I have a daughter about your age. If some man were beating the crap out of her on a regular basis, I'd want someone to step in and give her a means of escape. That's all."

Her eyes misted over and she closed them, but tears crept down her cheeks anyway.

A truck whipped into the parking lot and stopped short of the plate glass window. The man jumped out with a wad of bills in his hand and crashed through the diner door.

Terror covered Shamira. Perfect timing. No one had to announce Doug.

He crossed the room in a few steps and grabbed the young woman's shoulders. "What is this?" He slapped her with the money. "What have you got up your sleeve? Huh? Hiding this from me. You wasn't planning on walking out on me, was you?"

Selma picked up the telephone. He whirled in her direction.

"Put it down. This ain't got nothing to do with you, b..."

Shamira interrupted him. "Doug, let's go outside and talk about this. It's all a big misunderstanding. You're right. It isn't anyone else's business. We can go out to the truck."

Soured whiskey from his clothes mingled with a fresh round of cheap bourbon from his breath. His bloodshot eyes landed on Drake and the accusation in them hit before the words spilled out of his foul mouth.

"You trying to protect this jerk? You shacking up with him – maybe making a little money on the side? Is that where you got all this?"

She pushed him to the door. "You know better, babe. C'mon. Let's take it outside."

Selma waited until they cleared the door and picked up the phone again. Drake rose and crossed to the counter.

"What good will that do? Call 9-1-1 and they'll lock him up for a little while, but he'll come back. I'll handle this."

He walked outside as Doug threw the money into the truck and hit Shamira on the side of the head. She fell against the vehicle. He grabbed her arm and hit her again across the cheek with a closed fist. As he started to hit her for the third time, Drake slid his arm around the young man's neck and jerked him backwards. He regained his footing and swayed forward, his hands flailing against air.

Drake laughed and jabbed an already red nose. Blood streamed from one nostril. He hit him again, this time on the side of the head, then brought up the opposite hand and shoved his fist against the jawbone. He waited for the crack and repeated the motion when he heard none. Doug fell hard onto the pavement. Asphalt dug into his temple, blood oozing from the wound.

Drake reached out his hand to Shamira. She cowered beside the truck for a few seconds, accepted the hand, jumping over Doug's unconscious body, and sobbed into the older man's chest.

"It's okay now. It's all gonna be okay."

He peeled her away, retrieved the money and put it into her hands. Alex burst through the door with a baseball bat in hand, Selma behind him. She wrapped her arms around the shaking girl, and gently led her inside. Drake followed.

Selma handed him a wet towel for his hands.

Drake's tone remained even. "Honey, you have a little while. He's drunk – probably would have passed out even if I hadn't hit him. He shouldn't have hit you in front of me. My offer still stands."

Shamira's voice quavered. "I...I'm not sure. I appreciate what you did."

Alex said, "You can always stay with Selma and me. Ain't no way you're going back home to that animal."

Drake seethed at the sudden show of protection. "She'll be safer far away, where he can't find her."

Selma eyed him. Questions hung in the air without a word, but she asked them anyway. "She doesn't even know you. How do we know you'll take care of her, and not do something worse than Doug did?"

He tilted back his head and sighed. "You don't know. Maybe you'll have to trust me—put a little action to your faith."

He pulled out money for his breakfast.

Selma refused. "It's on us. You didn't have to get into it with Doug, but he would have really hurt her if you hadn't stepped in and stopped him."

Alex pouted. "I would have stopped him. Just didn't get my baseball bat fast enough."

Drake patted him on the shoulder. "You had my back."

He handed a business card to the girl. "I'm in town for a few more hours. I sincerely hope you'll take me up on my offer."

He headed for the door.

"Wait."

Drake turned back around. She clung to the older woman.

"I have to go, Selma. This is my chance to get away from Doug - start over fresh. I can't wait any more, not after he found my money. It's the only way. I'll be fine. I told you things would change."

"I know." Selma wiped a tear from the girl's cheek with her apron. "I don't feel right about you going off with a total stranger."

Selma looked at Drake, suspicion coursing over the hard lines of her face. She turned to Shamira. "You better call me or I'll send the law out looking for you."

"I will as soon as I get settled. You've been a mama to me. I can never repay all you two have done for me."

The young woman hugged her surrogate parents, removed her apron and left the diner. As they passed Doug, he groaned. She stomped his stomach.

"I wanted to do that for a long time."

Drake chuckled. "Glad to give you the opportunity."

She shivered. Her momentary courage visibly deflated as she climbed into the passenger's seat and melted into a puddle of tears. The skies opened up. Rain pelted the windshield as the car turned in the direction of Nashville. Lightening trailed through the sky in front of the car, and the peal of thunder roiled with the plans churning in his mind.

Chapter 25

A cacophony of birds ushered in early morning outside Charissa's windows, their song an ironic blend of sounds. Doves cooed, blackbirds squawked, and a myriad of other birds joined the chorus with an assortment of inflections. She snuggled down deeper into her bed. Sleep beckoned her to linger, refuse facing the day.

"Ugh. Not yet. It can't be morning." She opened one eye. Stupid birds. The dim outline of a large tree infuriated her. The sun hadn't even risen, yet those blasted bird songs pulled her from a night of restless sleep, disturbed by Haniel's words and the way he left. She shut her eyes against the dim light and willed herself back to sleep.

She drifted between dozing, anger and shame. What did Haniel have against Drake anyway? She mulled over his motivation. He had no right to tell her what she should or shouldn't do. His friendship meant the world to her. He looked out for her and many times pulled her from the claws of despair, influencing her perception. But Drake certainly didn't look dangerous. Haniel gave her no real reason for not going. She hated being pushed to the limit of choosing between the two of them. Besides, it was one date, a simple day at the lake.

So easy, and yet, apprehension taunted her as it did all during the night. Drake, charming and attractive, wanted to spend the day with her. Was that so bad? For some reason, Haniel detested this man. She disliked him too at first, but dinner turned out okay. Maybe, just maybe, for once in his life Haniel was wrong. A possible future with Drake both terrified and exhilarated her. She draped her hopes all over this date even to the point of risking a precious treasure of friendship.

Why couldn't life be easy?

She trusted God for so long and now, facing this day, she cried out for direction and peace. Neither came. She heard only Haniel's voice as she dragged out of bed and into the kitchen for coffee. Mug in hand, she slumped on her sofa and eyed the Bible on her table. She should read it. Lately the words meant little, tasting like dust in her mouth—mere words. If God was real, why did He leave her to face this world without a husband? He promised good plans for her, but trouble accompanied her most days.

What difference did today make anyway? What did Drake want? The questions picked at her brain until her head hurt.

Rusty laid his nose in her lap. She wrapped her arms around her faithful companion. His soft fur gave way to her fingers and she slid to the floor beside him, burying her face next to his. He responded with an eager, wet kiss to her cheek, a welcome assurance of his love. She evaporated into the warmth of her dog.

Everything would be okay. No matter what happened today, Haniel would forgive her. He always did. Drake couldn't be so bad, but she'd watch for hints. If she saw even a tiny red flag, she'd run from him, far and fast.

∞∞∞∞∞∞∞∞∞∞∞∞∞

Charissa finished braiding her hair, checked the mirror again and debated over the swimsuit. She looked fine, but maybe the two-piece was too suggestive even with a tank top covering it. She decided to change again and grabbed one of the other suits from the bed as her doorbell rang. Too late. Five minutes early — normally an early arrival wouldn't bother her, but today she didn't appreciate it at all. Her stomach lurched as if she stood at the rail of a giant ship with the sea rolling beneath her.

"Just a day at the lake," she whispered to herself. "No big deal."

She opened the door and met Drake's eyes, then watched as they consumed every inch of her body. He started at her eyes and moved down to her painted toenails then back up again. She swallowed down the visual ravaging and resisted the urge to slam the door in his face.

His lips curled upwards into lazy approval as he raised his eyebrows and said, "Wow. You look incredible."

Her face tingled.

He laughed."Sorry. I didn't mean to embarrass you. You took my breath away."

She rolled her eyes. "What a line."

"Well, I never claimed originality. Seriously, you caught me off guard. I've never seen your legs before."

He laughed, and she felt heat sweep up her face. She wondered how to wipe away sweat from her upper lip without being conspicuous. Behind her, Rusty growled in his most aggressive tone. She scolded him. The growl dropped to a less threatening level, but didn't dissipate completely. For a moment, she thought Drake snarled back at him, but when she looked at the man, he still wore the same goofy smile.

He said, "Are you ready? I'm famished. I hope you don't mind. I picked up some food for us instead of going out to eat. The day is too gorgeous to waste time inside, don't you think?"

"I hadn't really thought about it, but sure, that's fine." She stepped out with him and locked the door behind her.

Her spirit welled up inside of her, fought against her brain. Everything in her demanded a change of heart.

Don't go.

She pushed down the feelings. For once, she refused to let her distrust of men ruin a perfectly good day.

She turned and said, "Let's go."

Rusty's growl turned into ferocious barking.

Chapter 26

Water lapped against the small boat. Charissa looked at Drake. She imagined her father in the tan skin and hard jaw line, but this man's face lacked the pure pleasure and joy of the day. The wind left a scowl where she expected elation. Disappointment replaced her mind's portrait. She shrugged off the feeling. He wasn't her father, and maybe that meant something. Maybe he wouldn't walk away from her.

The boat picked up speed on the open water. Charissa hung tight to the railing. He hit a wave and her teeth clamped down on her tongue. He kept his eyes straight ahead, but she got the impression he watched with his peripheral vision.

She put a hand on his arm and shouted, "Slow down."

Without looking at her, he pushed the throttle forward and shot across the lake with a triumphant look covering his face. As they approached a cove, he pulled the lever back so hard she lost her balance and almost fell out of her seat.

He looked at her for the first time then. "Honey, you look pale. I thought you liked fast boats."

"I love boats, but they don't have to move like a freight train. This was supposed to be a nice, relaxing day, not a high-speed race."

He frowned and mumbled, "Sorry. I wanted to get to this place and have some food. I get a little cranky when I'm hungry."

"Okay, but going back can we keep it under 90?"

They laughed as he docked the boat at the cove's shoreline. He pulled out a large beach blanket and enormous picnic basket. She peeped inside. All her favorite foods. She didn't remember telling him she liked any of this stuff.

He pulled out a cooler filled with drinks including beer, juice, water and a bottle of champagne. His eyes dropped with an apologetic look.

He whispered, "I hope you don't mind. I see this as a celebration. We can at least make mimosas can't we?"

"I've never had one, but okay."

"Are you really innocent or playing with me?"

"My mom hated drinking, and I never wanted to displease her, so I chose not to drink. It's simple. Besides, you forget I see the aftermath of drunk driving and boating accidents where people had too much alcohol. It changes your perception."

"Well, I hope you don't mind if I have a few beers. I promise not to get drunk on you. But if you want to throw back a few, this is your golden opportunity. Relax."

"As long as you limit them, I'm not offended."

They ate in relative silence and lay back on the blanket to let the food settle. The warm sun beamed down, easing away tension. Drake poured more orange juice and champagne into a glass for her and moved so close his skin brushed hers. Disturbed by the closeness, she suggested a swim.

Without thinking, she drained the glass and slipped out of her shorts and tank top. She sprayed sunscreen over her body and offered it to Drake. He declined, but sprayed and rubbed the concoction onto her back. His touch sent sparks down the length of her spine and produced shivers in spite of the heat. She jumped up and ran to the water, not knowing whether she wanted him to follow or not. Little sirens wailed through her brain, but light-headedness blocked out their meaning.

Drake followed her into the frigid water where they played like children, oblivious to the passing of time. The sirens silenced as they swam and splashed each other. He touched her more frequently, but not in a suggestive way. The last traces of stress eased into complete relaxation. Exhausted, she leaned back into a floating position and gazed up at a blue sky. Not a small dot of a cloud messed up the perfection above. Any sense of fear she'd felt earlier disappeared when he emerged beside her and scooped her up in his arms.

He bent his head close to hers. "Tired?"

"A little."

His strong arms wrapped around her as he maneuvered through the water back to the beach. He laid her on the blanket and sunk next to her. She welcomed his touch this time. He brushed back hair with his fingertips. She strained against the overpowering look in his dark eyes. The cold black stare mesmerized her, simultaneously pulling her world to a standstill while everything spun around her. She dared not breathe as he spoke her name and softly pressed his lips against hers. When she didn't resist, he kissed her again with more force and passion. She squirmed and resisted a little as he moved his hands over her stomach and upwards. She placed a hand firmly on his.

Dark eyes flashed and fear pounded against her as the sirens returned with a gale force wailing. Then he pushed back from her. The huskiness in his voice cut through the wails.

"I won't make you do something you don't want, honey. I lost my head. The way you kissed me and gave in to my touch..."

"I'm sorry, Drake. I didn't mean to indicate I wanted more. I mean I do, but..."

"It's okay."

But the smoldering of his eyes and the tightness of his jaw left a boatload of doubt. She sat up and stared at sky blue toenails, fighting back tears. She ruined this perfect day. A warm hand touched her shoulder.

"Really, baby. I understand. Let's have some more to eat."

He brought out food she missed earlier and poured her another drink. This one contained more champagne and less juice. He held a strawberry to her mouth and waited for her to bite into it. When the juice ran down her chin, he wiped it away before sticking a finger into his mouth.

The image of her perfect day returned as they finished the food, moved the blanket into some shade and settled back for a nap. He laced his fingers through hers and kissed the tips. The earlier fears faded into a swirl of mental numbness. Drowsiness overtook her in the warmth of the afternoon, and she drifted off.

She came to full attention with a dream fresh in her mind. She hadn't slept long, but it was a hard sleep. The memories born out of her subconscious slumber ran through her brain— Haniel cautioning her about Drake. He was wrong. This man didn't seem dangerous. She leaned up on her elbow and looked into deep, black eyes. He smiled at her.

"That was a quick nap."

"Sorry. I didn't sleep well last night."

"You're even more beautiful when you are sleeping." He pulled her close and pressed his mouth against hers.

She succumbed and clung to him as he kissed her again. He rolled over and caressed her face with his hand as he continued covering her mouth and neck with his lips. His hands roamed again. She should stop him, but the exhilaration of his longing rippled over her. She didn't want the moment to end even when his hands moved close to inappropriate places. A touch high on her inner thigh slapped her back to reality.

"Drake. Please stop. We're going way too far."

"You're making me crazy, woman. You either want me or you don't."

She sobbed. "That's the hard part. It isn't because I don't want you, but I made a promise to God and myself. There are some lines I can't cross."

He pulled back as she tried to touch him. She shouldn't have let it get out of hand. She'd led him on, and now the price hit her with the repercussion of thunder. They sat in silence. His jaw flinched and he looked away from her.

Maybe Haniel really did know this man and danger lurked below the surface. Anything became a very real possibility. Panic crossed over her as she surveyed the deserted cove. He brought her out to this secluded spot with one thing on his mind. The solitude and alcohol all made sense.

What seemed an eternity passed before his shoulders dropped, and he turned his full body back. She braced herself for raging anger, in all probability a fist pounding her into the beach, but instead he wore a soft understanding.

"You're right. Women don't usually reject me – even for a good reason. I'm not used to it. Don't hold it against me for desiring a beautiful woman."

She sighed with deep relief. "I'm not beautiful, but thank you for saying it and for understanding."

"We should head back. It's getting late."

They packed up the food and blanket and climbed into the boat. He kept the throttle midway on the return trip. His face remained emotionless. He would never call her again after such an awful day.

Neither spoke as he loaded the boat and helped her into the truck. Her throat tightened as they pulled away from the docks.

Charissa's head pounded and her skin felt hot. She guzzled water from a bottle and immediately regretted it when her stomach lurched. She laid her head back against the seat, ready for a barricaded door and Rusty's watchful eyes.

"Are you okay, Charissa?"

"Too much sun and not enough water. My head hurts."

Drake reached into the console, removed a bottle of pills, and poured two into her hand. "These are for migraines. I get them sometimes."

Charissa hesitated.

Drake looked offended. "What? You think I would drug you or something?"

"No, of course not," she said.

She slipped the pills into her mouth and washed them down with the remainder of her bottled water. After all, they spent the entire day in a private spot where he could have done anything he wanted. The thought sent chills through her body. Still, she should have looked at the bottle. The pain made clear introspection impossible.

Trees and hills drifted by as the sun dipped below them. The eagles' nest would appear any moment, indicating she was almost home. As they drove, the nest never appeared. She glanced at the clock in the car and realized an hour had passed. Odd. Inks Lake to Llano normally took less than thirty minutes.

She looked out of the window. Unfamiliar surroundings stirred confusion. This didn't look like the way home. Where was Drake taking her? She started to raise her head and say something, but nausea bounced around her stomach and intense pain crashed against her skull.

She fought against the urge to protest and instead succumbed to sleep as the car drove into the night.

Chapter 27

The peaceful scene sprawled before him spurred Drake forward with one intense purpose, to replace peace with sorrow.

The cheerful songs of birds usually irritated him, but in the light of his purpose, they grew tolerable. He preferred stormy skies, but the sun's warmth intermingled with cool breezes didn't detract from his mood. Normally, any beautiful garden agitated him, but the euphoric aftertaste of capturing Charissa lingered. Approaching Haniel's garden, sheer happiness puffed out his chest as he sneaked up on his foe, ready to surprise him and deliver the news.

The scent of jasmine mixed with fresh cut grass wafted on the breeze. A stone pathway wound through a vast array of flowers and bushes, while well-placed trees shaded benches and tables strategically placed throughout the garden. Haniel knelt beside a tree where he spread colored mulch beneath it. The sun glistened off the waves of his hair.

Haniel rose. "Hello, Drake."

Annoyance surfaced from the failed attempt at surprise, but faded quickly. "I have her."

Haniel faced him. "You forget nothing gets past me. I know all about your game."

"Humpf. Do you know she chose me over you?"

Haniel stared into his eyes. "Did she?"

Drake shifted his weight and cleared his throat. "Well, perhaps not a conscious choosing. She knew we were headed the wrong direction, yet she said nothing. She chose by not choosing. A little sleep, a little slumber, a little folding of the hands to rest..." He sniffed and scratched his nose. "And she did rest. She fell into my arms and compromised herself with me. Tell me, did she ever do that for you? Well, did she?"

"And her deep sleep wasn't induced with a little something extra in her drink was it, Drake? I know you too well. You are a liar and always have been. I have an intimacy with Charissa you can't comprehend. You want me to believe she gave herself to you, but I know better. She is still faithful and soon will see the truth. Then she will choose, and it won't be you."

"Ha. That's what you hope. But where is she right now, Haniel?" Drake spat on the ground at his enemy's feet. "She sleeps in my dungeon with shackles cutting into her skin and chains binding her. And there is nothing you can do about it. I told you I'd take her from you, like I did Zoe."

A slow smile crept across Haniel's face. "You don't learn, do you, Drake? So long ago. Have you forgotten already? Do you think for a minute I wasn't prepared for this? I will bring her out of your dungeon, and your mischief will only make her stronger. So what? You won a little skirmish – not without trickery, I might add. Your tactics don't change. You did the same with me, didn't you? But I won in the end, and so will she. I told you she belongs to me. You couldn't stand it when Dad put me in the position you thought should be yours."

"I worked hard for him. It should've been mine. I earned it, and could've run things far better than you ever dreamed. But you were his only son, so whether you deserved it or not, he positioned you to take over. I'll never forgive either of you."

Bile rose in Drake's throat as his heart raced. Heat filled his chest and moved up his body until sweat flowed down his temples. He wiped it away and stared at Haniel, but the piercing brown eyes intimidated him. He closed his eyes and blew hot air through his nose, willing away the discomfort.

Haniel's controlled and calm voice irked him. "Forgiveness is your choice. I'm sorry you feel you must hurt other people to get back at Dad and me. You know I will not stand by silently while you destroy Charissa."

Drake strained against the desire to yell. His self-control waned as he looked at the calmness in his rival's face. "We'll see about that. My game isn't finished, and in the end she will choose me."

Haniel crossed his arms and planted his feet firmly on the stone pathway. The confidence on his face added to the anger in Drake's heart. "Give it your best shot."

"As if I need your permission."

Haniel raised his eyebrows. "Are you sure?"

"I've already taken her. Try to save her." In one motion, Drake grabbed a small bird from the feeder and bit off the head.

Haniel didn't flinch, but his brows narrowed and the challenge in his eyes held Drake captive. Moments passed as the two men stood, frozen in a mental battle.

Drake hurled the bird's body and spit out the head. "I'd rather kill your precious girl than let her go."

Slowly a roar rose from his throat. Unable to contain himself any longer, he turned and fled from the garden with a low snarl drifting behind him.

Chapter 28

Dull throbs radiated through Charissa's hip. She struggled between deep sleep and full consciousness. A low moan broke through the last traces of sleep with an uncertainty whether the sound came from herself or someone else.

Nearby sobs broke through, easing her mind into reality. Pain reverberated, a dull hammering behind closed eyes, accompanied by a musty dampness in the air. Cold stone pressed against her body, begging for a shift away from pressure on her hip. Knots squeezed against the base of her skull. Stiffness in her neck pleaded for a quick stress-relieving pop, a remedy learned from many tense nights in the ER.

She tilted her head to one side, stretching her neck, and stopped cold. Her eyes shot open into utter darkness. Mind reeling, both hands flew to her neck where cold metal greeted icy fingertips. She jerked to an upright position. Steel cut into her neck a split second before something yanked her backwards. A gasp escaped followed by a dull thud as excruciating pain split through the back of her head. She reached behind her head and steel slapped her face. She recoiled and screamed only to hit her head again.

A snicker cut through the heartbeat hammering in her ears. The sobs ceased. Sounds bombarded her from different directions and bounced off the walls—voices, growls, hisses. Shivers ensued at the uncertainty of what surrounded her.

She touched her wrists. Shackles? On her wrists and neck? She moved her hands upwards, tracing the cold links of a chain to her neck and criss-crossed around her body. A cry rose slowly, but caught before erupting into a full-blown scream. As she turned away from them, the chains grew tighter. Standing was out of the question. Panic surged as she switched directions and twirled so the chains untangled, allowing more movement.

A raucous "CAW" swooped across the stillness. She jumped and shrieked, looking upwards toward the sound. A patch of first light trickled through a small, round opening high above her.

As she watched the opening, the shriek of the crow dissipated. Without warning, several small creatures dove through the hole. A scream and rush of clanking chains drove several bats racing through the air straight into her chamber. The small creatures swept against her hair amidst screams and flailing hands. They screeched back at chains swung in their direction but hitting only her head and face. The headache intensified as her body tensed.

Confusion descended like torrential rain. Was she dreaming? Surely, she'd wake up on the beach beside Drake and… Wait. Her mind drifted back. They left the beach, loaded the boat and headed away from the docks.

Think. You have to remember.

A bottle of water, medication for migraines and unfamiliar scenery, and then…

But, what was all of this? Where was she? Did Drake bring her here? Why shackles and chains? Haniel's warning stabbed her heart.

"He's dangerous. If you go, it won't be good."

Charissa shook her head in a vain attempt to clear the fuzziness.

Wake up now. This is all an insane nightmare. Wake up. This can't be real.

In answer to her confusion, something slithered across her leg. Blood-curdling screams erupted. Every muscle strained against the chains. Chills coursed over her clammy skin. Evil laughter flowed from the walls. The rush of blood in her ears grew louder and left the room spinning. Short, quick breaths did little good.

Don't faint. Not now. Keep it together.

The adrenaline coursing through veins overpowered her mind as she thrashed around, ignoring the voice of reason.

A beam of light filtered into the room. Her eyes widened and strained against the remaining darkness. Through the dim light, cave walls came into view. Along the walls, several flat, hollowed out areas housed bodies. In the darkness, they resembled corpses left to rot, but shackles and chains held every one of them captive too. They must be alive—a corpse didn't need chains, but why weren't they tugging against their imprisonment?

She yanked at her chains again and screamed. "Help! Can any of you hear me? Please help."

In one of the closest chambers, a small creature lay curled into a tight ball of a human…at least it appeared human. She saw no movement from the chamber, but a slight whimper came from the ball. She scrutinized the other chambers in bewildered silence. No one seemed aware of her presence. Impossible. These women, bound as captives, rested without a care. The reality of the situation hit with the force of a sledgehammer.

I have to get out of here before whoever put me here comes back.

She clawed at chains around her body without success. A knot formed in her stomach and climbed to her throat. Shallow breaths quickened. She tugged against the chains, trying to loosen them from the wall, straining until muscles shook. Perspiration soaked her forehead and crawled downward, dripping to the chamber bottom.

Rats scurried past adding to the horror.

Lord, please keep them away from me.

Desperation drove her eyes upwards where rings the size of saucers and at least two inches thick attached the chains to the wall. She scanned the chamber and floor below it for a rock or anything she might use to loosen the rings or break a chain.

Nothing.

Looking at the rings, she grasped a chain with both hands and pulled as hard as possible. She grunted and strained against the force of the chains, kept pulling in spite of the wasted effort. Sobs broke out as muscles spasmed. Hopelessness and despair settled like a thick shroud while tears intertwined with sweat.

A bitter female voice from behind made her jump. "It's no use. Give it up, stupid. You can't break free so you might as well accept it."

She turned and scanned the room. "Who said that?"

Another voice broke the silence, "Now, Dierdre, you don't have to be so mean. It ain't nice to call someone stupid. None of us asked for captivity. We don't particularly want it, but we have to trust God to get us out of this mess."

A third voice shouted, "Can all of you shut up? Some of us are trying to sleep. Between the whimpering coward and a thin mattress, plus the drunken entrance in the middle of the night, I couldn't sleep at all. How am I supposed to think clearly without sleep?"

Charissa blinked. Had they all gone mad? They could have been a group of women with conflicting personalities on a retreat. How long had they been there to become so nonchalant about the situation? They cared more about sleep and manners than their captivity, wearing chains and shackles without a thought, ignorant to any danger.

Fresh terror zipped through her and spurred another frantic yank of the chains.

Dierdre said, "Oh brother. Give it up already."

Charissa pulled harder until blood dripped from hands and wrists to the floor of her prison chamber. She sank onto her knees and sobbed. Frustration and exhaustion crushed harder than ocean waves, starting low and building until they engulfed her. Everything about this place was real, but the scene appeared from the viewpoint of a spectator looking down from somewhere else.

Her mind searched for some semblance of reasoning, warding off the fear of insanity. Had she been drunk? A vile taste lingered. Still, she only drank a couple of Mimosas. Questions burned in her mind. Where was she, and how did she get here?

She searched her memory again. Drake drove the wrong direction. She knew it but did nothing to stop him. The headache, some medicine and deep drowsiness; but sleep didn't land people in a dungeon. He couldn't be behind this, could he? But, if not, where was he? Her mind struggled as she curled up into a fetal position on the stone bed.

Movement from the closest chamber caught her attention. The human ball shook, her moans muffled by the torn clothes she clutched. Unhelpful in the curled position, at least this one woman appeared to understand the danger.

In the depths of her despair, somehow Charissa's heart ached for the tortured woman. An overwhelming desire to hold the creature nagged until she lifted her head and started to move. Chains clanged as a reminder – she couldn't reach the woman. Pain darted through her head and forced it back down.

An unnatural chill swept across her back as a whisper drifted over her. "That could be you, Charissssa. The ripped clothes, rocking back and forth – you know what happened to her don't you?"

Tears filled her eyes and slipped across the bridge of her nose and down her temple.

What did I do to deserve this? Maybe I'm not perfect, but I shouldn't be here. I didn't do anything but fall asleep.

The whisper returned. "Save that woman and yourself…if you can."

She shuddered and one thought overwhelmed her with grief as she succumbed to sleep.

I can't save anyone – especially myself.

Chapter 29

Charissa awoke to a jab in her side. Her heart pounded and her breathing came with short, shallow gasps as her eyes adjusted to the dim light. Strange smells, dampness, and the rough coldness of stone surrounded her. Reality swept away the insulation of sleep, when Drake's face appeared, the distinct smell of whiskey pouring from his breath.

A pointed beard joined a thin mustache at the corners of his mouth. His face resembled dried-up leather instead of smooth, rich dark tones. Black hair wisped across his forehead and lay in uneven layers down to his shoulders. The unchanged eyes still held deep, black coldness. They betrayed his identity regardless of all the other changes.

Her throat ached and the dryness made speaking difficult. Whispers reverberated off the walls. Amidst the unintelligible words, a sinister overtone sent chills deep into the pit of her stomach. A hollow pain replaced a gnawing queasiness. How long had she slept? In this dungeon, time meant nothing. Trapped and bound by shackles and chains, utter despair and hopelessness hung in the air beside the condemning murmurs.

Drake jabbed her side again. "Wake up." He placed a hand over his nose and shook his head. "You stink."

He threw a bucket of water over her and then tossed a bottle of water. "Drink this."

Charissa sat up. Hesitant, but driven by thirst, she took the water and drank it. Dull aches invaded her back with stiffness creeping over every limb. Several men stood behind Drake while others approached the women around the cave. Their taunting reverberated off the walls.

She swallowed the lump in her throat. "Drake, what's this all about? Who are these women? Where are we, and why do you have us all chained?"

"So many questions. It's a game—just for you. Everyone came here of their free will, except for Valorie. She's my special little pet - brought her to this place full of fear for my pleasure. The chains, rather unnecessary to prevent escape, are simply a reminder you all belong to me. In time, I will remove them, but only when I'm certain of your allegiance."

He pointed at the woman with a thicker mattress. "Edna over there is close. She has already earned privileges as you can see, but she isn't quite ready to concede all power to me. She still wants full command for herself without sharing. Learn from her, and you might survive."

"I don't understand. You have no right to hold us captive. I don't know about Edna or the others, but I certainly didn't agree to come with you and let you chain me in some dungeon. I'm not your little pet."

"Oh, but you are, my dear. I brought you here because you didn't care. You chose me by not choosing." His raucous laugh cut through her courage. "That's what I told your precious Haniel too."

"Haniel knows I'm here?" She brightened with hope.

"He knows I have you with me. Not that it matters. If you think he'll save you, give up now. I told him you chose me over him, and he believed it. He said you told him to go away, so he did. He won't be coming to our little party."

Laughter recoiled off the stone and encircled the twinge inside her head.

The lump in her throat hardened. Shame swept in like a wave.

Still, she spoke as if the words made her statement true. "He'll come, even if I don't deserve it."

Drake slapped her. "Well, you don't. Look what you've done. You who would save the orphans. I brought these other women here to prove that Haniel doesn't love you. You can't depend on him. All this time, you've hoped for something imaginary and now, the only real thing you have is me. Think about that for a while, my priceless emblem."

He turned and beckoned his associates to follow him. They trailed up a long winding staircase. A heavy thud and the sliding of a bolt confirmed imprisonment even without chains. What had she done? She looked around the room at the other women.

Edna stared back. After several minutes of silence, she spoke. "He's right you know. This game is a power trip for Drake. I understand. I came of my free will or so I thought. I wanted his power and wealth – still do."

"I don't understand." Charissa said. "Why did he bring us all here? I don't know about the rest of you, but I have no desire for power and, as for wealth, I have all I need."

A bitter voice spoke from one of the other chambers. "Most of us trusted him when he promised exactly what we wanted. He lied, but what else do you expect? He's a man – they're all liars. And I'm betting you were naïve enough to believe he loved you, weren't you? So how stupid does are you? Maybe instead of worrying about how and why we got here, you should help us figure out how to break free from this mess. Of course, you can join little miss complacent Shamira over there and do nothing. Do you even have the guts to take control of your life? Or maybe you'll sit around full of fear, taking your cue from Valorie."

Edna said, "Dierdre's right isn't she? You thought he was your very own Prince Charming, didn't you? Then you went right along with whatever he said. He told me about his plan, although he left out key components. I'm not sure exactly how you fit into it all, but this is somehow about you. You're a weak, sniveling coward and if not for you, I'd be sharing his power instead of sitting in this stinking hellhole of a cave."

Charissa hung her head, full of shame. Did the others blame her as well?

From across the cave the large woman spoke. "Edna, we aren't s'posed to judge others."

Edna snapped, "Shut up, Ariana, you fat slob. I'm sick of your Bible thumping mouth. Don't you dare try to tell me what to do."

Her glare at the other woman sent tremors down Charissa's back.

"And none of us wants to hear about how Drake tricked you into coming here, so sit back and shut up. This is my conversation with the star pet. Keep your self-righteous nose out of it."

Charissa looked at Ariana. In the dim light, she couldn't tell if the woman cried or not, but Edna's words left handprints across a slapped heart. Charissa detested this power hungry woman who wore the common expectations of a successful woman. Even in the dungeon, her designer label clothes remained crisp and clean. She slept here, but obviously did whatever Drake wanted in return for favors that apparently included basic hygiene. She doubted Edna spent much time in the dungeon with the others and vowed not to trust the woman.

Edna's defiant stare returned to Charissa. "Make no mistake. You will not mess up what I have going here. Give Drake whatever he wants so we can all get on with our lives."

Charissa's back hit the wall, and still she drew farther into the chamber, pressed against rock. Pulling her legs up into a defensive position, she readied them to extend fully into a hard kick. This woman scared her almost as much as Drake did. The two of them together terrified her.

Chapter 30

Drake leaned back, propped his feet on the desk and sipped a drink. Smitty entered, clutching a teddy bear the size of a newborn baby and tossed it across the room into his boss's lap.

Drake picked up the stuffed animal and studied it. "Soft and sweet — this will do."

Confusion swept over Smitty's face, but Drake scowled at him. He was in no mood for brainless questions about plans. He trusted no one, least of all this stupid little man whose power hungry look kept his superior on guard around him. While he never worried about Smitty defecting to the enemy, he seldom trusted his loyalty. The man and all his counterparts fought constantly for a right hand position. Given a chance, any one of them might slit his throat in an attempted coup. Few of them were stupid enough to try such an inane move. Nevertheless, he kept motives and plans to himself.

He drained his glass and stood. "I'm in the mood for a cake. Let's see what Ariana can do to satisfy my hunger."

Without any protest or comments, Smitty followed through a secret doorway and down the stairs as if pulled by an invisible leash.

Valorie pushed herself back against the wall when they entered, but Charissa sat up as they approached. She hid emotions well, despite the fear pooling in her eyes. Not quite enough visible emotion for his satisfaction. The seeds planted about her beloved Haniel required watering. Maybe her hero would come eventually, but not today. In the meantime, he needed a touch of restored trust from her; woo her back into a position of favor.

He climbed into the chamber with her and stroked a cheek. "Honey, I'm so sorry about slapping you earlier. Your confidence of Haniel's love drove me crazy. You have to wake up to the truth about who really loves you. I had to bring you here, to convince you."

Distrust oozed from every pore as she stiffened against his hand. She wasn't buying it.

He held out the toy bear. "Here. I bought this for you as a peace offering."

She eyed the bear with suspicion.

"Go on. Take it. There isn't anything wrong with it. He's very soft and cuddly. You desire soft caresses."

Smitty leaned in and whispered, "Haniel never gave you any soft touches with the tenderness Drake did. You remember how nice it felt."

Drake closed his eyes and appreciated memories of the lustful moments at the lake hoping her mind also returned to pleasurable feelings. Not one to leave things to chance, he whispered his thoughts.

"Ummm…yes…the warm sunshine and soft kisses with the waves crashing against the rocks. The passion between us. It hurts me you would choose another man over what I offered."

An angry yell from across the room forced him out of the moment and back to reality.

"Drake. How dare you give her a teddy bear? Why not me? I've co-operated with you from the beginning—even though I knew better than to trust a weasel of a man."

Drake turned his attention to Dierdre. Such an odd reaction to a teddy bear, but he delighted in the opportunity to patronize the bitter one of the group. Surely, Charissa held some anger in her soul, although she suppressed it well. An unexpected twist bringing great delight. He pictured the two of them fighting over the bear and bitterness growing all around them.

"Dierdre. Tsk, tsk, tsk. Do we have a soft spot in your little heart?"

She glared at him and spoke through gritted teeth. "Of course not. But he would make a great little pillow."

"Oh really? Then why didn't you ask me for a pillow, my miss non-congeniality?"

Smitty snickered. Dierdre turned away in defiance, tossing her hair.

Drake turned back to Charissa. "She's right, you know. Even if you don't want my gift out of love, accept him as a small comfort."

He placed the bear in her lap and kissed her forehead. She remained unmoved but he caught a glimpse of softening in those big brown eyes.

Drake stood with an overstated sigh of relief. His voice echoed off the walls. "Ladies, we're much too solemn in this room. I think a party might be in order. After all we have a nice little group of women and nothing but time on our hands. Besides, we must celebrate Charissa's arrival. Don't you agree?"

With the exception of Dierdre, all eyes turned in his direction. None looked enthusiastic. One or two of the women looked more in favor of clawing out his eyes than celebrating. Most of them still needed short chains.

Edna crawled out of her chamber and moved toward Drake. "I can help you plan your celebration, darling. Whatever you want. Perhaps you prefer a party for two?"

Drake scowled at her. "Not this time."

She sneered at him and crossed her arms. He didn't trust her much, either. Her eyes shone with a hunger for power so strong, she'd betray herself to get what she wanted. He frowned at her and turned his back.

He walked instead to Ariana. "Okay, Big Momma, this is your million-dollar chance. Let's see what you can do in the kitchen."

He motioned for Smitty, who leapt across the room and unchained her. The woman moved slowly out of the chamber and almost fell when her feet touched the ground. He hoped she made it up the stairs and finished cooking before a heart attack claimed her life.

He pulled Smitty aside and spoke in hushed tones. "Unchain Dierdre too."

"What? Are you crazy? She wants to cut you in half."

"Just do it."

He surveyed the room. Charissa stared at him with bewilderment. He offered Ariana his arm and forced a smile as he glanced in Charissa's direction. He patted the older woman's hand and moved slowly until she reached a level of steadiness. Then he ascended the stairs with her, his voice soothing yet loud enough so the echo filtered down to the others.

"Now what I have in mind is a splendid assortment of treats, but especially a big, luscious cake. If all is suitable, we'll share it with your friends down here. I might even move everyone outside for a little garden party. How does that sound?"

Ariana spoke with a slight quiver. "That'd do fine. I'll do my best, sir."

"Good. We wouldn't want to let your friends down."

As the two left, chains hit the floor, and Drake smiled to himself.

Chapter 31

When the door closed behind them, Drake moved away from Ariana so fast she almost fell. He surveyed the kitchen. Everything stood ready for this part of his game.

Ariana's eyes bulged. "I've never seen such an amazin' kitchen, Mr. Hannibal."

"Please, dear. Call me Drake."

Indeed, the kitchen rivaled the designs used by the greatest chefs in the world. An island stood in the middle of the large room, perfectly placed and lighted with a pot rack hanging at the right height for this woman. A barstool waited beside it for her to sit and work if she desired. Broad counters and cabinets with see-through doors lined the walls, revealing neatly placed dishes.

Ariana walked around the room and caressed the smooth top stove. The great chefs preferred gas for better control. He purposely chose electric instead. He couldn't allow perfection in this meal. She ran her hand over pure granite countertops and eyed the pristine appliances with glee. At the sight of the heavy-duty stand mixer, she gasped and clasped her hands together.

Her voice quivered with excitement. "Oh, Drake, this is the most wonderful kitchen I've ever seen. I always wanted a kitchen like this, but we never had anything so nice."

Drake looked to the ceiling and shook his head. "It's a kitchen. Come. Sit with me for a moment."

He led her to an exquisite cherry-wood dining table lavished with dishes of fine food. A servant stood at attention, prepared to serve the meal. The aromas of steak, coconut fried shrimp, potatoes and a dozen other dishes merged and made his mouth water. Ariana's eyes grew so large they might burst from her head. The thought amused him; perhaps later but he had other things on his mind.

"Are you hungry?"

She nodded and reached for some of the food. He slapped her hand.

"Not so fast, my dear."

"I'm sorry, sir. We haven't had much to eat since we've been here."

"Yes. I can see you are wasting away from lack of food."

The enthusiasm in her face disappeared as the jab about her weight hit as intended, but then again he needed her cooperation so forcing down sarcasm and ignoring her size, he changed his tone.

"I know you must be hungry, Ariana. So I have a proposal for you."

Uncertainty replaced enthusiasm. "Okay."

"I have a menu with a few little treats for your friends, but for the grand finale you will make the biggest, most ornate cake you've ever baked. I want all the frills and pretty little decorations you can possibly imagine, and then some." He pulled out a brown paper sack. "In this sack, I have some splendid rum and a few other choice ingredients. I want all of it included in the cake."

She looked inside the sack and withdrew items – Syrup of Ipecac, Opium, and several unmarked bottles. She furrowed her brow. "You want all of this in one cake?"

"Yes."

"Just one of these bottles in a cake will make the ladies puke all the way to dry heaves."

Drake swept his hand over the food. "All of this can go to waste and you can protect the wenches downstairs, or you can feast, and do as I wish. Your choice."

She swallowed hard. Spittle formed at the corners of her mouth as she eyed the luscious looking food. "I don't know, Drake. It seems so mean."

"I have my reasons you can't possibly understand."

"What if it kills one of 'em?"

"Ariana, do you really think I'd kill one of my precious pets? Trust me."

"But Syrup of Ipecac? That stuff makes ya throw up bad."

His patience wore thin. Must he justify everything? For the sake of his plan, he devised a reasonable explanation.

"It will cleanse toxins out of their bodies. They may get a little sick at first, but then they'll be healthier. Besides, you can bet every one of them at some time in their life made themselves throw up. Look how skinny they all are."

"Still...it ain't right to knowingly put somethin' in the cake that'll make 'em sick. It would be... Sinful. That's what it'd be."

"Wouldn't it be sinful if you don't help cleanse all those impurities out of their bodies?"

Drake picked up a piece of shrimp and bit into it. "Mmmmm...this coconut shrimp is delectable."

He took two more bites to finish it and then licked his fingers before selecting another larger piece.

Ariana eyed the food and licked her lips. She blinked repeatedly as her mouth twitched. Her brow furrowed while she considered the options.

"I want to help these women, but I don't know..."

"Oh c'mon, woman. Look at who you're protecting. Dierdre? The bitter man-eater and the little whore, Shamira, who has slept with every man she ever knew. Or Valorie who is a woman so scared of everything, she wouldn't know faith if it wrapped itself around her. Of course, you could save Edna. Never mind she is a power hungry witch who would betray anyone and wouldn't hesitate to sell you out. And let's not forget Charissa who caused all of you to be here because of her selfishness and complacency. Why should you protect them? Enjoy the goodness on this table set before you in the presence, well almost in the presence, of your enemies."

She spoke sheepishly. "It hardly seems fair, but I do need strength to cook for them." She wrung her hands and bit her lower lip."Okay. But please don't tell them I agreed to add the drugs to the cake. They'd never forgive me."

"Of course not, dear. Your secret is safe with me." He winked at her for good measure. "Enjoy the feast and then get to work. I'll be back in a few hours."

He rose from the table. As he reached the doorway, the sound of smacking and near grunting drifted from behind. Without turning, he envisioned the pig-like event at the table and only hoped she didn't bite the servant as he ladled food onto her plate.

Chapter 32

Charissa curled up clutching the stuffed bear, like a child afraid of the dark. The soft fur comforted her, then left flashes of Rusty snuggling close. Her chest heaved and ached. She left him with food and water for the day when she ventured out to the lake. Her choice would cost his life, too, if she didn't get out of this dungeon and back home. A cold fist closed around her grief-stricken heart.

Dierdre jumped down from her chamber and stretched. Her chains, loosened from the wall, left her free to roam. Thick shackles surrounded her neck, wrists and ankles. The chain around her waist and attached to both wrists looked strong enough to tow a car. More chains wrapped her chest, with some larger and others smaller than the middle one, but all equally as confining.

Charissa looked at her chains. In comparison, she wore fewer around her body and the shackles holding her looked smaller than those of the other woman. She yanked the chain between her wrists in hopes it might break. If two of them were unchained, perhaps they could find a way out of this place.

Dierdre dragged her chains over to Charissa. "It's no use. They may look flimsy, but you can't break them. We've all tried. The longer you're here, the thicker both the chains and shackles become."

"So, what are you saying? Give up and sit here waiting for Drake's next move? The man is pure evil. I'm not sure why I didn't see it before."

"At least he gave you a soft teddy bear; a little pretend pet for Drake's favorite." She stroked the fur with longing in her eyes. "I have one of these. I packed it when Drake invited me to come with him." The hollowness in her eyes held an ocean of despair and sorrow. "If you give me this one, I'll help you plan an escape. We can work together and overpower him. I'll give the bear back when I find my own."

Charissa held the animal close to her body. "No. He's mine. I won't give him to you."

Laughter rang against the walls. The myriad of tones echoing back belonged to more than Dierdre.

Impossible. My mind is playing tricks on me.

Pinpricks raced down her arms as she pushed the sound from her conscious mind.

Dierdre's tone switched, mockery dripping through every word. "Awww...little baby. Are you afraid of the dark or something? You need a teddy bear to hold in the night?"

Charissa gritted her teeth. She pictured Ann, taunting and mocking her dreams. Charissa respected authority, which kept her from fighting a supervisor, but this woman meant nothing. She held no power or authority.

I don't have to sit and take this.

She lashed out. "Maybe you are the one who's afraid."

Dierdre bristled. "Not at all. I want him for a pillow. Give me the bear."

"You're scared, aren't you? A pitiful being who'd rather tear people down with words than treat them with kindness, because then you lose power over them. And the sick part – you don't really have any power at all."

"I'm not afraid of anything. They call me Madagascar you know. I eat men like Drake as a morning snack. I've not gotten everything I want from him yet, but I will and then you'll see a different Dierdre."

"What I see is a bitter, angry woman."

"Really? Maybe you see your reflection in my eyes. Now give me the stupid toy."

She lunged and grabbed for the bear. Charissa screamed and moved away so the other woman touched only cold steel. Dierdre grabbed the chains and pulled her off the stone bed. The wall scraped her back as she tried to get her feet down first. Nails dug into flesh. Her head yanked back with a forceful jerk as the hair pulling began. A chain came down on top of her head; the room spun. She clung to the small bear as teeth sunk into her hand. She screamed as the other woman took hold of the prize.

A tug of war game ensued with the little bear. Pulling, kicking, biting, and clawing from both sides, time dragging with neither quitting. She would not give into this woman. Not here – not now. This wasn't her supervisor, and she could fight back without fear. Anger burned deep within her. Not only regarding Dierdre, but coupled with memories of Ann as well. Every sting of her flesh brought back constant comments born without a word of retort. Then her mother's nagging about her failure at finding a husband flitted through her mind, and flames raged as if someone threw gasoline on them. Fire bubbled up within her and spilled out into each blow, every kick and the fiercest claw marks.

Sweat and blood poured from the two women and mingled together on the floor. Dark glass eyes shined up at them from the little animal as they tugged. Dierdre lost her grip and Charissa scrambled back to her chamber, only to feel a yank on her hair and the rock floor meet her back. She rolled away but the chains wrapped around her. As she rolled back and tried to stand, the other woman grabbed the bear again, and the tug of war continued.

The other women yelled at them, spurring them on or begging them to stop. Like two animals fighting over a piece of meat, both kept fighting, not holding back growing rage. Then, a loud rip silenced both women as they tumbled to the ground. Each woman clutched part of the bear in scratched and bleeding hands.

Dierdre broke. Deep sorrowful moans racked her body as she clutched ragged pieces of the toy. Charissa wanted to feel sorry for her, but she didn't. She felt no remorse for the fight or torn bear.

Maybe you see your reflection in my eyes.

Emptiness gnawed at her belly with the possibility of her bitterness, but rage overpowered conviction. Scrambled viewpoints raced around and left no room for anything but confusion.

Howling laughter rolled over her with the intensity of a deep boom of thunder. She looked up at the dark figure above them. Drake.

Chapter 33

Charissa slouched against the dirt-laden floor. When did he come in and how much had he seen?

New fear settled. He planned this. He purposely left the other woman unchained and relished every moment of the fight. The acidic taste in her throat rose higher until she wanted to vomit. Instead, she forced it down.

"Ladies. It's only a bear. Now it's gone, and neither of you can have it." The sickening sweetness of his voice changed abruptly. "Get back to your chambers and quit disturbing things down here."

Both women moved back to their stone beds and scowled at each other across the room. The senselessness of the fight nibbled at Charissa's conscience, even while the anger singed the edges of her heart. Determined to remain mad for a little longer, yet uncertain over the object of her fury, she alternated glares between Dierdre and Drake.

He motioned with his head. Flanked by servants, Ariana entered the middle of the cave. Each servant carried large restaurant-style trays covered with sumptuous foods, along with stands to hold them. A rich aroma filled the cave and almost drove away the stench of death and decay.

A rumbling rose from her gut, mounting slowly and changing to an intense growl. How long had it been since she ate? She eyed the other women. All stared at the meal. How long had they gone without food? Ariana's face gleamed with pleasure as she directed the servants to set down the trays.

Smitty went to each chamber and unlocked chains. None of the women needed an invitation. Even Dierdre forgot her anger and plunged for the food. He reached Charissa last, but when he unlocked her chains, she sat still. Even if Ariana cooked everything, Drake controlled her. For all any of them knew, he might poison everyone. She started to yell – urge them to stop and think, but Drake spoke first.

"Charissa, honey, please come and eat with the others. Ariana worked hard on this special meal. Surely, you don't think she would do anything to taint such wonderful fare do you? Come. Eat."

The trays beckoned her as the other women stuffed food into their mouths. From a distance the symphony of meats, vegetables and fruits, lined with different types of bread lured her from the chamber. The others seemed famished, a sure sign their captor gave little thought to a need for food. If it didn't kill her, this meal might be the last for a long time. She yielded to the temptation with a quick prayer it wasn't poisoned.

She bit into a strawberry first and the juice ran down her chin. The taste exploded in her mouth, knocking everything else out of her mind. She joined the other women, snatching whatever her hand touched. Any fear of poison dissipated into exquisite flavors bursting together against taste buds. Not stopping to wipe away traces of food, she crammed more until her cheeks bulged and chewing became difficult.

The feeding frenzy lasted only a few minutes before Drake clapped his hands. The door above them banged open, and two more servants appeared at the top of the stairs carrying an oversized cake.

Three tiers of pure ecstasy descended the steps. As the men entered the circle, all the women gasped.

Thick white icing flowed over the top and down the sides, while large, full roses of all colors covered half the top. Smaller rosebuds trailed down the cake and dotted the sides with a pink icing bow joining them all together. Charissa's mouth watered in spite of herself. Not one to indulge in cake often, this one moved her almost to tears. Ariana belonged in the finest, world-class bakery.

Stunned by the intricate detail, the women all froze in silence for a full minute before the first oohs and aahs escaped from one and then another. Drake handed Ariana a long, dull cake cutter. She smiled, but something troubled Charissa. The woman's eyes reddened against the painted smile reminiscent of a doll's plastic lips. Suspicion bubbled up again. The sweet smell of rum mixed with hints of vanilla and almond wafted through the stale air and caught her breath. Not wanting to exhale, she licked her lips.

The older woman carefully cut saucer-size pieces and handed them to each woman who took a single small bite. Charissa watched as each of them closed their eyes and deep sighs convinced her of the goodness waiting in the first taste. She bit off a mouthful and closed her eyes as the full flavor enticed her into wide-eyed, repeated mouthfuls even before she finished the previous ones.

Drake cut off a small bite of cake and gently placed it into his mouth. Without chewing, he spit it onto the ground and raked the entire cake into the floor.

"Phulf. Ariana! How dare you poison my guests? Pure rum is one thing, but I can taste traces of opium and castor oil, among other things I dare not mention. Did you rummage through the medicine cabinet and pantry or limit your selection to under the sink? What were you thinking, you wretched woman?"

Ariana's eyes bulged and her mouth dropped before she regained some composure and stammered a response. "It was...I....I...you made me."

Drake slapped her. "You would lie against me? And after I fed you an exquisite meal before you prepared all this? Perhaps in your greed for food, you planned to kill these other women. Or maybe you thought they deserved it because they aren't as holy as you."

Ariana fell to her knees sobbing. "No. It's not like that. I wanted to please you – to do as you wished. I only meant to help you cleanse them. Isn't that what you said?"

"Hurting my guests doesn't please me. You are a selfish woman full of pride and unrighteous 'holiness' using me as an excuse for your sin. I will cleanse you."

Drake took a small whip from his pocket and brought it down across her back. He hurled insults at the woman as he swung.

"You fat greedy slob." *Crack.* "No wonder your husband wanted another woman." *Crack.* "You're worthless." *Crack.* "Betrayer." *Crack.* "Liar." *Crack.* "Selfish hussy." *Crack.* "Self-righteous hypocrite."

Charissa flinched with every blow as the other woman wailed and begged for mercy from Drake. Stunned by both his cruelty and Ariana's betrayal, fuzziness covered her mind. She wanted to stop him, but fear gripped her throat, and then anger descended as she considered the woman's betrayal. She blamed Drake, but he denied it. Which of them lied? He had saved them from eating more, but how did he know what she put in the cake? Had she put it in the other food too? How much and what? The conflict banging against her senses shrieked with the terror of many possible outcomes.

Ariana whimpered and said, "You're right. I've judged these women, and I see my sinfulness." She turned her face upwards and said, "Lord, I'm so sorry. Please forgive me. I knew better than to listen to this man. I was so hungry. I fell into temptation and sinned. Jesus, please make him stop. I won't let him deceive me again."

Her body shook as she wept and collapsed on the stone floor.

The beating stopped. Drake's face contorted. His eyebrows narrowed and the veins in his neck popped. Rage shook his entire being. "Don't ever mention that name in my presence again, or this beating will be nothing."

He flung the whip to one of the servants and flipped the tables holding the remainder of the food. He turned and raced up the stairs. The servants followed, leaving the mess on the floor.

Charissa's heart pounded. She studied the single bite of cake in her hand against the half-eaten pieces the other women still held and threw it in the floor. The other women followed suit and spit out pieces remaining in their mouths.

Her insides gurgled as she swallowed hard with nothing left to spit.

Chapter 34

Charissa grimaced as Ariana pushed herself into a sitting position on the floor, her legs sprawled in front of her. The woman clasped her hands, intertwined her fingers and bowed her head, a child saying bedtime prayers. The rolls around her middle proved she seldom went without food for very long. No doubt, gnawing hunger drove her to do what Drake wanted with the food. The fact didn't ease Charissa's disgust. How could she betray them all for such a low price?

Nevertheless, she either prayed or wanted the appearance of prayer. A twinge of guilt assaulted Charissa. She should pray too. Why would God listen to her? She hadn't exactly spent much time on her knees lately. She loathed this other woman for daring to pray after what she did to them. Nevertheless, self-condemnation chastised her for a serious lack of prayer time.

Grunts and groans rose as Ariana rolled over to reach a kneeling position. She looked around for something to steady herself. Her eyes begged for someone's help, but none of the women moved.

Edna's stern voice broke the silence. "You should stay down there with the rats. I'm sure they will join you since they don't care if food is poisoned."

"Please," Ariana begged. "I know what I did was wrong, but I promise I poured half the bottles out when the servants weren't watching. It isn't as bad as Drake wanted it. He made me do it."

Edna's voice held an edge to it. "Nothing but your fat selfishness made you do it."

Shamira said, "Seriously? You sold us out for a meal?"

"No. Drake said it wouldn't hurt y'all – just clean ya out good. You know, a cleansin' thing. I'm sure some of you've used one before."

Dierdre said, "What would you know about cleansing? From the looks of you, all you ever put in your mouth is junk."

The remarks brought tears to Ariana's eyes. Uncharacteristically, Edna walked over and offered a hand. When Ariana took it, she kicked the older woman in the stomach and laughed.

"You thought I wanted to help you?" Her crazed laugh raised goosebumps on Charissa's arms. "I want to hurt you as much as the rest of us will hurt when this crap hits our intestines."

She began hitting and kicking the woman and motioned for the others who joined in the assault. Angry words hurled through the air and struck the older woman, fiery arrows piercing the heart. She covered her head and screamed for mercy and forgiveness. Caught up in the moment, Charissa joined in the word volley. But the idea of physically hitting the woman made her cringe.

The rest of the women held nothing back. They hit, spat at and kicked her. She fought back little and accepted the blows. She cried out with many of the punches. Guilt gnawed away at Charissa along with queasiness that chased back the shame. A more frightening thought crept up on her.

Drake planned this. He gave her the stuff and told her to put it in the cake. Then made sure we knew so we'd all be against her.

First the teddy bear and then this. His little game became clear. A tiny light pierced the darkness of her understanding. She wasn't playing along.

She backed away from the group of women and watched. As they continued the assault, wrath cast shadows on each face. Even Valorie, who cowered in fear most of the time, lashed out against the other woman. With each blow their shackles thickened, and new links appeared in the chains as they grew and wrapped around arms and legs binding the women more. Charissa drew in a sharp breath.

Fresh anger bubbled up to her throat. "Stop."

The women glanced up. Edna spat in her direction and then turned back to Ariana. They weren't listening.

Distaste for confrontation held her back. No one ever listened to her. She hated being in the center of attention or leading anything, but this had to stop. Taking another deep breath and exhaling loudly, Charissa stepped in front of Ariana and held out her hands against the onslaught.

She yelled, "You have to stop. Look at your chains and shackles. They're growing."

The women looked down at themselves. All of them except Edna stepped back from Ariana. Horror filled each of their faces as they examined the chains around their bodies. Edna smirked. Her chains grew too, but she maintained composure. She wore her chains loosely as if she took pride in their growth. Charissa recognized the power-hungry look in her eyes. A dagger-like flash shot from the coldness of the woman's light gray eyes. As she spoke, the color of her iris darkened with a smoldering flame.

"Stay out of this, Ms. perfection unlimited. You're so much like Ariana with your holy, judgmental attitude. I have this under control. Go back to your little corner and look the other way if you don't want to join us."

Beneath the well-controlled surface of the woman's face, vehemence seeped through her eyes. Deep breaths hinted at her struggle for composure, while the glower directed at Charissa shouted for obedience. If Drake meant this for intimidation, he planned well. With the personality combinations of Ann and her mother, Edna scared her. She pushed down the urge to cower and sprint to her chamber in spite of a racing heart.

"No. You want her, you'll have to come through me."

Shamira stepped beside Charissa. "She's right, Edna. We're only playing into Drake's game. He wants us fighting against each other. What good is beating Ariana? It's making our bonds worse."

Edna fumed at both of them. "So you'd stand with her instead of me? She's the reason we're all here. Don't you know that? I, for one, intend to use her to my advantage. Drake promised me wealth and power, and so whatever his reason for wanting this little wimp, I'll play along. In the end, we'll see who's imprisoned and who becomes ruler over this little kingdom."

Charissa clenched her teeth. "Maybe so; but not today and not at this woman's expense. She's been used and beaten enough."

She turned and offered Ariana her hand. Shamira helped as they pulled the large woman up from the kneeling position she reassumed during the argument. Without another word, she scurried off to her chamber. The other women backed away.

Charissa waited for Edna's first strike; instead, the other woman lunged, hissing at her.

"You'd treasure fighting me wouldn't you?"

Charissa stood firm. "No. But I'm tired of backing down from controlling women. So c'mon. If you want a fight, let's get it over with." Her shoulders tensed.

Edna blew through her nose. "You're not worth my time." She turned and flounced to her chamber.

Unaware she'd been holding her breath, Charissa released air from her lungs. Her shoulders relaxed slightly. Still unwilling to leave her back unprotected, she felt her way, glancing only long enough to avoid running into the wall until she reached the chamber. She sensed this confrontation with Edna was only the beginning of a bloody war.

Chapter 35

Drake sipped golden liquid from a fluted glass. He preferred scotch, but Edna liked expensive things and, with her limited tastes, she considered champagne the ultimate drink of celebration. So far, she pleased him. Her desire for the finer things in life drove her to compromise herself. Her presence in his home proved the truth of Smitty's assessment of the woman. Nevertheless, he fingered the financial portfolio on the bedside table. A little insurance never hurt.

Edna entered the room behind a servant. A black lace covering left little to imagination. Her short hair fell perfectly around her face. She flaunted the shackles like fine jewelry, as if she secretly enjoyed wearing them. She slithered onto his bed, his favorite shampoo, body wash and perfume drifting from her body.

She moved closer and spoke in a seductive tone. "How can I please you tonight, Drake?"

She untied his robe. The mixture of smells exuding from her body drifted over him raising his pulse and body temperature. He pushed aside desire and maintained control.

"Business first, my dear, then we'll move on to my pleasure."

He pushed her back and filled a glass for her.

She sipped champagne. "Are we celebrating?"

"Depends on your response to my proposal; but if I know you, we'll celebrate all night."

"Good. What do you want from me?"

Straight to the point, no less than he expected. So predictable. Yet he didn't trust her for one minute. The yearning in her eyes rattled him; she'd stop at nothing. Still, he needed a dependable ally and she was his best bet. Dierdre had enough bitterness, but she hated men, which made her unreliable. She might as easily betray him to Charissa simply because of his gender. He stroked his goatee and kept Edna waiting. Let her sweat for a few minutes. Finally, he detached himself from the surroundings and scent, and took on a business air.

"I want Charissa's loyalty."

"Yes." Irritation filled her voice.

"You don't like her."

"No. Why do you want such a sniveling little wimp?"

"She isn't a wimp at heart. She carries potential for great power capable of demolishing my plans. She can't ever know. Besides, my biggest enemy loves her, and if she figures it out and returns his love, I won't be able to stand against the power unleashed in her."

She sniffed. "Love doesn't have that much power."

"In this case it does."

"Okay – for the sake of argument, I'll go along with your paranoid assessment. How can I help you gain her loyalty?"

"Do what you do best. Persuade her that she needs to stand with me."

"How?"

"I don't care. Debate with her, beat her, pretend to be her friend and manipulate her. Use whatever tactic works. You're the top-notch attorney. I'm sure you have all kinds of tricks to get exactly what you desire."

Edna took a gulp of champagne and ran a finger over her lips. "And in return?"

"I'll give you what you came for—wealth beyond your wildest dreams and power no one can overcome."

"Look me in the eyes and make that promise."

Drake laughed. "You don't trust me, my dear?"

"Write it down and sign it in blood. Then I might halfway trust you. You're a liar, and we both know it. But I can hold you to a legal contract."

Drake picked up the portfolio. "You aren't really in a position to bargain, are you, Edna?"

Her eyes smoldered, but she didn't grab the papers.

Drake refilled her champagne glass. "Oh, come now. You need the money, so you'll have to trust me on this one. But if it makes you feel better, I do have a contract for you."

He removed a single sheet of paper and held it out to the woman. He drew a small knife from a drawer in the bedside table and took her hand in his. He cut a small slit in her right index finger and placed it on the paper. She signed her name with the oozing blood. When she finished, Drake took her finger and placed it in his mouth. He handed her the knife and held out his right index finger. The sting of the blade drawn against his skin surged up his arm and through his veins all the way to his loins. He signed his name and threw the papers on the floor along with the knife.

Business finished, he grabbed her glass, finished the champagne and in a demonstration of power, threw her onto her back. He grasped her wrists and attached them to short chains bolted to his bed. As he chained her ankles, she squealed with anticipation. The rip of lace sent a river of quaking beneath him, but she didn't fight. A gentle kiss transitioned into a nip, and exploded into a full-blown bite when the action brought a nervous giggle from her. He wanted fear and submission from this power-craving woman. He clamped down harder with his teeth until salty iron burst against his taste buds. As her playful squeal became a painful shriek, he laughed with delight.

"Drake! Stop. You're hurting me."

"I intended for it to hurt – and it's nothing compared to what you're about to endure. Don't forget any power you have comes from me."

His blood fired up again as he moved to prove his power over her. The scents from her body heightened his level of lust. He ripped the sparse clothing from her body. With full intention of inflicting the most agony possible, he embraced the struggling under him. The more Edna fought, the rougher he grew. Delight washed over him while she screamed in anguish and he howled with pleasure.

Chapter 36

Darkness settled over the dungeon. A lone torch cast an eerie shadow across the floor and danced around the room providing some light for the prisoners. Charissa looked across the room at the other women. Drake's summons of Edna removed the last knots from her shoulders. An unnatural quietness intensified in this prison and left her with too much room for troubled contemplation.

Edna wanted power and wealth, making her as much of an adversary as Drake. She pictured the two of them together, plotting an unimaginable fate for the rest of his captives. She still didn't understand the motivation. Although she longed for answers, could she really trust these other women? Ariana turned against them and, given the right circumstances, perhaps the others would as well. Nevertheless, they needed a plan, and at some point, one of them must take a leadership role. Dierdre seemed the most likely for the position. She certainly had a mind of her own and knew how to take control. Besides, the bitterness dripping from the woman gave her an edge in fighting Drake.

Charissa understood the anger directed at him, but Dierdre seemed to hate all men. The other woman looked about forty-five. Pretty, but lines of hardness burrowed deep into her face. Cynicism and sarcasm laced her words and voice.

Madagascar – home of the first man-eating plant. What turned her into such an angry man-hater?

Charissa ran fingers over her face, searching for lines. Beneath the grime, smooth skin remained unwrinkled. But in another twenty years, her features might reflect years of disappointment and loneliness. With every failed relationship, she dug deeper for hope. Sometimes on sleepless nights, she hugged her pillow close and wept bitter tears of desperation, the semblance of an orphan with no one to love her.

Charissa's mind drifted back to the incident with the bear. She looked at the chamber where her opponent sat, knees drawn into her chest, arms wrapped around them. She appeared so insecure, a little girl, in a vast chamber with cold stone for a bed. The thick manacles and chains held her captive even unattached to the wall. The façade of a tough exterior melted into the image of a frightened child.

She thought of one girl—only ten, yet with a face hardened and despondent. For a week, she chipped away at the wall around the her heart, but the self-protective barrier against everyone grew thicker. No one could blame such a child—abandoned and then rejected all of her short life.

Deep yearning swept through Charissa. Sorrow surged, like a tidal wave out of control. Dierdre took on the appearance of the orphan with the same empty, frightened look radiated from her face. The unimportant teddy bear represented security to this woman who somewhere along life's way lost control and no doubt constructed her foot-thick heart fortress.

A voice inside said, "Like the orphan. Like you."

Charissa shivered at the realization. She saw her emptiness. Hadn't she experienced those emotions? The same fear and loneliness covered her far too much of the time. She lived in the same mindset of a orphaned child, fully aware her mom and stepfather loved her deeply. Her father abandoned her, though, so she lived in the shadow of rejection, expecting the same from all other men. Up to that point, she received exactly what she expected—perhaps what she subconsciously caused.

Looking at Dierdre, she regretted not surrendering the bear.

The woman snapped. "What are you looking at?"

Charissa searched for inoffensive words. "You, Dierdre. I'm looking at you and seeing myself. You were right. I do see the reflection of my potential future." She paused. "I'm sorry for not giving you the bear or at least sharing it with you. I should have seen you needed it more than I did."

"Whatever. It was a stupid bear."

"It meant comfort to both of us. I get that."

Irritation rose in the other woman's voice. "I don't care. It wasn't important."

"Can I ask a question? Do you hate everyone in general or men in particular?"

"All men—only women with big, naïve eyes trusting everyone."

"I don't trust everyone. Especially not men, but I keep hoping someday I'll meet one who proves me wrong and shows me I can trust him." She sighed. "Actually I do know one, but I pushed him away and didn't value his friendship."

"Good for you. Better now than down the road when he betrays you for someone else or beats and then abandons you. Then again, I didn't shed many tears when they found my sorry excuse for a husband. He killed himself in an abandoned building way back on the edge of our property. The cops actually accused me. Wish I'd thought of it. Suicide was the only good thing he ever did for me and my kids."

Charissa's heart throbbed for this woman. "He shouldn't have treated you like that. You deserved better."

"He wasn't the only one. I grew up with things you don't want to know." She sniffed. "Anyway, it's no big deal. It all happened a long time ago. I'm over the whole, stinking mess. Now, I make sure no man will ever hurt me again."

"Sounds almost as bad as being in this dungeon."

A soft voice broke into the conversation. "There are worse prisons than this dungeon."

Charissa turned. Shamira sat in a nearby chamber. So young and fragile, wearing defeat as makeup. Pain and sadness covered her entire being. A conflicted soul of ironic proportions, she couldn't be more than twenty, yet moved with the effort of an eighty-year-old. The determination mingled with defeat coupled with a mixture of hope against despair on her face confused Charissa.

"What do you mean?"

"Dierdre gets it. The beatings, every single day, for no reason. What do you know? I bet you were daddy's little girl, and he never let anything hurt you."

Charissa drew in a deep breath. She didn't like talking about her daddy. "No one ever beat me, but my daddy hurt me more than anyone. He up and left one day, and I never understood why. We were close. I thought I was his precious angel, but he forgot about me after he left. I seldom see him even now."

Shamira's voice quivered. "I wish I could hate men. Instead, my boyfriend raped me and then I gave in every time afterwards until I got pregnant. The shame about killed my parents. I ran away and ended up going from one guy to the next, until each of them grew tired of me, or I got sick of being hit. Then I finally met Doug. He seemed so different from all the others, until I moved in with him. He beat me more than all the rest put together. Dierdre, you deserved good, but not me. I'm here because Drake offered me a better life in spite of my worthlessness. At least he isn't hitting me."

As she listened, Charissa choked back tears. Slight movement over Shamira's body caught her eye. She blinked and then rubbed her eyes. She squinted in disbelief. The chains around this young woman grew thicker with every word.

In panic, she jumped off her chamber and paced. "We have to get out of here. This place will consume us. Don't forget Drake did beat Ariana, and he'll beat the rest of us too—or worse." She shuddered.

Dierdre jumped to the ground too. "How? We've been here for days, and trust me, there isn't a way out. Even unchained from the walls, how far can we get with these shackles?"

For the first time Valorie spoke. "No. We can't try to escape. He'll catch us and do something awful."

Charissa swung around to the woman backed all the way into her chamber, curled up as tightly as ever. "Something more awful than waiting to see what he'll do next?"

Dierdre said, "I want out, but you're the key. I don't know how or why, but it is you he wants to destroy."

Charissa's shoulders slumped. "Why? I don't get it. I'm nobody - nothing."

Ariana whispered, "Yes you are, honey. You're the one chosen to lead us outta here."

Chapter 37

Charissa froze. How could she lead anyone?

Dierdre grabbed her shoulders. "Look, we'll back you up and do what you say, but you've gotta figure this one out, girlie. Or we'll all die in this stinking hole."

"I can't." The chain around Charissa's waist grew thicker. Fear gripped her heart as she watched it expand.

Ariana spoke with new boldness. "You can do all things through Christ who gives you strength. You know Him. I see His presence in you."

"Don't go throwing scripture at me. I've never led anyone. I don't know how."

Dierdre said, "Forget about the Christ thing. Focus on why Drake brought you here and how we can use his game against him. I'm not dying in a dungeon."

"I don't want to die here either." Charissa sighed. "Why? Great question, but I don't have an answer. You all seem so sure this is about me."

"It is." All four women chimed in.

Oh, Lord. What have I done? Why am I here?

A whisper drifted across her mind. "The enemy demanded permission to sift you as wheat, my daughter, but

I've prayed you remain faithful, and when you find freedom you will lead your sisters to me."

Me? I'm nothing.

The whisper returned. "You are a child of the King, a daughter of the Most High God. Stand firm."

Charissa fell to her knees, trembling hands covering her face. How could she lead anyone when she felt so weak?

A firm hand touched her shoulder. Dierdre pulled her up from the floor. "You have a quiet strength about you. I don't understand it, but you need to set it free, girl."

Still trembling, she said. "Okay, I'll try. But you all have to help me. Tell me everything you know about this place and Drake. Oh, and Edna can't hear one single thing we discuss. She's too deep under his control." Her chain receded a little.

The women gathered around Charissa and started talking in chorus, pouring out ideas, comments and fears. Even Valorie ventured from her chamber and joined in the discussion. When Ariana approached they eyed her with suspicion, but she too entered their circle. As they shared stories, many of the chains grew and a few new ones appeared on all of them.

The night passed quickly with no resolution or plan formed. Day broke through the hole, and diving bats sent Valorie back to her chamber in a torrent of yelps. Too bad the hole wasn't bigger, but the distance from floor to ceiling made it an impossible escape route anyway.

The bolt in the door slid back, and Edna appeared at the top of the stairs unescorted. She made her way down in somewhat obvious pain, yet with a smirk on her face. At the sight of all the women together, her demeanor changed.

"What's this? A meeting of the minds to discuss an escape plot perhaps?"

The group of women backed away a little, but didn't run this time. Charissa stood in front and spoke with utter calmness. "We were bonding. Nothing else much to do down here."

"I'm a New York attorney. I know when someone hides the truth. You better not be leaving me out of any plans you're making – as if you could really pull anything off. You? Lead these women? Well maybe Valorie, except she's too scared to even pee without permission. Ariana would do anything you say if you tell her God said do it—and of course promise her some food. The rest?"

Edna broke into a fit of laughter for several minutes. When she finally regained composure, she continued. "Come now. Tell me what you are planning. I have power over Drake, and I can lead all of these women far better than you can dream of doing. When we get out of here, I'll reward you. I do have money you know."

"I'm good really, but thanks for the offer. I'll let you know if I get any bright ideas."

"Liar."

Edna's eyes flickered with hatred. She brushed back her hair and sniffed. Charissa broke the stare by dipping her eyes. The faint scent of shampoo and soap sent her mind reeling.

Oh to wash away the stench of this place.

Her eyes lingered for a moment longer. Bruises lined the older woman's throat; those on her breast peeked out from her silk gown.

He beat her.

Sorrow for the woman welled up and as the tears almost burst from her eyes, Edna touched her cheek with a soft caress, almost like a lover.

"We can do this together, honey. Give Drake what he wants, dear, and this will all be over." Edna leaned in. Realizing the woman's intent, Charissa flipped her head so the kiss landed on a cheek.

Charissa's stomach bolted in disgust. Heat rushed through her body and sweat popped out on her upper lip, but the words racing through her mind stuck in her throat. She pulled away from the woman, wiped her face and spit on the ground.

Edna raised her hand. Charissa shrunk back from an anticipated slap, but it never came. The door above opened, and Smitty lumbered down the stairs. Soured whiskey lingered on his body with an odor so strong it reached her nose even before he came close.

He grumbled, "Back to your chambers. Now!"

He pulled bread and water from a basket and thrust it at the women as he chained each to the walls again, all except Edna.

He said to her, "You pleased the boss last night. You remain free."

After the pronouncement, he provided not only water, but also a thick chunk of cheese, some grapes and a bottle of wine along with bread far more appetizing than what he gave the others. The bonds still covered her body, chains long and thick dragging the floor behind her. No matter how much she pleased Drake, the shackles remained.

As Edna climbed into her chamber, the gown slipped up revealing large bruises on her inner thighs. A fresh wave of momentary compassion swept across Charissa as she imagined the amount of force Drake must have used on the woman. The possibilities of what he planned for her slammed against the recesses of her mind. No matter how much she fought, he could overpower and force himself on her - take what she vowed to save for her future husband. Yet she sensed he wanted something far greater. His purpose for bringing them all here confused her more than ever.

A hand of apprehension gripped her heart and wrung away hope. Edna's words rang across an expanse of despair originating in her belly and working its way up, passed her heart and throat to her brain.

Give Drake what he wants.

Uncontrollable shaking overtook her.

What does he want?

She glanced around the room wondering about the other women and their place in Drake's game. Ariana sat in her chamber with folded hands and fingers touching her lips. She pictured the woman kneeling beside a bed.

Amusement bubbled up as she imagined Ariana trying to get up off the floor from a prayer time. The woman weighed at least 350 pounds. Memories of her struggling to get up after Drake's beating fed the momentary distraction from reality.

A twinge of guilt assaulted Charissa. If ever she should pray, this was the moment. Instead, she sat and judged another woman who spent her time praying in the middle of this insane place. Ashamed of her lack of prayer and faith, she diverted her eyes. She got herself into this predicament with bad choices over Drake. If she listened to Haniel, she wouldn't be here now. Stubbornness and rebellion led to this imprisonment. How stupid could she be?

She blinked back tears and scanned the other chambers. Most of the women sank into their self-centered worlds, seemingly accepting their situation or too afraid to confront it, waiting for a savior. From across the room, Edna stared at her. She focused on the sophisticated woman. The blackness in her eyes consumed any boldness Charissa felt earlier. Foreboding moved down her spine. She scooted back farther into the chamber, hugging her knees close. A consuming fire in those darkened eyes said she best prepare for a fight if Edna came near.

Chapter 38

Drake slumped on the sofa in his study. So far, nothing broke Charissa. He felt her fear, but she hid it well. A worthy adversary indeed. He hadn't anticipated such inner strength or boldness from a woman so afraid of chasing dreams. If she figured out his weakness…

Never happen. He'd break her first.

Smitty brought Shamira into the room. Bathed and changed into clean clothes, she looked so small and vulnerable, a veritable little street urchin. He saw no fear, only intense sadness that echoed his emptiness. The sunshine streaming through the window bounced off her shackles as she turned her full body, absorbing every ray.

He spoke softly to her. "Come over here, little one."

She hesitated for a few seconds and then obeyed. He patted the sofa. As she sat next to him, a stiff coldness hung between them.

He touched her shoulder. "What is it, sweetheart? You don't have to fear me."

"You beat Ariana. I don't want another beating."

"She was bad, Shamira. She wanted to hurt all of you. I couldn't let her go unpunished, could I?"

"I suppose not." Still, she kept a foot of space between them.

Drake pulled her closer. She didn't struggle, but tiny vibrations played against his arms. "I won't hurt you. Let me show you pure love, sweetheart."

He picked up a brush from the table and ran it through her long hair. The softness of the curls fell against his hand as he caressed the auburn locks and breathed in the fresh scent of baby shampoo. With each stroke, she relaxed a little more. He continued brushing and caressing her hair without words. With every gentle touch from him, the rigidity fell away until she gradually settled back against him. Had any man ever showed her love without hurting her?

After several minutes he said, "How did you end up with such an abusive boyfriend, my dear? I bet Your daddy never brushed your hair. He must have beaten you too."

"No, he never beat me—barely spanked me, even when he should have. Daddy was a good man." Sorrow filled her voice. "I messed up so much."

"Oh, come now. You couldn't have been so bad."

"Yes. I was." Her head dropped.

He kept brushing. "What happened?"

She took a deep breath, but her voice remained flat and numb. "I was young…only fifteen. The high school quarterback caught my eye from the first day of ninth grade. I couldn't believe it when he asked me to a party. Daddy said my skirt was too short. I didn't listen. He was so old-fashioned. I swore I wouldn't do anything with this boy, especially on a first date."

"I'm sure he wanted to protect you."

"I guess. At the party, they offered me a beer, but I opted for soda. Then something weird happened. After a little while, my head started spinning. My date took me upstairs to lie down. I'm not sure what happened then. I remember saying no, but he didn't stop. I felt so ashamed; I couldn't even tell Mama or Daddy what happened."

Drake clenched his teeth. "No little girl should have that happen to her. But surely your parents wouldn't have blamed you."

"He warned me about my clothes. I should have listened. I never told them what we did. From then on, whenever we went out, our dates always ended up without clothes. I loved him. At least I thought I did, and I'd already given myself to him anyway. He told me not to deny either of us the pleasure of being together. Within two or three months, I got pregnant. I hid it from my parents as long as I could—all the time the weekly dates continued. When I finally told them, Daddy exploded. He confronted my boyfriend, and when the stupid idiot hit him, Daddy let him have it. He beat him so bad. To be honest, I felt relieved—as if he freed me from ever having to see the guy again."

Drake placed his lips next to her ear, speaking with the tenderness of a gentle breeze." A girl needs a hero."

"Those feelings didn't last though. A week after my sixteenth birthday, I had a beautiful little boy, but Daddy made me give him up for adoption. Supposedly an open one, but I ran away." Her voice broke and sobs from deep inside rose to the surface. "I disappointed my parents and failed as a mother. I found plenty of men who wanted a sweet young girl for their pleasure, so I went from one to the next until each grew tired of me or beat me so bad I couldn't stay any longer. Doug was the last one, and you saw what he did to me."

He fingered the scars on her arm. "Is that why you cut?"

"I can't feel pain inside any more - nothing but numbness. The cutting convinces me I'm not dead. I feel pain." She lifted her shirt slightly, revealing a long scar across her stomach. "I learned the sweetness of cutting when one of my boyfriends got drunk and angry, then came after me with a knife."

"I understand, sweet Shamira."

He held the key to her weakness. One simple suggestion, the right tool and her weakness became a delicious weapon in his plan. Tears tumbled down the face lined with years of torment and sorrow — more years than her actual age.

He considered his next words. Chosen carefully, and placed within her thought process, she offered great value to him. If she took the words wrong, though, it jeopardized his entire plan. He squelched the sense of pleasure from his voice.

With great tenderness, he turned her face toward him. "It's okay, little one. If you need to cut so you feel alive, it's okay."

He pulled a small pocketknife from a drawer in the end table. She eyed it with suspicion and balled her hands into tight fists. He nodded. Her fingers reached for the handle, stopped, tightened into a fist again. She shook her head, a quick, one time shake, her eyes never leaving the knife. Slowly, her fingers unfolded and then snatched it from his hand. Both hands wrapped around the treasure and dropped to her lap.

Drake spoke again. "You know, it might do the others some good to feel a little pain too…especially Charissa. She looks alive, but I think she hides things well, don't you?"

"Maybe. Are you saying you want me to cut them?"

"Yes. Teach them to feel pain like you do. Let Charissa watch while you cut the others first so you bring all her feelings to the surface. It's for her good."

She winced and turned her head slightly. "I'm not sure I can cut someone else, Drake."

Drake touched her cheek. "Sweetheart, I won't hit you. Please don't be afraid. Do what I'm asking, and I'll reward you with anything you want."

"I'm claustrophobic. The dungeon is making me crazy. I'll do what you want, and afterwards, I'll give you whatever you want. Let me live up here with you instead of down there. Please."

Wild fear jumped from her eyes and ran through his veins. Euphoria filled his blood, coursed the length of his arm, and traveled to his heart, where it exploded and raced through his body all the way to his brain. The sense of sheer power and pleasure mixed there as he drank in the extent of his hold over this girl.

"Done."

He pressed an intercom button and waited for Smitty's response.

"Yes, boss?"

"Return my precious Shamira to the dungeon, and leave her unchained."

Chapter 39

The distant sound of a door bolt sliding back woke Charissa from troubled sleep. She welcomed the sunlight as it peeped through the small window high above them. When Smitty pushed Shamira through the door and then slammed and bolted it behind her, the implications rang louder than the lock. Frazzled nerves from the tension of Drake's games along with nights of restless sleep left a deep well of suspicion and irritation.

Shamira descended the stairs carrying the heavy chains wrapped around her body. They hit each wooden step with a thud as her shackles clanged against the iron rails. Her steps resembled a tired old woman. She wore fresh clothes and long curls of hair hung loosely about her shoulders, clean and brushed.

Heat simmered in the pit of Charissa's stomach. Her nostrils flared involuntarily. She closed her eyes and imagined hot water flowing down over her body. The scent of soap wafted over her in a mingling of reality and imagination. She succumbed to the memory with deep longing. Oh, how she desired such a simple pleasure.

The clunk of chain on stone snapped her mind back to reality. She eyed the youngest of her fellow captives. Unlike Edna when she returned, Shamira looked much better than when Smitty took her the previous evening. At least Drake didn't hurt her. Nevertheless, Charissa found looking into her eyes impossible. The pool of pain overwhelmed and reminded her of precious orphans. The same hollow emptiness shone from their eyes.

She doubted seriously Drake alone produced so much agony in this young woman, unless he'd kept her in this stinking dungeon for a lot longer than the rest of them. In this sick place, adding more pain to a wounded soul left a vulnerable woman open to his power. She shivered at the thought.

What did she promise Drake in exchange for the shower and clean clothes?

She pushed aside the last traces of envy and spoke as gently as possible. "Shamira, are you okay?"

She nodded, pulled a small knife from her pocket, flicked the blade open and held it up. "Look what I have."

Charissa blinked. "No way! How did you get a knife?"

"Drake gave it to me." The flat tone of her voice unnerved Charissa.

She recovered quickly and jumped down to the floor as Shamira approached. "We can pick the locks and free ourselves from the shackles and chains. Bring it over here, and I'll help you with yours first."

Excitement crackled through the dungeon. Edna and Ariana sat up. Valorie ventured down from her chamber. The scene captivated Dierdre's attention, although she barely moved.

Shamira sat down on the floor in front of Charissa. "Then what? I have no place to go. So maybe I'll stick with my plan."

Dierdre flew from her chamber and shouted, "Don't be a fool. Charissa is right. This is our chance to escape - maybe the only one we'll have."

Charissa eased down in front of Shamira, and sat cross-legged. She started to reach out and touch the other girl's hand, but stopped cold as the younger woman drew the knife across her left arm. Shame joined the pain on her face and then melted into an almost euphoric picture of relief.

Charissa held her breath as she watched. Scars lined Shamira's arms. Horror, repulsion and compassion alternated as Charissa frantically processed the situation. She'd seen signs of cutting many times, but never watched someone do it. She fought against confusion while bright red blood appeared on the girl's forearm as she drew another line with the knife, and then a third and fourth.

"Stop!" Charissa screamed. "Shamira, what are you doing?"

The girl's eyes rolled back, then she shut them and continued cutting. Her body relaxed more with every slice of the blade against skin. Trickles of blood pooled around the cuts while the girl remained silent.

Charissa grew frantic, but controlled her voice like a mother addressing a frightened child. "Shamira, you don't want to do this."

"Yes, I do. You don't understand."

With those words, she stood and abandoned the methodical ritual.

Charissa breathed a sigh of relief. She detested this cutting thing and agreed—she didn't understand. How could someone cut herself? Shamira seemed finished with the scenario. Relieved, Charissa stood. They still had a chance to break free by using the knife.

She started to speak, but Shamira turned and walked over to Valorie, grasped her arm and slid the knife across it.

Valorie's eyes widened as the woman sliced through her skin several times. She seemed paralyzed by shock at first, then attempted to jerk her arm away from the other woman and hit at her with the free hand.

Shamira said with the same monotone voice, "Give into it. You'll feel so much better." She clung to the wrist and cut Valorie's arm a few more times.

Valorie yanked her arm away."Stop it."

Shamira grabbed the other arm and made a few cuts on it before turning away. The others stared at her, the wildness in their eyes matching those of the woman holding the knife. Stunned, Charissa wanted to stop the attack, but her legs wobbled. The air stifled her breathing. She fought against lightheadedness, wondering if the new game was a bad dream.

Shamira approached Ariana who scooted far back into the chamber. Shamira grabbed one of her legs, though, and sliced through the skin. Ariana kicked at her, but with amazing strength, oblivious to the foot beating against her, the younger woman held on and cut the leg repeatedly.

The other women screamed at her to stop, while they took defensive positions as the young woman spun from Ariana. Dierdre looked ready to fight, but her agression didn't slow Shamira. In a frenzy, she climbed halfway into the cave's hollow chamber and slashed away to hit whatever body part came near the knife. The flurry of hands and feet shortened the attack. She spun in Edna's direction and lunged across the floor.

Edna yelled, "Don't even think about coming near me with that knife." At an advantage with her longer chains, Edna took an aggressive position. She used one of the chains as a whip, swinging it around and down across the younger woman's back. When the hits didn't stop the advance, she flung chains from both sides over the other woman in a failed attempt to ensnare her. Shamira twisted away from each thrust and avoided capture in spite of red marks left from chains slapping against her body. She landed several cuts on the woman before she backed away.

The surreal feeling of the moment faded into reality as the cave cleared and rushed against Charissa's senses. She yelled, "Why are you doing this, Shamira?"

She had to get through to her. Drake must have triggered something, or maybe he promised a favor as he did with Ariana. Either way, this attack had to stop. She scanned the chambers. None of the cuts looked deep, yet all of the women bled. Her breath came in shallow spurts now as she anticipated the next attack. She was the only one yet untouched by the knife.

If I can withstand the attack and somehow gain control of the knife...

Shamira whirled in her direction. The girl's eyes glowed red and yet possessed an ironic coldness that replaced the pain and shame from earlier. Charissa's heart pounded like horse hooves on a racetrack. She retreated until her back hit the cave wall. Shamira pounced on her and drew the knife across Charissa's stomach. She raised the blade and aimed for Charissa's face. Moving quickly, Charissa blocked the knife and cringed at the sting of metal slicing her forearm. Nausea tumbled as each cut felt deeper than the last. She cried, screamed and kicked frantically, twisting away, but the assault continued.

The cave blurred around her as she fought against chains and the continued slashes of the knife blade. Muffled voices from the other women mixed with an unintelligible chorus of unknown sounds. Pleas for mercy mingled with encouragement for Shamira baffled her. Confusion bore down heavy as endorphins released into her body and dulled the pain of each slash. Her body grew heavy as it reacted to the attack with its volition to remain upright. She revolved in various directions and darted in between chains, the cave walls and floor in avoidance of the knife. The mesh of her chains tangled with Shamira's and hit against her face and body. The cave twirled around her with increasing speed until she wondered if she spun or if only her mind tumbled in confusion and dizziness.

The blade raked across her abdomen with greater depth and a fresh wave of pain swept over her entire body down to her toes. The endorphins lacked enough strength to drown the intensity of the last cut. She glanced down at a dark line of red on her shirt. Death's reality breathed down on her as the line widened. Adrenaline pumped through her veins. Without thinking, she slammed her arm down across Shamira's hand and knocked the knife to the ground. Both women leaped downwards toward the clattering of thin metal against stone.

Chapter 40

"Enough." Drake's voice boomed above the clamor.

Both women stopped and collapsed on the floor, their lungs laboring for breath. Charissa eyed the surrounding blood splatters and dared not look at her body. She glanced up at the man towering above them.

"What are you doing, Shamira?" A thunderstorm brewed in Drake's blazing eyes.

"You told me to cut them," she shrieked.

Fear consumed her face as she cowered beneath their captor. With a deep breath, she moved to a semi-standing position, but he knocked her down with his fist. He yanked her up by the hair and hit her again. She fell, pushed herself up and took another blow to the face. She stood only to meet his fist before she gained her balance and fell hard against the stone. She pushed up again, meeting a kick to the shoulder. Propelled to the ground, she hit the side of her head. Blood dripped from her nose and oozed into her hair from the scrape on her head.

Stay down, girl.

Charissa's confusion and anger melted into sorrow. The cutting came from Drake's orders and now he punished her as if he had nothing to do with it. Her anger at Shamira shifted to him. Fury mounted slowly, ash-covered coals fanned into glowing embers.

He spoke with a biting tone. "I told you to let them experience the release of pain through cutting. I did not tell you to kill her."

Shamira sobbed and stood up again. "I'm sorry, Drake. I don't know what happened. I lost control. I didn't mean to hurt them so much. Please..."

Drake answered by grabbing her arm and punching her repeatedly in the stomach and face. She fell forward into him and slid down his body to her knees. He released her arm and kicked her.

Charissa couldn't hold back any longer. "Drake, stop. You'll kill her."

He turned his attention to her. The flicker of hatred in his eyes forced her backwards. Still on the floor, legs propelled her bottom away from his fists of fury. At the same time, the embers in her heart ignited and the flame fueled ferocity. She didn't understand his game, but somehow she caused this. Guilt mingled with the growing fury inside. Groans from the other woman acted as an accelerant thrown on the fire burning out of control in her soul. She sprang to her feet and stepped between him and Shamira.

Fear and wrath collided within her soul, but she pushed down her emotions so her voice came out controlled. "You've beaten her half to death already for doing what you ordered. I know your game. For God's sake, leave her alone."

Drake glared at her, "Stay out of my way with these other women. You can't save them any more than you can save yourself, you pitiful excuse of a woman."

He turned and stormed up the stairs as a roll of thunder boomed down from the small window. Smitty moved from the shadows, jabbed Shamira with his foot, retrieved the knife and followed his boss.

Charissa's knees buckled. She grasped the edge of her chamber to keep from falling. Shamira lay still at her feet, curled up, bleeding. Charissa pulled a small bottle of water from her chamber. It held precious liquid, but the other woman needed water more than she did. She knelt on the stone floor and gently stroked Shamira's hair.

"It's okay. He's gone now."

Dierdre and Edna both said, "Leave her alone. She deserved a beating."

Charissa stared at one and then the other. "Don't you see what he's doing? He'll use all of us against each other if we let him. I'm not playing his sick game."

Edna frowned at her. "You are the game."

Tears spilled from the corners of Charissa's eyes. "I know, but I don't understand why." She fought back a sob. "One thing I do know – I won't surrender to him."

She turned her attention back to Shamira and helped her sit up. "Here's a little water. Drink it."

Shamira shook her head. "No. They're right. I deserved it. I'm so sorry. He promised to let me move upstairs."

Charissa wrapped her arms around the other woman. "I understand how he talked you into it, but why cut?"

"I do it all the time. My life has been out of control for so long. I told you, so many men beat me, and I couldn't stop them. Cutting is the one thing I get to choose. I control when, where and how much pain I experience. It's at least some form of control in my powerless life."

Charissa sniffled. "Control is an illusion. We have choices, of course, but ultimately, God is in control of everything. Any control we muster – well, it's a sick imitation the enemy uses to make us trust ourselves instead of the Lord. In the end, we gain control only through trust in Him. I know it seems strange, but it's true nonetheless."

Ariana offered a weak amen.

Valorie said, "But why cut the rest of us? I don't like pain; it scares me."

Dierdre said, "Everything scares you. She already told us. Drake promised her a reward. He's a liar, the same as all men, and personally if this is God's control, I don't like Him much either."

Tears slipped down Charissa's cheeks. "I don't blame you – any of you. I'm sorry you all ended up here, especially if I caused it somehow." She held the water out to Shamira. "Please, drink this."

The younger woman wept. "I'm so sorry—all of you. I don't know what got into me. This place terrifies me—it's a tiny closet shrinking around me. I want to go home."

Charissa patted her shoulder. "We all do, and somehow we will."

Valorie's voice shook. "Before he kills one of us?"

Charissa fixed her gaze on the frightened woman, but she had no answer.

Chapter 41

Drake fumed through the house into his study. How dare she mention that name in his presence? *For God's sake...* He hated those words — despised the very thought of God. Yet somehow, the mention of the name always seemed to stop him cold, which angered him even more. What did he care about God?

He grabbed a bottle from the shelf and filled a glass to the top. The liquid burned going down. He filled the glass again then started to yell for Smitty only to realize the man already stood by the door waiting for him.

His scowl challenged Drake's foul mood. "What was that all about, boss? Why didn't you let Shamira kill the troublesome little wench?"

Irritation simmered under the surface. "You still don't get it, do you? I don't want Charisa dead. I want her under my control with total allegiance to me."

"Doesn't seem to be working too well for you, does it?"

Flames burst through Drake's veins and his skin tingled, but he remained in control. Who was this imbecile to challenge him? "It's progressing as I planned."

Smitty cocked his head to one side, jutted out his chin and raised his eyebrows. One blow to the arrogant ingrate's jaw – that's all he wanted, but the matter at hand pressed his anger down. He neglected the creation of a contingency plan in case Charissa didn't bend to his will.

She fought back much more than he anticipated, not something he'd admit to an employee. Too many holes in his plan, her potential power against him only poured frustration into a wounded soul.

He narrowed his eyes and thrust his chin forward before speaking. "I suppose you think your plan's better? I'm sure you've mused about how you'd handle this situation – perhaps even discussed it among your comrades."

A grin started at the corner of Smitty's mouth and spread across his entire face. The power lust on his subordinate's face seeped into the bubbling mix of emotions making control harder to maintain.

Finally, Smitty said, "So far, you've been much too mild with the woman. She doesn't fear you, and why should she?" He winced as Drake took a step closer. "Your plans have been impeccable, but you grow impatient and stop them. You gave one a knife but no one died. If you hadn't stepped in…

"I told you, I don't want Charissa's death. I want her on my side, not against me, you fool."

"I didn't say anything about Charissa's death. The others, however, are expendable. Are they not? She'll never turn to you willingly without fear driving her. What? You think she'll grow to love and trust you?

The simmering expanded and boiled over into uncontrollable rage. He leaped across a chair and knocked the snide grin off Smitty's face. "Much more than you ever will. Get out of my sight."

He needed another drink. As he turned from the liquor cabinet, Smitty pushed himself up from the floor, shook his head and moved across the room like a kicked puppy.

At the door, he glanced back over his shoulder. "Raise the stakes, boss. Make her choose life or death. It's your only way now."

Smitty slammed the door as a glass crashed against it.

Drake watched the liquid run down and contemplated his next move. This game grew wearisome and not as easy or fun as he imagined. Amusing at times, none of the women proved as strong or helpful as he expected. The game should have already ended.

He turned on metallic rock music and cranked it to a deafening level before he opened a door to the balcony. He stepped out, closing the distance to the rail. Sultry night air drifted across him as thunder rumbled. A single lightning bolt streamed from a cloud to the ground, ending with a loud crack.

Some marveled at such a sight, calling it a show of God's power. God meant nothing to him. He spat in God's face long ago, and would do it again, given the chance. He needed nothing from God. He chose to make his own power. Those who trusted in God for anything were simply fools, and he delighted in proving it. His enemy, Haniel, lived for God, which was precisely why he chose Charissa. She loved Haniel and the God he served. Before this ended she'd see his way though. He clung to confidence.

Haniel. No other man brought such hatred out in him. The favored son, always perfect. Their rivalry went back longer than he dared admit, from early in his life. He, the servant, did everything right. He worshipped old man McCrae with the devotion of an adoring son, instead of some poor foster kid. He never considered the only true son as a rival. When the time came, "Dad" gave Haniel authority over all of it, including him. Bitterness swept across his body as the unleashed memories consumed him. His intestines burned with an insistence of control.

The private garden stretched out below him, returning his mind to memories of long ago. He won Zoe in such a place.

She believed everything he told her without question. She fell under his charm, and turned her back on Haniel without hesitation. He closed his eyes and relished the moment when the man and his precious father learned the truth of their favorite woman. Pleasure soothed his stomach for a minute.

Yet in another garden, at a different time and place, he challenged Haniel in a fight to death. He almost won. How the man survived, he never understood. He quaked with anger as the events flooded over him as if no time passed.

Not this time.

Charissa held the same favored place. He suspected it, but the first night at the hospital, Haniel confirmed how much he cared for this one. Why else did he butt in and command him to stay away from her? That tempted him more to take her and gain allegiance. He slammed his fist against the rail. If she just gave in to start with...

But then, he expected some resistance, hence the capture and enticement of the others. Still, he grew impatient. She needed to break. Soon. Perhaps Smitty had a point. Had he gone soft? These women meant nothing to him. Sacrifice one for the many, for a final victory and the rapid end of this tiring charade. He tried playing nice, didn't he?

He closed his eyes and drifted into a vision of his next plot. Yes, his next target was expendable if necessary, but it depended a lot on the reaction from his prize toy. What difference did it make really? One sacrifice meant nothing to him. He didn't particularly want a dead body stinking up the place, but Charissa needed a reminder of his power. So if it happened, too bad. He must show her he held life and death in his hands.

Boom. The glass door behind him shook, windowpanes rattling from the repercussion. Sheets of rain poured from the sky, while gusts of wind blew it onto the patio, stinging his face as he yelled into the night.

"Is that your answer, God? You trying to scare me as if you can stop me from continuing what I started? You know it's her decision. She can choose me. She will and that scares even you, doesn't it?"

He laughed as his body shook with an array of emotions. Fear, anger, and pride choked the laughter, rolled with the sound from his throat and drifted into the blackness surrounding him.

He would win no matter what it cost. He must.

Chapter 42

A low rumble far above drifted down into the cave. In an ironic way, the thunderstorm comforted Charissa. Water ran through the small window, adding to the dampness of the dark walls surrounding the room. Yet the trickling sound soothed her soul. Strange. Storms always brought a sense of peacefulness.

Haniel once said she saw God's power in the storms and loved them so much because of it.

If only I'd listened to him. I'd give anything to go back — forget about Drake and drown myself in one of Haniel's hugs right now.

His strong hugs always left comfort in their wake, as if the whole world worked in her favor. She curled up in her chamber and closed her eyes against hot tears escaping amidst regrets. Her chest heaved as sobs of deepest sorrow fought to the surface, held in check by sheer will power.

No use in crying or wishing I'd made a different decision.

'What if' dreams did no good in this terrible place.

With effort, thoughts shifted to Drake. Who was this man anyway? She knew little about him, yet he knew Haniel well. Could that be the connection? Was this to get back at her friend for some reason? As she grew still in the darkness, she considered the days since she first woke in the dungeon.

The chains and shackles intrigued her. As unbelievable as it sounded, they changed. With every situation, they thickened and new ones appeared as anger and fear grew.

How absurd.

The confinement messed with her mind—a much more plausible explanation. Still, the constant whispering in the atmosphere left her wondering, etching constant stress within. Fear palpitated below the surface of her mind with an uneasiness she couldn't quite place. She didn't usually feel such things, except for her last camping trip. She felt the same way then, as if some creature smothered her, or sat nearby waiting for an opportunity to pounce.

Maybe Drake concocted some exotic sound system, placed in the walls, creating a torture chamber designed to drive them all mad. With the constant hum, the imagined presence of an enemy came easily. Then again, she didn't rule out the possibility of a supernatural force. The evil arising from her captors opened all kinds of doors to the unknown. Tingling trickled down her arms.

As more time passed, survival appeared less likely. Surely, someone missed her by now, but no one knew her well enough to know where to start a search. No one but Haniel, and after the way she treated him…

She pushed the guilt away.

I'll deal with it later.

Did she imagine it, or did one of her chains thicken? She shook her head and focused on the small window and the sound of water running down the cave wall. Her breathing evened out, relaxing the tension a little.

I've got to get out of here before I lose my mind completely.

But how? Prisoners often came to identify with their captors. She'd heard stories of kidnap victims actually falling in love with the men who took them. Drake nearly deceived her into believing she wanted a man like him, before his true character emerged. She'd never love him. But maybe if he thought she did…

At least she might discover why he brought her to his dungeon. If she pretended, would he see through the act? So many questions without answers.

She let the sounds of thunder and running water wash over her weary mind. As she drifted off to sleep, the beginnings of a plan formulated. There must be a way out. If she broke free, somehow she could help the others too. If Edna was right, if she caused the entire bizarre game Drake concocted, she owed them all.

Chapter 43

Charissa ran through a hilly forest. The sound of footsteps pounding from behind drove her forward. Chains swallowed her, like vines encasing her body. They weaved their way around, tighter and stronger with each second. Yet she moved forward, fighting against the fetters. Screams pierced her from every side. Cries of terror and pain, followed by shrieks of horror and appeals for mercy, ate at her core. Chains of guilt entangled and tripped her. Escape became impossible.

Charissa bolted upright. Tears streamed. Sobs wrenched her body while sweat teemed from the pores, and chills exploded down her back. Her heart pounded with the vibrancy of the footsteps in the dream. As the fog of sleep lifted from her brain, terrified screams shook her fully awake.

Valorie!

Sheer terror came from the direction of her chamber. Charissa jumped to the cave floor as Shamira limped up beside her, shouting at Drake. Still shaking from the dream, she forced herself to focus. Valorie trembled before Drake, expressing her fear through grating cries. A sinister light from his torch cast shadows on the tiny woman and in the dim light, her nakedness screamed louder than her voice. As he threw her to the cave floor, Valorie kicked and scooted away from him. He merely laughed and dragged her back.

Shamira yelled, "Drake. Stop it. Leave her alone."

He glanced over his shoulder for only a moment. A fierce glow from his eyes sent a fresh wave of chills through Charissa. He returned his attention to Valorie.

Shamira's voice squeaked as she spoke again, but this time calmness laced the apprehension. "Drake, please don't do this to Valorie. She doesn't deserve the humiliation or pain. Take me if you must have someone. I deserve to be used this way. She doesn't. Please stop."

Drake spoke without looking away from his target. "Why would I want used goods from a worthless slut? Besides, I'd rather see the fear in Val's eyes." He pinned Valorie and looked into her eyes. "You've been waiting for this since I brought you here, haven't you, my pet?"

Valorie answered him with wails of sorrow and pounding of fists against his chest.

Hatred overpowered Charissa. How cruel could this man get? She looked at the shame covering Shamira and then at the terrified woman fighting against the monster she once saw as attractive. Remorse inundated her.

This is my fault and I can't stand by and do nothing to stop it.

She slipped from her chamber, took a deep breath and placed a hand on Shamira's arm.

Boldness rose from somewhere deep inside. "You have great value, Shamira. Don't let him take the truth away from you."

Drake turned toward the two women. His eyes still glowed.

What choice did she have?

She stared into the glow and without emotion said, "Drake, let her go. I'll take her place. That's what you want anyway isn't it? Let these other women go. Send them all home, and I'll give myself to you."

Drake howled with laughter. "I'd rather you watch from your chained position where you can't do anything to stop me. It isn't your body I want."

The blaze in his eyes deepened, then he turned back to Valorie and threw off his robe.

The strength of her screams grew to an unbearable level. All of the women, even Edna, joined in the pleas for mercy. But Drake showed none.

Charissa watched in horror as the rape proceeded. Her throat constricted and breaths came in short, raspy gasps. Her wails united with Valorie's. She begged Drake to stop, but her pleading did no good. The more she implored him, the more violent he became not only with the rape but also in beating the woman. Her soul cried out in despair for the innocent woman enduring the attack. Sympathy grew deeper and more intense.

Unable to watch any longer, she closed her eyes, but the weeping from the others exploded through her mind and all the way down to her belly. She dropped to her knees filled with anguish beyond anything she ever experienced before that moment.

Filled with wretchedness, she whispered, "God, please make him stop before he kills her."

Valorie grew silent. Charissa's eyes shot open. The attack continued but Valorie lay beneath him still and silent. Blood covered her face and swelling already appeared around her eyes. Fury mounted, and the accompanying adrenaline pushed Charissa to her feet. She strained at the chains, yelling, yet unaware of what she said. The shackles holding her back cut into her wrist and ankles.

"You devil! Get off her now!" She pulled harder against the restraints until her strength gave away and she fell into a heap on the dirt floor, helplessness giving way to earthquake level sobs. Her heart pounded through her head until she thought it might burst.

Then, silence.

She looked up. Drake stood over her. The glower in his eyes subsided, cold blackness returned.

He said, "You couldn't save her could you? Valiant try, my dear. Valiant, but not good enough."

He turned and moved up the staircase. Smitty appeared from the shadows and followed his boss as usual.

Drake spoke over his shoulder, "Bring Charissa now."

She considered fighting the little man, but her arms and legs wobbled, as flimsy as jelly. She hoped she could stand without help.

Chapter 44

Hot water ran over Charissa's head and down her body. Aching muscles drank in soothing heat, but the knots in her shoulders and neck remained tight, unrelenting. Throbs slammed against her skull.

She stood under the stream of water in hopeless despair it might somehow wash away the memories, but Valorie's screams haunted her. The silent, still form she left in the dirt as Smitty pushed her up the stairs tormented her unlike anything she ever imagined. More than Bubba, and even more than the little boy in Dallas.

A fresh wave of sobs engulfed her as guilt trickled with the water. Torment burnt every inch of her body, as if she climbed a mountain and ran a marathon on the same day. Scenes from the early morning hours became unbearable in spite of eyes squeezed shut. Weariness overcame her. Unable to stand any longer, she placed both hands on the wall and slid down to her knees.

"Why?" She asked herself. "Valorie didn't do anything to Drake. He should have taken me instead and let the others go free."

Grief bore down hard. Heaviness deeper than any amount of chains pressed against her body, zapping every ounce of strength. The depths of her soul searched for an outlet until, having found none, resigned itself to a place beyond reach. A flaming arrow seared the open wound and left numbness in its wake. A self-constructed wall closed around the spot.

She knelt for another minute or two, and then forced weary legs into a standing position. With great effort and determination, she made her arms move, picked up the shampoo and washed her hair. She scrubbed her skin with a bar of soap. The scents ran together and filled her nostrils, but the stench of the predawn hours lingered in her mind. Not even the heavy chains weighed her down as much as pictures flashing in her brain.

∞∞∞∞∞∞∞∞∞∞∞∞

Drake paced in his study. Charissa caught him off guard with such a bold offer of sacrifice. He anticipated begging and even a possible fight, except he made sure all of them remained chained during his display of power over Valorie. Rage over the audacity of her and Shamira spurred him on and definitely encouraged greater force with the woman.

Not satisfied with offering to take the other woman's place, she dared to speak encouragement to the youngest. The image raised his blood pressure as he fumed. Surely, she judged the younger woman for her lifestyle. In all her righteous choices about sex before marriage, how could she not judge Shamira? Instead of putting her down and agreeing the younger woman should take Valorie's place, Charissa comforted her and confirmed the girl's value.

Comfort and encourageent could not happen again. Not in his dungeon.

Of course, he regained the upper hand. The sweetness of guilt and pain throbbing through her being as she begged him to show mercy pleased him immeasurably. He adored the memory of Charissa on her knees before him, with the shackles and chains growing thicker and stronger as she succumbed to his power. Yes, she lost her steam rather quickly. The end of his monumental game neared. He smelled victory in the air. He needed only her vocal surrender. Only a short delay while she finished cleaning up stood between him and sweet triumph. His skin tingled, and he almost giggled like a schoolgirl at the prospect of her arrival.

Impatience settled over him while late morning shadows danced across the silk Karastan rug. He rehearsed his planned lines as he moved back and forth across the room. Blame her, pour on the guilt, and fill her up with shame. He suspected she already stood under the shower letting the piercing screams and images flood over her mind. Her sorrow worked to his advantage. He only needed a few well-placed subtle words with half-truths dropped beside them.

His favorite method of manipulation—the sprinkling of a few twists, believable enough to cast doubt. The same plot he used with so many other women in his lifetime. Amazingly simple, yet so effective. When he finished, she'd fall at his feet, consumed by the imprisonment of her emotions. His mind echoed with imaginary sounds of heavy chains as they brushed against the magnificence of the room. The sweet savor of victory melted in his mouth like rich chocolate.

Comforted by the inevitable, he relaxed into the moment as he strode to the sofa and sunk into the deep cushions. He closed his eyes and rubbed his hands together contemplating the scene he fully expected when Charissa arrived. His annoyance subsided somewhat. A craving for the final winning blow shot through his arteries and boiled his blood on the way to his heart. The assurance of the impending euphoric release soon to come heightened the longing and calmed his senses. He waited, the mirror image of a junkie pausing while the injected drug kicked in and brought relief.

A few more minutes until his game ended, and he took possession of his prize.

Chapter 45

Smitty led Charissa into the study by the chain shackled around her neck. Her mind drifted back to the prisoners jailers brought into the emergency room sometimes. Even the most horrendous ones wore fewer chains than those surrounding her body. She lost count from the many places where they intersected and crossed each other as they wound around and choked out hope.

In spite of the hot shower, her body hurt. If not for the man's constant tug, she doubted whether her legs possessed the ability to move on their own. Struggling, she picked up one lead filled foot and placed it in front of the other. Smitty cursed and yelled at her for moving at the speed of a slug. She thought about glaring at the pitiful man, but dismissed the idea. He wasn't worth the extra effort a look required, much less a glare. She assumed their little journey ended at Drake's feet where he expected groveling.

She should be more alert — prepared for whatever Drake planned for her, but the numbness of heart consumed so much energy. Numbness consuming physical strength made no sense. Somewhere in her mind, the answer played with consciousness in an unclear way making her brain ache. She didn't want to think. If she thought, Valorie slipped into the picture, and if she allowed the memories, she'd break and he'd win.

Vanity of vanities! All is vanity. What difference does it make now? What if he wins his little game? Even if he doesn't and I somehow escaped, I can't forget what he's done — what these women suffered because of me. And I still don't know why.

The senselessness of this whole game bothered her most. The unanswered "why" infuriated her, as it did any time she questioned circumstances. Over the years, she prayed and asked God why so many times. His silence deafened her. Seek Him. Why? He didn't answer either.

They reached the end of the hallway, and Smitty opened the door, shutting out her thoughts.

Classical music flowed over the room with a dark sound, resolved into perfect harmony and a lighter mood, then moved back into the darker tones. The rise and fall of the music grated against her nerves as the intensity waxed and waned. The notes shifted from sweet to a ferocious crash of sounds all coming together — much like she felt even before the dungeon.

Drake leaned back on a plush sofa with his eyes closed and brows furrowed. His bare feet stretched across an expensive area rug. He rubbed his hands together in what appeared as serious contemplation. The furnishings, wall hangings and décor in the room screamed luxury and wealth. Standing on the edge of such an expensive setting, she longed for her little apartment with its mismatched, hand-me-down furniture, where Rusty disobediently parked his furry body every chance she gave him. Drake probably shot dogs for less of an offense; then again, maybe he enjoyed animals more than he did people.

Her mind drifted back to the day Drake picked her up for their lake date. Good old Rusty growled a warning, but she ignored it, abandoning him in a locked apartment. Had anyone missed her and rescued him, or must he pay for her choices too? She dropped her head in anticipation of more tears, but not even a sting in the corners taunted her, every available drop already expelled. The aching disappeared behind a cloud of numbness, leaving nothing more than fatigue in its place.

Smitty pushed her across the room. She tripped on the rug and almost fell, but somehow kept her balance and came to a stop within inches of Drake's feet.

He spoke from the sofa. "That will be all, Smitty. Close the door behind you."

He held out his hand. She didn't move. "Come now, my dear, sit with me."

"I'd rather not."

"Are you afraid?"

Oddly, she felt only repulsion of this monster. "No."

"Really?" He raised his eyebrows, and then laughed loudly. "What then?"

"I don't like or trust you."

"All the same, come and sit with me. Let's end this game, shall we?"

"Why don't we start with you explaining what this game is all about?" She fought against the rising tone of her voice.

Stay calm. Keep your head straight.

"Sit. That isn't a suggestion, my dear."

She looked into his stern face with the black eyes gleaming. She moved to the sofa and sat as far from him as she dared.

"What is your game, Drake? Tell me or throw me back in your dungeon now."

"What spunk. I like it. You really don't understand yet, do you?"

She looked for some clue in his face. Nothing. "No. I don't."

He reached across the space and ran his finger down her arm. "It really isn't about you. Admittedly, you as an added prize pleases me more than you can imagine. But the game...

See, my dear, you are quite strong in character. I need you. Imagine what we might accomplish together." He gestured around the room. "This is nothing compared to what I offer. All the power and riches you can ever imagine."

"What about Edna? Isn't she your partner in the power department?"

"Edna serves me well, but she lacks loyalty. Don't you think I know she'd stab me in my sleep given the chance?"

"I don't care about power, and wealth means nothing to me."

"Aw yes, your precious little orphans; your dream. My dear, think how much you could help those children with money. Join me, and I'll make sure you have all the orphans you want."

Intense anger shook and fought against control in a sudden desire to tear him apart with bare hands.

"Join you? And what about the others? What you've done to them is despicable. Why would I be a part of someone capable of so much evil?"

His eyes smoldered as his hand wrapped around her upper arm. She flinched and clenched her teeth. Visions of Valerie grabbed hold of her stomach, twisting it into tight knots. Drake lightened his grip but didn't let go. He pulled her off the sofa.

"Perhaps we should take a stroll and let some fresh air cool us down a bit."

He led her across the room to French doors that opened onto a spacious patio. A gentle pathway led away from the house into a perfectly manicured lawn lined with immaculate gardens. Beside the patio, a five-foot waterfall cascaded down large rocks and swirled into a pool where a fountain shot the water back into the air. A soothing spray drifted through the wind into her face.

Trickling water usually soothed her, but anger and fear tugged at her heart.

Fight or run?

She scanned the perimeter with its brick wall twice her height. Running was a pitiful option. Valorie's screams played through her mind. Fighting seemed even more impossible than the possibility of scaling the brick wall.

Drake moved behind her, wrapped his arms around her waist, and whispered. "You did it to them. If you gave yourself to me willingly, I wouldn't have needed the other women. But you fought all the way. You hate me right now, don't you? Dierdre showed you so well how to hate men. You look at Edna and envy her power and composure. Nothing stops her. She takes what she wants, unlike you. Fear keeps you frozen – almost as much as it does Valorie. The very thing she feared most happened. You stood powerless to stop it. Just as you couldn't stop Bubba's death the night we met."

The words stung, and she had no answer.

"Your pious religion gained you nothing. Ariana judged you all and agreed to help you purge yourselves of sin, but you are no better. Didn't you sit in judgment of the others – made up your mind about them without knowing their stories? You see me as evil. You are no better. If you held a knife in your hand, you would forsake the treasured Ten Commandments and commit murder. You're full of hatred directed at me. I feel it in your quivering body."

He tightened his hold and pulled her closer to himself. She balled her hands and pressed the fists against her chest.

He continued, "I watched from the darkness when Shamira cut you. I saw the euphoria on your face. You are as worthless as she is in spite of your self-righteous purity. And in exchange, no one wants you. Your father abandoned you along with every man who got close to you, because you're too good for all of them, yet really without any value."

Anger dissipated into hollowness. She spiraled into a pit of desolation, dropping her arms like massive pieces of lead pipe.

"What do you want from me, Drake?"

"Surrender completely to me. Kneel and kiss my feet. Deny your God and denounce the despicable Haniel you so dearly love."

A spark flickered in her heart. "What does Haniel have to do with this?"

"He and his father took everything from me. They cheated me and threw me out of my home. For some reason, he loves you. But he holds out on you, as he did with me. They learned it from your God. Don't you see? Supposedly, he wants the best for you. Tell me, Charissa, do you have the best? Do you have those things you desire so much? Where is your husband or the dream—the desires of your heart? So, you see, my motive may seem like revenge, but I'm really saving you from them. Let me be your god from this day forward, and I'll give you the desires of your heart."

Water trickled down the rocks, but instead of peace, the sound roared in her ears with the roar of a massive waterfall. Confusion swirled around her head, filling her mind with a thick foggy mist. Could Drake be right? Had she completely sold herself out to God only for Him to let her down? She wanted His presence with an ache deeper than anything she'd ever known or imagined, but she felt only a great chasm of empty space in the deep places of her spirit.

God, where are you? Why can't I feel you?

She looked up into a sky filled with clouds. The shape of one reminded her of an angel with big wings and a sword stretched out before him. The sun passed behind the cloud and the edge of the sword shape shimmered with a silver outline. The fog in her head cleared and the spark leapt into a tiny flame. She shook uncontrollably. The muscles in her body froze into utter loss of feeling while the quaking of her body continued.

With a trembling voice, she squeaked out a response. "No."

"What?" Drake's voice drowned out the trickles of water as he spun her around to face him and grasped both arms in a vice-grip. "Did you say no?"

She prayed silently for strength. "I will not deny a God who has been with me through the most difficult times of my life, and Haniel tried to protect me from you. I didn't listen."

His eyes bore into hers as they first smoldered and then burst into a red glow. "I'll kill you for this."

Her heart beat against her chest with such force she wondered whether a heart attack might take her before he delivered a single fist to her face. Still, something rose up inside of her. Boldness poured from her soul.

"Go ahead. I have no fear of death. You may kill my body, but my soul belongs to God, and you can never touch that part of me. I fear God much more than I do you. If you kill me, it will place me straight into His arms, and He still wins at your game. You lose, Drake."

Shrieking vile curses, he slapped her across the face. She winced but kept silent. More slaps jerked her head left and right as the blows continued and knocked her off balance. Grabbing a fist full of hair, he flung her to the ground and then spat on her. His bare foot rammed against her stomach. She gasped for breath as another kick landed higher than the others did. She grabbed his foot but he yanked it away and kicked her in the head. A fuzzy, dark mist blanketed her. He pivoted and ran into the house screaming for Smitty.

Charissa pushed herself up and fought the spiraling fog of her mind. The clouds darkened the sky, shutting out the sun. Wide spots of brown dotted the lush green lawn and spread from the center outward. The flowers wilted and dropped from their host plants. The fountain gurgled, sputtered and died away. The cascading water stopped flowing.

She fell to her knees and then bowed her face to the ground.

Oh, God, what have I done? Please forgive me for getting myself into this mess. Protect the other women from Drake's anger. Please, please, save us.

She screamed and grabbed the back of her head as a large hand grabbed her hair and hauled her up from the ground.

Chapter 46

Smitty pushed Charissa through the door and down the staircase. Each step tugged at tender joints and muscles. Near the end, he shoved hard. She tripped and stumbled down to the landing. He laughed, but around the room, loud gasps came from the chambers.

He bellowed across the room. "Not a word."

At her assigned hole, he clicked the chains back into their rings and pulled to check whether they held her securely. He pulled out a bottle of whiskey and took a long drink. "I sincerely hope Drake will let me have fun with you before he kills you."

She turned her head away as he tried to kiss her, and then shoved him. He wasted no time in slapping her hard enough to send her tumbling to the ground. She hit the floor hard but rolled away to avoid his foot.

He cackled, took another drink, and then turned away from her. "I'll deal with you later."

He stumbled away, the bottle at his lips. The thud of the door confirmed his departure. Without the sliding of the bolt, she wondered if he waited at the top of the staircase. She squinted upwards, but the top landing stood empty.

With a deep sigh, she climbed into the confines of her chamber and coiled up. Dark shadows chased away the last traces of light. The fuzziness in her brain retreated with one remaining sunbeam, but her body rippled involuntarily. The cut across her stomach stung. Her ribs and face punched out a steady beat as dull reminders of Drake's threat. Death seemed rather merciful at this point. Escape appeared hopeless.

She glanced over to Valorie's chamber. Still naked, she hid in the corner, a knot no one could unravel. The bloodied body jerked occasionally, but not even a soft whimper escaped the hole in the cave wall. Condemnation assaulted Charissa as she relived the moments of the attack. A flood of tears washed over her. Drake meant it as a lesson in fear. A formidable enemy, yes. Yet she stood up to him didn't she? So his experiment failed. She wasn't afraid.

Yes, you are. You fear the most important things in life.

Her heart spoke so loudly she wondered if the others heard it. No one stirred. She didn't have to ask for clarification. She knew. Relationships terrified her because she feared abandonment. The thought of pursuing dreams vanquished her, cowering into a corner. She always found reasonable explanations, but in the dungeon, truth met her face to face. Every reason offered was nothing more than an excuse. Fear of failure overshadowed hope for fulfillment of any dream or desire.

A cough across the room drew her attention to Dierdre. If ever a woman hated men and wanted others to as well…

But she didn't hate men. Drake – yes. At the moment, she dared not deny how deeply she detested his vileness. Not all men acted like him. In fact, she never met any man so filled with evil.

Her hatred comes from bitterness, and you harbor the same thing deep in your soul – even against God.

What? No way. A fresh wave of tears streamed down her face. Her throat burned with caustic spit as she considered all of the men who left her. Why didn't God give her a good husband? If He had, she wouldn't be here now. A pang of self-reproach tripped through her stomach and tightened her chest. In the middle of declaring God's greatness to Drake, she held Him responsible for her circumstances in the dungeon – and in her life.

Not looking at Ariana or Shamira, she didn't wait for a voice. No arguing there. She repented of judgmental attitudes on a regular basis, confessing her weakness and turning around to criticize some little thing. She judged her fellow captives too without realizing it, but the snootiness hung as a thundercloud above them.

You know all about the Lord, but sometimes you want the things of God more than you want Him.

She already agreed with everything. Did there have to be more?

She sighed, and teardrops fell without check. Admittedly, she read her Bible all the time, but more from a sense of duty and the ability to check a task off her daily list. When had she grown so cold spiritually?

Edna moved and a rustling of paper came from her direction. At least Drake was wrong about her. Power-hungry people nauseated her. Edna reminded her of Ann—always controlling every tiny aspect of life including those who stumbled into their worlds. But she wasn't like them.

Not power hungry, but the control thing – definitely you.

What was it with this internal voice? She wanted to shut it off. The truth in what she heard, left no doubt where the voice came from.

You asked God to help you, didn't you?

She sighed. This one puzzled her.

You've surrounded yourself with non-threatening people where you don't have to risk your heart. You have everything planned out for yourself, but you won't trust God with even little things much less the big ones.

Relationships. How many boyfriends in the past told her they couldn't stand her control. The very suggestion angered her every time, but in the musty air, she understood. Her insecurity and lack of trust drove those men away.

Guilty of all these things plus a whole lot more, she deserved this dungeon.

But grace...

In a soft whisper she prayed, "Lord, please forgive me. I deserve this place, but you don't always give us what we deserve. I confess my sin to You. Please help me. I really don't want to die here."

She fell into a deep sleep and dreamed of meadows and waterfalls where she splashed and played with abandon. The sweet smell of freedom drifted over her with a peaceful sleep unlike any she'd known for years.

Chapter 47

Charissa startled awake. The dungeon remained dark. A sweet smell floated in the air, surrounded her producing the same peacefulness of comforting dreams. Until she noticed a shadowed form standing near her chamber.

She blinked her eyes and squinted. Her pulse raced, vibrating through her head as she willed her vision to clear. The man stepped closer. The scent grew stronger.

She gasped. "Haniel?"

Was she still dreaming?

Lord, please don't let me wake up. I want to stay right here in this dream, die here in this peacefulness, secure with Haniel.

"Yes, Charissa. It's me." Haniel's voice drowned every fear.

"It is you. I knew you'd come. How did you find me?"

She jumped down from the chamber and wrapped her arms around his waist. She clung in desperation and wept.

"I'm so sorry ..." The words choked in her throat as sobs leapt to the surface.

He touched her cheek with the gentleness of a butterfly. "Charissa, what are you doing here?"

"Drake—you were right about him. He kidnapped me. I think he drugged me, but I fell asleep after our trip to the lake, and I woke up here."

He offered her a bottle of water. She gulped the cool liquid. It ran down her throat and soothed a rawness she didn't know existed.

He asked again, "What are you doing here?"

"I told you. Drake kidnapped me."

The moon glistened off his eyes. Blasted piercing look. When he used it, everything stripped away. A soul bared of all masks gave way to those eyes. She trembled even holding tightly to him.

The moon peeked through the small window and hit his white shirt. Light illuminated the dingy cave. In the place where she slept for days, the filth of her existence became evident. Rat droppings lined the edges of the chamber. Dried blood spotted her thin mattress among rings of urine stains. A swarm of cockroaches crawled over the walls and ceiling. Spider webs covered the corners. Bits of food and wrappings strewn in the chamber held worms and bugs of every shape, size and color. A snake curled around one of the posts where her chain remained secure. The stench of human feces, urine and blood suffocated her as she looked around the room. Rats scurried close to the cave walls in search of crumbs.

It wasn't all Drake. He couldn't touch you without your willingness.

She stood frozen in time. The revelations from earlier in the evening rushed from every direction. The filth of the cave mirrored the garbage of her soul. Shame engulfed her. She looked back at him and then down at the floor of the cave.

Her voice came out as a mere whisper. "It was me, Haniel. I put myself in a position for Drake to bring me here. I should have listened to you. I can't blame him, you or God any longer. I'm guilty."

She poured out her heart, then, sharing all she experienced after the beating. Between tears and quivering breath, she finished with an admission.

"I asked God to forgive me and to help me so I don't die. Then I woke up, and you were here."

Haniel cupped her chin in his hand. She looked into a pool of tranquility. A twinkle across the brown irises danced in the soft moonlight. He spoke with complete tenderness. "You are forgiven." He held up empty hands. "No stones. If you're ready, I'll lead you out of here."

"I am. But what about the shackles and chains?"

"Baby Girl, the chains around your heart held you more as a prisoner than these. And I believe you broke those when you took ownership."

He held out a hand, and she didn't hesitate in grabbing it.

The clank of chains and thud of shackles against stone resounded in her ears.

Chapter 48

Drake descended the staircase with Charissa's sudden flare of courage draped around his shoulders. An anchor of defeat weighed down each step, yet anger simmered below the surface, ready to flame into rage.

He contemplated killing the other women and leaving her to writhe in shame, die on her own. On the other hand, he could kill her and secure control over the others. Perhaps the enslavement of five compliant women to do his bidding was better than killing them to hurt her.

Either way, she chose, and he demanded her life for choosing against him. He couldn't simply return her to civilization as if none of this happened.

He reached the bottom landing. Prickles raced along the back of his neck. The torch held high into the air lit the dungeon as he reached for the knife, sheathed loosely on his belt. He sensed an emptiness in the chamber before he saw it.

How? If Smitty took her for his pleasure…

"Smitty!"

Edna stirred in her chamber.

Drake grabbed her arms and shook wildly. "Where is she?'

"Who? What are you talking about?"

"Where is Charissa? Did Smitty take her?"

"How would I know? I *was* sleeping. The last time I saw her, she was in her chamber, curled up, crying – maybe even praying for help. Guess she never learned God helps those who help themselves."

Drake slapped her. "Don't mention that name in my presence – ever again."

Edna blinked. "Sorry. Didn't realize G…" She paused. "…a simple saying about some non-existent being would offend you."

"But he does exist; and I loathe him." He spat on the floor. "Wake the others. If Smitty doesn't have Charissa, one of them better know what happened to her."

He raced up the stairs and bolted through the door, not bothering to shut it. He stormed through the house, yelling and cursing. He half expected to find Smitty ravaging Charissa, hoped for it. Foreboding gnawed at his gut. He opened Smitty's bedroom door where the man lay, passed out across the bed alone. Dread swooped down on him like buzzards on a dead animal.

He controlled his voice in spite of the rage swirling through his body. "Where is she?"

Smitty mumbled something in his sleep, but never moved. Drake kicked him.

Smitty roused, rolled over and grumbled. "What was that for?"

"What did you do with Charissa?" Drake's veins pulsed against his neck as he fought for composure.

"I chained her in the chamber – half dragged her there. Left the wench curled up, crying like a baby."

"Then why isn't she there?"

Smitty shot out of the bed. "What? I swear, boss. I left her chained up."

He raced through the house and down to the dungeon. Drake ran behind him, more certain of his intuition.

In the dungeon, all of the women sat in their chambers wide-eyed. Even Valorie uncurled a little, but remained drawn up and as far back as possible. The chains lay in a heap beside Charissa's empty spot. Drake bent down and picked them up.

"Who helped her? Someone better tell me or you all die."

A soft voice came across the cave from the recesses of one chamber. "God helped her. She prayed for help and a man appeared. I saw him, and if I hadn't been so afraid, maybe he would have helped me too." Valorie retreated into her ball consumed by breaking sobs.

Drake bounded across the cave. "What did this man look like?"

Valorie looked up. "I don't know, except his face shined. He might have been an angel."

"Which way did they go?"

"Up the stairs maybe. I couldn't see, but she's gone."

Drake slammed his fist against the wall. Dirt and rock fell around him. He cursed and stomped around the cave. He kicked a scurrying rat to the other side of the room. Fury burned. It had to be Haniel. He found them somehow. Or Smitty lied and hadn't chained her at all, then left the door open.

"Smitty, get the dogs and a few men. I'm not giving up so easily. If Haniel took her, they'll both pay for it."

∞∞∞∞∞∞∞∞∞∞∞∞

The dogs strained against leashes and pulled Smitty along behind them. Drake sniffed the air, seeking his prey. He moved down the trails and kept his eyes opened for any possible hiding place. The fury mounted with every passing moment, but he slammed a lid on the emotions, saving release for when they found the escapee.

Small rocks tumbled beneath his feet as he rushed along the pathway. He didn't know how long ago she escaped and whether Haniel really helped or if Valorie dreamed about a man. He seriously doubted Charissa left alone. The fact she didn't take the others surprised him a little, if indeed she had help – especially from Haniel. Maybe she lacked virtue after all and saved her pretty, little hide without a thought of anyone else. Selfish to the core – what a pleasant thought. And if she escaped alone... Reminding her of the selfish act provided the perfect weapon to win her completely. The possibility drove him to find and reclaim her.

The group of men and dogs rounded a corner. The animals barked as they sniffed the ground and ran in circles. Drake stopped. The rocks dropped off to the side, forming a steep cliff, but pseudo trails drifted down to the bottom of a ravine, treacherous in the early morning dew, yet maneuverable. He scanned the shallow riverbed. A large outcropping of fallen rocks formed an overhang and a somewhat secluded area hidden from most trails – the perfect shelter for a woman fresh from a dungeon. Water trickled down the side of one rock. He looked over every crack and tiny crevice for a hint of clothing or hair, but saw nothing.

He sensed a presence in those rocks. Against the early morning light, a large shadow crouched on one of them as if standing guard over the area. Drake shifted his position and looked again. His spine tingled as he peered deeper into the hidden places below. Still no sign of one person, much less two. If they spent any time there, he saw no evidence of it.

Drake moved away from the edge. "Let's go. They're not here."

He picked up the trail again with Smitty close behind tugging at the silent dogs. Drake looked back one last time when the light shifted as the sun peeked over the hills. The shadowy figure dissipated. He blew out a breath, disgusted at his inability to distinguish between reality and imagination. He loved games of deceit, but not when he became the recipient. The uneasiness in his stomach lifted a little, but he scanned the area once more in case he missed something.

Still nothing.

He hurried forward. Anger at a distraction which put more distance between himself and the prey bubbled up and spilled over in the form of cursing. He silenced himself as quickly and stepped lighter with greater speed.

One thought moved him forward.

He will not defeat me this easily. I will find them and win this game.

Chapter 49

Charissa followed Haniel along the trail, almost thankful for the constant darkness of the dungeon. After the hours and days of dim lighting, her eyes adjusted easily with the moonlight shining through the last hours of night.

They rounded a corner and reached an area where the rocks dropped off and formed a cliff. Below, large rocks hung over a shallow riverbed. A small path led to a sheltered area. She drew in a deep breath and held it as Haniel moved onto the small path. He turned slightly and held out a hand. She released the breath as anxiety fell away like the tiny pebbles slipping beneath her feet. She held tightly as they climbed down the rocks into the riverbed. She slipped several times, but Haniel's firm hand steadied and kept her from falling.

Her heart raced, but instead of apprehension, a sense of excitement overtook her mind. Far from fun, she still found this escape exhilarating. The cool pre-dawn breeze revived her tired body. Her breathing grew rapid as they reached the end of the trail. Shallow water ran between the large rocks, fed by a small stream descending from the rock overhang. The half-cave formed a perfect temporary shelter. Large fallen rocks surrounded it, providing perfect covering.

She climbed onto the rock and looked up. If she scooted beneath the rock, the overhang hid her from most views. The only possible vantage point for discovery existed where they just traveled. If Drake followed the same trail…

They must remain alert. If he came, they could move down behind the big rocks, but still might need to maneuver, matching any shifts he made—especially if he arrived after daylight.

She scanned the trail. In the moonlight, only the swaying trees moved on the pathway, but in the distance, dogs barked.

Lord, please let them take a different trail. Don't let them find us.

The barking drew closer as the night sky shifted into dawn.

She looked back at Haniel. He placed a finger over his lips, stepped behind the rocks and pulled her behind him. He nodded toward the big rock. She saw nothing, but a strong presence calmed the thundering of her heart. She trusted this man, who pursued, freed and now protected her at the risk of his life. The knowledge helped fight mounting fear. Peering over his shoulder, she waited. The barking grew louder until a group of men rounded the corner on the trail above.

Run.

But her legs refused to move. She scarcely breathed. Drake stepped to the edge of the trail and peered down. She glanced upward and noticed an open spot directly above them. Haniel reached back, wrapped an arm around her, and stopped the trembling. She wouldn't return to the dungeon without a fight. Planting her feet firmly, she stood still behind her protector.

Drake shifted his position and looked straight at her. The breath caught in her throat. At any moment, he'd release the dogs and let them attack. She braced herself. Instead, the dogs sniffed the ground in circles and grew quiet. Agonizing moments passed as she alternated between holding her breath and trying to control it. Her heart returned to thundering and she prayed more fervently for protection. Then, the men turned and moved back onto the trail. As the sun peeked over the hills, Drake looked back in their direction before moving on at a quicker pace. Cursing echoed against the rocks surrounding them.

The two of them remained in the same position as the sun rose higher into the sky. In spite of the nearby danger, the burst of pink fading into gold captivated her. Awed by the beauty, tears welled up. She held her breath again, this time not wanting to interrupt the glory of the moment. When was the last time she watched a sunrise? She didn't recall one that meant as much as this one did with newfound freedom. She exhaled slowly and tension flowed from her body.

Haniel turned and spoke softly, "They're gone. You're safe, Baby Girl."

She searched his face, found assurance in the smile and twinkling eyes. She moved beneath the stream of water, letting it run over her face and trickle into her mouth. The cold, clear liquid ran down a parched throat. The sweet, pureness compelled her to drink deeply of water more refreshing than she ever tasted before.

A soft touch spread deep warmth across her back. A mixture of emotions collided as tears cascaded, mixing with the stream of water. She turned and buried her face in his chest. He stroked her hair as she wept quietly against him. Weariness crashed over her. When he pulled her down onto the hidden rock, she didn't resist. Strong arms wrapped around her until she fell asleep.

Chapter 50

Throwing a switch at the top of the stairs flooded the dungeon with intense light. The women squealed in the sudden brightness. Drake pounded down the staircase straight to Valorie's chamber. Sweat poured from him as he grabbed a foot and pulled her onto the floor without caring if he scraped her body against the rocks and hit her head in the process. She cowered before him and attempted to hide the nakedness. He snatched her wrists and forced them wide.

His voice boomed. "You have a choice. Choose wisely. Your answer will bring you a reward or another rape you will not survive. Now, tell me everything you remember about the man who helped Charissa and anything indicating where they went."

Valorie cringed, panicked terror written across her face. Her eyes darted around accompanied by body convulsions. She hesitated only a moment before answering in sporadic fragments.

"Tall. Broad shoulders — muscular. Long hair. White shirt. The moonlight reflected off it." She panted.

"How did he break the chains?"

"He didn't. The chains broke—not all at once. They talked...a link broke. Then she talked more...cried. I don't know what she said. Little bits fell...until, all of a sudden, they all broke."

"Why didn't you call out? Go with them?"

"I thought it was a dream. Besides, I'm naked. I didn't want them to see me naked."

"Well, you shouldn't want anyone to see you naked. You're a pitiful skeleton of a woman—not desirable at all with your bag of skin-covered bones. Where were they going?"

"I don't know."

"Think woman. I need to know where he took her – at least what direction."

"He led her out, that's all I know. The light softened and before I could see again they left. She wanted him to save her, and he did."

"Did she say his name?"

"I'm not sure. M...m...m...maybe."

"Haniel?"

"I guess--yeah. Sounds right."

"Figures." He turned to the other women and raced between them. "What about the rest of you? What do you know?"

None of them offered any information. All claimed they slept through anything that happened.

What a crock. More likely, they all watched and waited for a promise of rescue. The taunting image of Haniel plagued him and brought on a fresh wave of bitterness. The enemy, here, in his dungeon. A worthy adversary, after all; but how dare he breach security into this place. After going to so much trouble, freeing a lone woman didn't make sense. It wasn't his style. If he knew Haniel, and he did, the two of them would regroup and come back for the others.

Well, he'd be ready for them.

He grabbed Smitty by the shirt. "They'll be back, but we're not making it easy for them."

He looked around the cave. Shamira slumped in her chamber. The pallor of her skin contrasted against the dark bruises covering much of her body. She took shallow breaths. Every movement brought soft moans with furrowed brows and wrinkles lining her forehead. Dried blood dotted her arms and clung to the side of her head. She looked more like something out of a zombie movie than a living woman. Perhaps he'd been a little too severe.

Too bad.

He nodded in her direction. "Leave the whore here to rot."

He studied Valorie for a moment. She shook visibly and again attempted to cover her body. He shook his head in pity at the fear still pouring from her.

"You can unchain this one and give her a room upstairs – the attic one. She won't run any more than an unchained elephant."

Smitty laughed loudly. Drake gritted his teeth and took a step toward the assistant, grabbing his collar.

"Sorry, Boss. That was funny…comparing this anorexic wimp to an elephant."

"I'm not amused. She's disgusting though, so get something for her to wear."

He looked at Dierdre. She reminded him of a big cat, ready to pounce if given half a chance.

"Put her in one of the hidden rooms down here – be sure it's locked and keep the key with you."

He motioned at Ariana, who backed against the wall. "Put her somewhere – she's no threat either. Use another of the hidden rooms, but away from the bitter one."

Edna moved near. The hunger in her eyes intensified as he released Smitty and stepped in her direction. "Edna, my power hungry accomplice. Are you still devoted to me?"

Her voice dripped sugar laced with arsenic. "Of course I am, my dearest. I'll do whatever you want."

"Yes, I'm sure you will—as long as it serves your purposes." He turned to Smitty. "Unchain her. She'll stay near me so I can keep an eye on her."

Smitty's eyes moved over Edna with unhidden lust, undressing and caressing each curve without a touch. He bit his lower lip and started to comment. Drake narrowed his eyes and dared him without saying a word.

Smitty pasted a smile across his face and moved around the room following orders.

While he worked, he asked, "Do you really think they'll come back?"

"Count on it. Be ready before first light, when they'll come—right into my trap."

Chapter 51

Sharp pain in her hip woke Charissa. Afraid to open her eyes and find herself still in the dungeon, she kept them closed, waiting motionless. A cool breeze lured her back into restless sleep filled with dreams.

Running. Always running, through a hilly forest. The sound of footsteps pounded from behind and drove her forward. Chains no longer engulfed her, but they hung all around, clanging in the wind, taunting. She proceeded, fighting against chains that grabbed and threatened every step. Screams assailed from every side, followed by shrieks of horror and appeals for mercy.

As she raced down trails, faces appeared behind trees. Countless orphans reached out, crying for help. Her footsteps echoed. Bloodied, broken bodies fell beside the trail while she ran farther away. Valorie remained naked and in a tiny ball under a bush that kept pricking her. Dierdre, with all her anger, clung to a tree, a desperate child, hiding from pain. Edna, ever in control, peered at her from a hidden trail. Shamira reached out, blood running down her arms and splattering on the ground. And Ariana knelt in prayer, emaciated with hollow eyes.

Chains rose from behind and engulfed Charissa as she reached a wide, roaring river. An empty place within opened up and surfaced as a scream so intense, it echoed off canyon walls and drowned out the rushing water.

Haniel shook her gently. "Charissa. You're okay. Wake up."

The rock smacked her head as she bolted upright. Sweat poured down her back and dripped from her face. Breaths surged, fast and shallow with choked off sobs. Haniel rubbed her back. Her breathing slowed, but the vivid scenes played like a recording stuck in an endless loop.

He spoke softly. "Are you okay?"

"Yes. Really bad dream."

"It'll be okay." He retrieved a backpack from a crevice and pulled out a protein bar. "Here, eat something."

Under the dream's effect, her stomach tightened and lurched at the thought of food. At his gentle urging, she accepted the bar, removed the wrapper and chewed in silence.

"The dream bothered you more than you admitted, didn't it?"

"So much happened in the dungeon. You can't imagine and I..." she hesitated. "I'm not sure I can talk about it yet."

"It must have been terrifying."

"Yeah."

The silence between them, usually comfortable, grew awkward. The look in his eyes usually meant deep thoughts-- ones that challenged faith. Concern flashed in those eyes, and her heartbeat quickened, but not from fear. Or was it? She'd be fine--as soon as they got away from here and back to her dispassionate little world.

Where was here anyway? She considered asking, but something else in those eyes held her back.

The deep pools of brown drew her in, held her attention as he spoke. "You know we have to go back for the others, don't you?"

"No, we don't."

"Charissa, we have to save the others."

"I'm not going back there." Her throat tightened with panic.

"He'll kill them. It's not beneath him."

"I know, but I'm not sure how we even escaped. If we go back, he'll kill us."

"Maybe."

"He'll expect us to come back, and he won't make it easy to rescue them."

"Probably. But we have to try."

"No, let's get out of here. We'll get to a phone and call the police."

A thick mist covered his eyes. "It will be too late."

Groans swelled up and choked her words. "I don't care."

"You don't mean that."

"Yes I do. Those women—they... they..." She stood and paced.

"They what?"

"I broke my chains. They can break theirs."

"Of course they can, but not if they don't know. What if I hadn't shown you the way to freedom?"

Resentment bubbled in the pit of her stomach, mixing with the undigested protein bar. The tidal wave of nausea took her back mentally. She dared not think of the true filth where she spent the last days. Some choice he put before her. Freedom or the lives of other women—ones who didn't give a rip about her. Every one of them sold her out – beat, cut, poisoned her and the others. Why risk her freedom for them?

"I can't go back. You don't know what it was like. How dare you ask me and then make me feel so guilty."

The accusations of the other women pricked her conscience. They blamed her for their imprisonment, and Drake confirmed it. Whether she fully understood his reasons, she accepted responsibility. But ownership of her part didn't include going back to save them. Cops got paid for rescues. Let someone else save the others.

It might be too late already. So what difference did it make? Why die for nothing? Worse, why end up as a prisoner again? She was free and wanted to remain that way. Pictures from the dream ripped at her heart. The other women wouldn't be captives without her as the object of whatever stupid game Drake played. Guilt bore down on her, but not from Haniel's words. She condemned herself.

Fear crept up her back and entwined itself around her while compassion mingled into the flood of emotions immobilizing her. She pictured the pain in Shamira's eyes. Valorie—okay, she didn't do anything wrong, but still...

A determined voice interrupted the pondering in her head. "I'm going back. I can't leave them there to die." Haniel quietly filled a canteen with water trickling over the rocks.

"No! You can't leave me here alone."

"I don't have a choice."

"So you'll leave me to save women you don't even know?" The anger brewing boiled over and splashed onto her friend, her savior.

"I care about them. Deep inside so do you."

"I can't do this. You ask too much." She melted into a puddle of tears, sank back onto the rock and buried her face against her arms.

A gentle hand caressed her hair, then reached in and lifted her chin. "They need your help, Charissa, but it's your choice."

"I'm scared. I don't want to be his captive again. I can't go back to the dungeon and face those chains, and he may find me here, so if I stay..." Shivers ran over her in spite of the warm sunshine.

His eyes stabbed to the depths of her heart. Why did he do prick her conscience so well, as if he knew her better than she knew herself? He stared at her for a few minutes until she wanted to scream at him.

Say what you're thinking already!

"You're right, Baby Girl. If you go back, yes, he might capture you. I don't blame you for being scared."

"Then how can you force me to choose? I lose either way."

"I know you well, and you'll always regret not leading those women to freedom. The dream you had earlier pales in comparison to nightmares in the future if you let them die."

Tears streamed down her face. "I'm scared, Haniel. I've never been so scared."

"I know you are, but I'm not going to let anything happen to you."

"Isn't there any other way?"

"No."

"I don't want to do this."

"Charissa, listen to me. It's okay to be afraid, but will you let fear keep you from fulfilling your destiny?"

"It's worked pretty well so far."

"Yeah – and left you in a job you hate with a life of mediocrity."

She crossed her arms and leveled her eyes at him. He stared back. She blew air through her nose. Why did he always have to be right? For once, she'd love to catch him mess up. Muttering under her breath, she finally gave up. As much as she didn't want to admit it, she couldn't argue.

"That's what holds me back from pursuing my dream too, isn't it?"

He nodded. "You know, in many ways, those women could be the orphans you love so much. Their true bondage goes way beyond physical chains. Come fight with me. Show them the truth."

She contemplated his words as they dug into the deep places of her heart. If Drake imprisoned her, at least she knew how to break the chains off her heart. The others didn't. She shuddered at the thought of a giant chain wrapped around her no matter where she went. That future loomed before her if she walked away now.

What a choice: live caged with unseen chains, or fight for freedom and possibly end up in physical chains. She'd rather fight.

She forced a smile. "I have to go back, don't I?"

"Yes. But you aren't alone. I'm here."

"I won't let him shackle me again. I'd rather die."

"Personally, I'd rather set the other women free and go home."

She chuckled. "Thanks. I can always count on your perspective."

His smile illuminated dark apprehension as doubt gnawed away at reasoning. Her stomach tightened, but she pushed down the fear. Better to go down fighting.

She stood, washed her face in the cool water, took a long drink and then turned to face him. "Let's get this over with."

He stood, slipped on the backpack and moved to her side. A strong hand wrapped around her small one. "Lord, help us lead these women out of the dungeon and into true freedom."

He led the way up the small footpath and down the trail back to the dungeon.

Chapter 52

Drake entered Edna's room. She lounged in the expensive chaise, sipping champagne and nibbling caviar. Moonlight streamed in through the French doors leading out to an expansive balcony overlooking the hills. From there, the entire valley spread below them. She'd pulled back an elegant wine colored silk comforter embroidered with gold thread. It covered the oversized four-poster bed made from ebony wood, inlaid with ivory. Various Waterford, Lenox, and mango wood vases, interspersed between pure ivory statues, graced the matching nightstands and tables scattered throughout the room.

The dresser held small decorative gold and ivory chests filled with diamond jewelry, some of which she already lavished upon herself. She lost no time in perusing the closet and selecting one of the luxurious, silk lounge sets stored there. Although Smitty removed the chains, she still wore the shackles, and the effects of bondage remained. She appeared completely subservient, but distrust lingered.

The cold blackness of her eyes resembled much of himself. That should've offered comfort, but he sensed an ancient art of deception. She rivaled his abilities of manipulative half-truths and straightforward lies. She raised her eyebrows. A glint passed across her irises and he knew…she trusted him as little as he did her. Yet, he played the game with her still.

Forcing honey into his voice, he said, "I trust your accommodations please you."

"You should have put me here from the beginning. We could've achieved so much more than with me trapped down there in that stinking dungeon."

"But then you wouldn't know the other women."

"Oh, I would have managed, my dear. I still don't understand your little game. Of course, your prized pet is gone now, so what comes next?"

"You don't need to know my plans." Irritation laced the fabricated sweetness in his tone. "I need to know you are on board and willing to do exactly as I instruct you."

"That's not how I operate best." Her lips tightened, but she too applied a syrupy voice. She gestured around the room. "But if this indicates my reward for compliance, I'll adjust."

She smiled, but the gleam from her eyes suggested the highest bidder usually won undying devotion—at least as long as it suited her. In the quietness, she tilted the champagne glass and drained it.

"I suggest you don't overindulge tonight. You'll have plenty of time later."

"What exactly do you want from me, Drake?"

"I suspect my enemy, Haniel, helped Charissa escape. I know him well. He would never take only her and abandon the others. That isn't how he operates. Besides an unwillingness to leave any of them open to torture, he won't sit back and do nothing while I win."

"You go back a long way with this man, don't you? What happened?"

Suspicion covered him. Was this genuine interest, or fuel for a later power play? Still, she must see Haniel as an opponent; otherwise, she might fall to his persuasion.

"It was a long time ago. I don't remember much about my parents, except flashes of a drunken brut, fist in my face sometimes, a woman bloodied and bruised. I remember one time waking to the smell of coffee with him beating Mama because it was too strong. The last time I saw them, he lay in a red pool, and she held a gun in her hand. Police officers whisked me off to an orphanage."

Edna approached him, genuine sorrow replacing the power play face.

Familiar numbness encircled his heart as he continued. "The headmaster there didn't care for me. He reminded me a lot of the man from my childhood—left me looking like Mama."

Her voice softened. "I'm sorry. No child should endure beatings from anyone. But, what do those years have to do with Haniel?"

Drake hesitated. He seldom reflected on childhood. While he remembered little about the early years of life, the headmaster's face remained vivid. He choked back emotions.

"His father visited orphanages. He didn't approve of my treatment and took me to his home. He didn't beat me, but I never quite measured up to his standards. Haniel was always the perfect one, with me, standing in his shadow, trying to be half as good."

"I don't know Haniel, but I can't imagine he's so much better than you."

"He's not. After graduating, I worked in his father's business. His empire reached farther than you can imagine. He wouldn't share his wealth and power with anyone—other than his son. I gave up my entire life for him, studied to please him instead of what I wanted. I should've been an equal partner with as much respect and admiration as Haniel commanded. Instead, dear old "Dad" became angry when I asked for a little piece of his operation. I didn't want it all. Okay, maybe I did, but I earned it. He kicked me out and left me with nothing."

Bile filled his throat as the bitter memory embraced his mind and swept along his veins. Anger pulsed, inciting a rapid heartbeat. He clenched his teeth against the rage building inside.

Edna caressed him. "No wonder you hate him so much. It would be hard to walk away and not look back. But you have your own business now. Surely all you accomplished gives you an advantage over this man, or at least an equal amount of wealth and power."

"It isn't about the money any more. I've made my empire. This is a small part of it. I can't take his wealth or power from him no matter how hard I try. He has way too much fire power. But I can take revenge every chance I get."

The puzzled look on her face pleased him. Things always played out better when others remained confused around him. He sensed compassion from hearing his story and didn't hesitate to reel her in and drop her in his net. She'd do anything he wanted.

"So why do you need Charissa?"

"Haniel loves her. I've done it before — taken his favorite woman from him. Nothing hurts a father as much as watching his son with a broken heart and being powerless to change it. So when I come across him and can take away a woman or persuade a man to join me instead of staying in his service, I do it."

"But why? I mean, what's the advantage?"

"Besides the satisfaction?" He chuckled. How could she be in such a high position with her law firm and not get this? "Sometimes it doesn't add much for me, but it keeps them from gaining ground too. And there are times the target works very well for me. He'd prefer having you on his team - with a little refinement to his way of thinking. But me — I like the way you think. I don't want any changes at all, and you will serve me well."

"Okay. I understand, but you still haven't answered my question. What do you want from me?"

"When he comes back to rescue all of you, stay. Do not let him suck you into the escape plan with vain promises. He won't provide your heart's desires. He'll promise to give you what you want. Don't believe him, whatever you do."

"I'm not naïve, Drake. As long as you keep your end of the bargain, we'll be fine. You can count on me." She stroked his cheek.

He grasped the shackle around her neck and pulled her close. "Of course I can, my dear. But don't forget, if you bail, I will hunt you down and make you pay."

She slipped her arms around him and stroked his back. "That won't be necessary. Treat me right, and I'll never disappoint you."

He pushed her away. "Good. Get some sleep. I suspect they'll return at daybreak, and I must prepare a few little surprises for them."

As he closed the door, a cork popped behind it. At least if she got drunk, the chances of losing her lessened. It definitely improved the odds of her staying behind and not betraying him. Haniel might sway her, clear-headed, but with brain cells muddled from too much champagne, she'd sleep right through any attempted escape. Nevertheless, he'd return as soon as he checked on Smitty's progress. Someday, the ignorant fool might do everything right, but the preparations for dawn meant too much to risk trust tonight. He sauntered down the hall quite pleased with the renewed prospect of victory. The game wasn't over yet—not by a week's wager.

He'd visit Valorie too—put a little more fear under her skin. And Dierdre... In spite of her bitterness in relation to him, she needed a reminder suggesting Haniel held no more trustworthiness than any other man did. If she believed the enemy, it meant the end of deep-seated anger. However, if he fed the fire a little, the anger already burned enough for a slight move into rage; and rage always served him well. If he kept half these women on his side, and destroyed Charissa, triumph over his long-time rival waited easily within his grasp.

The sweet taste of near success lingered on his lips as his mind traced through the anticipated rescue attempt. Move fast. Relish the outcome later. And he would relish it alright. His entire body tingled at the thought of defeating Haniel. A matter of hours and well planned defense. He'd take the offensive and turn the tide against them. Anticipation quivered up his spine. With a little luck, he might even get Charissa back long enough to take great pleasure with her before he killed the little wench.

Chapter 53

The massive house loomed before Charissa, dark, except for lights in a few small windows. Memories gushed until a thick fog of despair descended.

Haniel grabbed her hand, pulled her across the yard and into shadows surrounding the house. He separated thorn-filled bushes, revealing a door. The entry matched the stone making up the house's exterior, invisible to an unsuspecting eye. It swung open with a light touch.

He flicked on a flashlight, and led the way into a narrow passage ending at a steep staircase down. At the bottom, they ventured into another tunnel toward the back portion of the dungeon. As they neared a wide crevice opening into the room where she spent so many days, she gagged at the stench of urine and human waste. Rats scuttled from the light while shudders ran over her. A foulness of bat guano added to the wrenching in her stomach. The instinct to turn and run back up the stairs waged war against logic and emotion.

Without a word, Haniel grasped her hand for the last few steps leading into the cave room. Stifling air constricted her lungs, left her panting, fighting to breathe, as if an unseen fist punched hard. The utter silence in the room tormented her.

No snoring, clinking of chains, or moans from sleeping women greeted them. An mental portrait of five dead women in their chambers held her back, yet propelled her forward.

The flashlight beam swept the room. She held her breath and peered around Haniel's broad back. The middle of the room stood empty, silent except for the unmistakable sound of rodents moving in darkness. The beam bounced off the walls into one chamber after another.

Empty.

They moved into the room. A soft moan came from one chamber.

The light hit a young woman's ashen face. Dried blood caked Shamira's head, with traces at the corner of her nose and mouth. Compassion compelled Charissa—drove her across the cave and into the chamber.

"You came back." Shamira said in a hoarse whisper. "Even after all I did, you came back. I'm so sorry for cutting you." A chain link popped.

Charissa whispered, "Shhhh. It's okay, Shamira. We'll get you out of here."

Haniel handed over the canteen and she held it to the younger woman's lips. She sipped the water, choked, coughed, and sipped again.

Shamira spoke softly. "I messed up so many times. I deserve to die alone, bruised and bleeding."

"No. You aren't gonna die, and you didn't deserve this any more than the rest of us. You can break these chains, but not if you believe the lie about your worth. We came back because you are valuable—to God and to us."

"You don't know what I've done."

"It doesn't matter. Ask God for forgiveness first, and then share whatever you want to tell us."

"What?" Shamira struggled to sit up. Haniel offered his hand. At the touch, her eyes brightened.

"It breaks the chains. You hold the key to freedom through admitting your sin and taking responsibility for it. Some call it confession."

She chuckled a little. "We could be here all night if I have to confess everything."

"Well, we don't have all night, so maybe offer a really broad one. We've got to get out of here."

Shamira sipped more water, and then spoke with a monotone voice. "I used to be good — Daddy's perfect angel. I messed up big time. I told you. I really was sorry and so ashamed. I didn't know how to stop what we were doing. I regret all of it." A few links popped. "But the worst part was the hatred I've carried around for my father. I never forgave him. I think he wanted what was best for me."

Her voice broke, but she maintained composure. Charissa stroked her hair thinking he probably talked her into an abortion. "What happened?"

Emotion spewed out as she continued. "The guy ditched me. Swore he wasn't the baby's daddy. He made me so mad, but somehow, it relieved me. No more sex, or shame from hiding the truth. Then Daddy made me give up the baby. I wanted my little boy — loved him so much. I hated Daddy and blamed God. I quit going to church with my parents, got a job and saved a little money, then about six months later, left. I tried to find the baby, but nobody would tell me anything."

"That really stinks. To lose your baby and the relationship with your father must really hurt."

"Yeah." She brushed away tears. A chain fell free and clinked against the rock chamber. She stared at it with wide eyes. "Did that really happen?"

"Yes." They must hurry, but she wanted Shamira free. "Go on. After you ran away."

"Met a guy, moved in with him out of necessity. Before long, he started hitting me. I got away from him and ended up with another one. He hit me too, so I left, and kept doing the same old thing until I met Doug who almost killed me. I kept making bad choices, and always blaming someone else. Then I met Drake. I thought he was different."

"Drake is different all right, but in a much worse way."

"I believed he wanted to save me."

"He deceived you."

"I know now. Oh, Lord, I'm so sorry I trusted him. I should have known better."

"You went to church as a little girl?"

"Yes. I loved Jesus so much back then." She broke into sobs. "I wish I still did. I miss feeling his presence."

"You can get it back. Simply ask the Lord. He's still there you know."

Shamira bowed her head. Tears poured down her cheeks as her body shook with emotion. As she prayed chains fell, a barrage of rocks cast into a vast sea. After several minutes, the torrent subsided. A smiled beamed from the pale face. She sipped more water from the canteen.

Haniel spoke quietly for the first time. "Shamira, we'll get you out of here. But do you know where they took the others?"

"I'm not sure. I was half-unconscious when Drake came back. He left me here to die."

"Try to remember," he said.

She closed her eyes. "Something about an attic room — I think for Valorie. He took Edna with him. The other two..." She paused. "Hidden cells — maybe close."

Haniel looked at Charissa. "There may be more passageways down here or cell type rooms at the top of the staircase. One of us has to take Shamira out the back way and to a safe place while the other looks for them."

"You take her. I'll see if I can find another corridor and then go upstairs. You won't take too long will you?"

"I'll be back before you miss me. Be careful."

He reached into the backpack and handed her a small flashlight. His touch lingered on her arm for a few seconds, but a warm glow remained long after his back disappeared into the shadows.

Chapter 54

Charissa drew in a deep breath. Bad decision. The smell made her eyes water.

Wiping them with the back of her hand, she made her way around the cave, carefully probing with a beam of light. Every sound penetrated and reverberated through her head, slowly raising her pulse. Several times, the passage to freedom beckoned, but not without the other women. Moonlight shone through the tiny window, growing dimmer, passing toward darkness before sunrise. When she found the others, they'd have to break chains much faster.

She searched beneath the staircase and noticed a hollowed out area. Not quite a passageway, and yet she felt drawn to the place. She stepped over a six-inch high threshold into a smaller room of the cave. Sweeping the area with the flashlight, a distant murmuring skimmed her ears. Three feet ahead, another threshold, and then a tight passage where the dirt gave way to a stone path.

As the area took on the air of a basement, the sounds grew louder and more distinct. Ariana's voice—soft, yet firm— recited the Lord's Prayer, and then the 23rd Psalm; "Yea though I walk through the valley of the shadow of death." Fitting for this place. It felt like death.

Charissa moved quietly along the path until a door appeared. Ariana's voice drifted through a small bar-covered window in the door. Confinement hung in the air, a stench indicating the original intent of the place. Several doors stood along the narrow hallway with tiny windows, big enough to peep through from either side lined with bars barely wide enough for a piece of bread and perhaps a small cup of water. She swung the flashlight beam over the walls hoping for a ring of keys hanging from a large hook.

Of course not; it looks like a Hollywood set, but this isn't a scripted movie. Still, keys would be helpful.

Harsh reality set in. In spite of the cool air, the dampness in this part of the dungeon produced a mustiness. It filled her lungs and tickled her throat and nose. She choked down the dryness and tiptoed to the door.

"...of death, I will fear no evil." A choked sob broke the soft voice. "I am fearin' though. I can't help it, Lord. I just..."

"Ariana?"

Silence.

"It's me—Charissa."

A slight grunt and cracking joints came from behind the door. Charissa tried to see through the window, but the other woman remained invisible. Perhaps she knelt sometimes after all.

Charissa waited for a moment and spoke again. "It really is me. Come to the door."

Ariana's face appeared in the small window. "Oh. You came back. How did you ever find me down here?"

"I'm not really sure, but I did. Are you okay?"

"Stiff and tired. I been prayin' since that ole snake sent us down here. I swear he's the devil hisself."

"He certainly acts like it anyway. Are you still chained?"

"Oh yes. But even if I wasn't, how would you open this door?"

"I don't know. Don't see a key anywhere out here."

"Smitty had them. But he'd been drinkin' quite a bit. I heard something thud when he walked away. I don't s'pose they could be lyin' on the ground?"

Wouldn't that be nice? A little far-fetched and too good to be true.

Charissa shot the beam downwards. So much dirt covered the stone pathway. She swept the dirt with the light. No use. Nothing there either. As she turned back to the door, the light brushed a glint of something on the opposite side of the walkway. Could it be? She crossed and bent, seeing a glimmer of hope. Half buried beneath the dirt, the top ring of a small key protruded. Nudging it with her finger, the dirt gave way and revealed a small brass ring holding about a dozen keys of various sizes, all of them the kind used to open ancient locks.

Maybe she needed a little more faith down here.

"Are you still there?" Ariana asked timidly.

"Yes, and you won't believe what I found." She held up the ring.

"Oh sweet, Jesus. Hallelujah!"

Charissa's fingers trembled as she tried the keys. One...two...three... None of them worked. Frantically she kept trying. Three keys remained on the ring when the lock slipped and the door swung opened. Both women released pent up breaths.

"C'mon. We have to find the others and get out of here fast."

"Dierdre is down here too. I think." Ariana stumbled through the door. The shackles around her ankles restricted the steps to inches. Not good enough. Charissa cut to the chase.

"Ariana, I know you believe in God. I heard you praying in there. But I think you are stuck in religion. Do you really know Him?"

The indignant reply popped out of the other woman with a matching glare and toss of her head. "What are you sayin'?

That I'm not as good as you? You still holdin' that cookin' incident against me, ain't ya?"

"No, no. It's not that. Look. We don't have time for details, but something keeps you all bound up with these shackles and chains. Only you can break them. I suggest while I look for Dierdre, you pray—not rote prayers you memorized either. Ask the Lord to show you truth and find out what's holding you. It's the only way. Hurry!"

"Why I never..."

Charissa didn't have time for an argument. She suspected the answer to the woman's bounds, but Ariana must discover it without her help. Besides, Dierdre didn't seem like the church-going kind of woman. Those chains of bitterness and unforgiveness took years to build—breaking them required a miracle and unfortunately, much of it depended on the woman. Convincing her to let it all go...

Find her first. Worry about breaking chains later.

Ariana's muttering followed her down the hallway, but the tone softened. Freedom dangled above her if she listened well. Charissa counted on the older woman's knowledge of the Bible and a desire for God to lead her to Truth. In the meantime, each flash of light and peep into a cell door window left her frustrated. Empty rooms taunted on both sides. Time reached up and choked her along with the dust and mustiness. Drake purposely separated the women in anticipation of a rescue attempt. Every second counted in the fight for all their freedom.

Only two doors left.

Please let her be in one of these rooms.

The light broke through darkness in the second to last cell. Nothing. Crossing to the last door she heard "Look again."

What?

Was she hearing things now? A faint shuffling near the doorway drew her back to the previous cell. The light bounced off the walls and caught a shadow.

"Dierdre? Are you in there?"

A breath caught on the other side of the door.

"It's me, Charissa. I'm gonna get you out of this stinking dungeon."

The sudden appearance of a face behind the barred window threw her heart into overdrive as she squeaked and jumped back, banging her head against stones lining the wall. Deep breaths heaved against her lungs. Hand on her heart or head? It didn't matter.

"You didn't have to scare me half to death." She said.

"Sorry. I was ready to pounce on Smitty and claw his eyes out. Get me out of here already."

Charissa fumbled with the keys, trying first one and then another.

Please. Not the entire set again.

On the third try, the lock snapped and the door swung open. Dierdre nearly pushed her down coming out of the tiny prison.

"The chains?"

Charissa shook her head. "There's no key for them. Only you can break the chains."

"What the…"

"Look. It's complicated, and I don't really know how it works, but it does." She told her story; how as she confessed sins and wrong attitudes to first God and then Haniel, the chains and shackles fell to the ground.

"Ludicrous." Dierdre responded. "Look. I'm no saint, but I'm better than most. Besides why should I trust this Haniel of yours? How do you know he isn't working with Drake and leading you straight to him? You could be free. What's in it for you – coming back here?"

"Peace. I chose freedom of my heart even if I end up in physical chains again. But trust me. That isn't my plan. I'll die fighting before I let him capture me again." She grabbed the chains between the other woman's hands. "Dierdre, if I took away every one of these chains, your heart still isn't free. I don't know your story, and unfortunately, we don't have time for it right now. But bitterness and rage ooze from you."

"I have reasons to be bitter."

"I'm sure you do. Did you ever consider forgiving the ones who hurt you?"

"Ha. Forgive? You have gone mad in this God forsaken place."

"God didn't forsake us. He wants to set you free, but only you can accept His forgiveness for your anger. And then, because you experience it, you can forgive others."

"I'll stay in chains."

"Suit yourself. You'll have a hard time climbing the stairs – not to mention the trails outside."

Where was Haniel? He'd make her understand.

"I'll take my chances, thank you. You can't imagine what I've been through – the way men let me down."

"No I can't. I had a father who abandoned me as a little girl and many men who rejected me later. But I caused a lot of it—not trusting them because I feared they'd leave me too. I see your fear, Dierdre. Behind the harsh exterior, you're a scared little girl. I was too."

Dierdre's face contorted, her teeth clenched. A single tear slipped from the corner of one eye, but the harshness remained along the creases lining her face and screaming against her silence.

Charissa shook her head. "C'mon. Ariana's waiting for us down the hall. We've got to get going."

Chapter 55

They clanged back along the hallway. So much for an element of surprise. She'd send Dierdre out through the back passageway and look for the others alone.

As they rounded a corner, a breathless Ariana skipped into the light, a bright smile beaming before her. She held up loose chains, laughed and chunked them to the ground.

Dierdre gasped. "How did you do that?" She grabbed Ariana's wrist. "Tell me how?"

Ariana giggled. "I listened with my heart. I saw my self-righteous judgmental attitude. I confessed my sins of gluttony, lack of self-control, and..." she paused. "Well the rest don't matter so much. But mostly, I admitted to spending a lot of time doin' all the right religious stuff and not much bein' a child of God. I fixed it. Jesus is real to me now."

Tears ran down her cheeks into deep laugh lines around a broad smile. Tears of joy and freedom glistened as shackles and more chains thudded in the dirt beneath them.

Dierdre's eyes grew wider. "It's true then." She sank to her knees. "I don't want this bitterness any more, but I can't forgive them. I just can't." She bawled into clenched fists.

Ariana spoke with the soothing words of a mother hurting with her child. "It's hard, honey. And at least you're honest 'bout it. Sometimes ya gotta start there – where you can't forgive yet, but you wanna be able to. When you pray, He understands ."

"I don't know how to pray. I know how to look out for myself. My abusive, cheating husband taught me , and the second one controlled and manipulated everyone around him, until he hung himself." Chain links popped as the hurt poured from her heart.

Filled with deep sorrow, Charissa softly touched her shoulder. A start—slight beginnings with promised hope for this woman kneeling in a dirty, musty dungeon. Not wanting to rush her, but conscious of the minutes ticking by, she prodded. "Keep going, Dierdre. Ariana's right. You have to start somewhere. Talk to Him, the same way you would with us."

A dam of emotions broke. Hurt, betrayal, bitterness from a heart cracking wider filled the little prison area as Dierdre confided in the other two women, releasing years of pent up anger and rage.

As she sought forgiveness, chains broke. Shackles clunked on the dirt. Peace slowly replaced harshness. A soft glow fell over her cheeks along with a glimmer of hope in the once cold eyes.

Charissa's heart swelled, tears escaped as she prayed over Dierdre and Ariana. Temptation to dance right there almost got the best of her, but two women still sat somewhere in this house, bound, and in danger. She had lots of ground to cover. Shudders moved down her spine in spite of the joy surrounding them.

"Rejoice later. Two women are still prisoners and waiting for freedom."

Dierdre's demeanor shifted. "Of course. How can we help?"

"Any idea where Drake took them?"

Ariana said, "He took Edna. She seemed willin' enough, but he don't seem to trust her much."

Dierdre joined. "Agreed. She's probably in his room or close, which could make rescue difficult. Smitty took Valorie. Something about an attic room."

Charissa shook her head. "Figures. From a dungeon to a tower prison. Let's go."

By the time they reached their former prison, deep pants lumbered from behind. Ariana. Maybe Dierdre really should get her out of this place. She prayed Haniel made it back.

He stepped from the dark passageway across the room. Relief rushed in like a cool breeze in a hot kitchen. He nodded at the two ladies and smiled, the twinkle in his eyes expressing pleasure at the sight of them without bonds. He touched Ariana's shoulder and the breaths grew shallow, calmer.

He listened intently as Charissa conveyed the locations of the last two women. He took her flashlight, handed it to Dierdre and then quickly explained where they'd find Shamira.

"Go. Stay in the shadows. When you get near enough, she'll flag you down. I left her near drinkable water, with some food. Wait for us there, but if we aren't back by sunrise, the three of you follow the trail. It'll eventually take you to the main highway."

He took Charissa's hand. Warmth and assurance covered her as they ascended the spiral staircase. Halfway to the top, calf muscles began burning, aching, screaming stop. But she kept going, pushing to the top. If not so dangerous, she'd enjoy the workout. Muscles begged for mercy, and produced an increased heart rate with sweating. Anxiety coursing through her body might have something to do with the setting, but blaming it on a workout sounded less threatening.

At the top, Haniel pushed the door gently. Nothing. Memories of the bolt sliding into the lock made her groan. No. Of all the times for Smitty to remember the lock.

Haniel pushed his shoulder against the door and leaned into it, pushing with more force. It gave with a slight creak of the hinges. They both held their breath as he urged the door open enough for squeezing through. He went first and peeked around. Without a word, he motioned. She followed. Other than the pounding of blood in her ears, everything stood in complete stillness with scattered lamps burning in the hall and study. Shuddering, she tiptoed past the big double doors half-afraid Drake lounged on the sofa waiting for her return. The cold, bare room mocked her, laughed at her fear. A sensation of chains tightening around her chest angered her.

No. I won't cower in fear. I'm finding the others.

They inched up the stairs, hugging the rail against the wall, watching every shadow, every sound magnified. A creak brought a gasp, cut off her breath, shut her eyes, and moved her to panicked prayer. Frozen, waiting. Deafening silence brought relief, accompanied by terror.

Half-expecting Drake to jump out and say boo, the steps seemed endless; Haniel so near she almost tripped him as they continued upward. Bedrooms lined the hallway. Which one belonged to Drake? Was he behind one of the doors, ready to pounce when they opened it?

He took Edna—willingly. The words beat across her mind. Maybe she wanted to stay with him, share his power and wealth. Finding her might be worse if she betrayed them into Drake's hands.

They crept down a long, thickly carpeted hallway. Silent footsteps protected their approach, but one creak of the old floor… A door opened as they slipped past. She turned, fists up, ready to fight. Edna stepped out and put a finger to her lips.

She pointed two doors down and mouthed, "He's in there."

She pulled them away from Drake's bedroom to an alcove at the end of the hall.

"Thank goodness you came back. He has a big trap for you, but doesn't expect you until dawn. Let's get out of here fast."

Odd. No chains; only a single shackle remained around her throat.

Haniel spoke her question. "How'd you break free from the chains?"

Smugness glittered over her face as she puckered her lips. "I know his kind – his games. I play them well. He thinks I'm on his side and won't go with you."

Haniel's eyes narrowed. Chills tumbled through Charissa's veins as she watched a cold, hollow blackness spread through Edna's eyes.

Charissa questioned her loyalty. "Are you? On his side?"

"Of course not," she snapped. "I didn't know whether you'd come back or not, but I'm sick of this place. Free tonight, beaten tomorrow. I'm not living that way. Let's go already before he wakes up."

"Not without Valorie."

Haniel nodded in agreement. "Where is she?"

"How should I know? I'm not her keeper."

The physical chains gone, Charissa still saw a myriad of bonds covering, choking the other woman. Selfishness, greed, lust all exuded from Edna. She might bolt and run or yell for Drake. Either way, they weren't leaving without Valorie.

"Too bad, because I'm not abandoning her. Go if you want."

"You..." Edna's face turned red, her fists balled although she kept them close to her sides; she clenched her teeth. If not for fear of alerting Drake, she might have stomped her feet too.

"Listen!" Haniel cocked his head to one side and looked up.

A faint sound drifted through a vent directly above them. A gentle breath of air rustled a thick velvet curtain enough to reveal a brown door at the bottom. Brushing aside the curtain, a tinge of light seeped under the door, drew Charissa. No knob, but a latch gave easily when she touched it. They all three slipped behind the curtain, through the door and up a short flight of stairs, following the soft glow of light and a haunting lullaby.

A soft thump of footsteps as their feet hit unfinished wood flooring startled Charissa. Stifling heat suffocated her; the fretful rocking of a human ball lying on a cot in a man's large shirt stole the little breath left in her lungs.

"Valorie."

Chapter 56

Tears coursed down Charissa's cheeks as she approached the tiny figure of a woman.

"We're gonna get you out of here."

At first, she cringed and drew away from the outstretched arms. Fear jumped from her eyes, drawing her as far away from them as possible. Charissa held out her hand, shook her head in response to the questions coming from Valorie's body language. Immovable, even without chains or shackles.

Lord, help us. I've got to get her out of here.

"Let me help you, Valorie. We've got to go."

Valorie shook her head. "No. He'll catch us."

She forced calmness into her voice. "Not if we go now."

Edna pushed past. "Oh for Pete's sake, woman. Get over it already. I'm not staying here another minute. Get up or I'll beat you myself."

Charissa cut her eyes at Edna. Anger pushed up from her gut and spilled out through flaring nostrils. Nevertheless, Valorie edged off the small cot. She gingerly locked hands with Charissa. It didn't soften the anger, but she'd deal with Edna later. They headed back down the steps.

Peeking from behind the curtain, they stepped into the alcove. A door down the hall shut quietly. On the opposite side of the alcove, French doors opened onto a balcony. She pointed.

Haniel opened the doors; Edna went through without hesitation. He held his hand out to Valorie who shook her head violently, her eyes growing wider. Charissa glanced around the corner. What had been Edna's door flung opened. Not good. Her shoulders tensed. Every sense screamed run, as curse words rammed through the hall followed by Drake's voice yelling for Smitty.

She wrapped herself around Valorie and pushed her onto the balcony. Haniel closed the doors behind them.

"Quick. Climb down the trellis," he whispered.

Edna didn't wait for a second invitation. He nodded at Valorie. She shook her head again, backing away from the edge. Beyond the doors, footsteps pounded the hallway. Doors opened and slammed. Unrepeatable curse words floated through the glass.

She took Valorie's hands. "If we don't go now, he'll kill us."

Valorie's chest heaved; her breath came in short gasps. Charissa's heart pounded so hard, it felt about to break through her sternum. Haniel remained calm, but his teeth clenched and concern covered every inch of his face. He moved between them and the door, facing the alcove.

Finally, Valorie nodded.

Charissa breathed relief. "Okay. I'll go first and guide you down."

Charissa climbed over the balcony ledge, found the trellis with her feet, took a few steps downward and motioned for Valorie who stood frozen far from the edge. Fear kept her glued to the balcony.

Haniel appeared above her, and pointed to the ground. How could she leave Valorie? Searching his eyes for assurance, she shook her head. He looked straight at her, filling her with peace. His gaze shouted *trust me*.

As she descended, he stepped over the rail with Valorie tucked under one arm. The muscles rippled and grew taut while her legs flailed.

Oh, Lord. Please don't let him fall. Please.

She reached the bottom and looked up. Two-thirds of the way down, Valorie kicked loose and tumbled to the ground. Haniel jumped.

"Let's go!" He shouted.

The grass beneath them blurred as hot tears coursed down her cheeks. Her arms and legs pumped hard as they sprinted toward the tree line. Valorie screamed as Haniel half-carried, half-pushed her across the yard.

Edna reached the trees and scrambled over the fence far ahead of them. Bright lights flooded the yard as Charissa reached the trees and pulled herself up and over. Sweat poured from her face, and down her back. Haniel pushed Valorie up into her waiting hands – pulling, tugging over the fence.

In the distance, shattering glass broke the silence of humid night air.

From the balcony, Drake's booming voice cursed and yelled. "I'll kill all of you before this night ends. Smitty, bring the dogs — and my shotgun."

Chapter 57

Drake fumed as he exited Edna's room. He assumed the worst, but not ready to concede defeat, he checked the other rooms. As he sprang from a room, movement in the alcove caught his eye. He raced down the long hall. Smitty bounded from a room and hit him square. Both plummeted to the floor.

"You no good imbecile. They're in the alcove."

"Sorry, Boss."

As he bounced up, Smitty moved, catching his back with a knee. Sharp pain raced up his spine. He glanced back and glowered at the other man, stood and started forward.

Smitty, somehow underneath him, caused a face plant in the plush carpet. He pushed up on all fours to a hand in his face. Slapping it away, Drake stood only to meet a dull thud as his cohort's head smashed hard against his temple. Sharp and dull pains alternated in his head as he stumbled into the wall.

Smitty held one hand to his forehead and reached out the other for him. Drake grabbed the hand and tripped over a big foot. He banged against both sides of the narrow hallway, but kept his balance. As Smitty pushed past in pursuit of the intruders, he almost tripped again. Smitty went down, and bounced back up.

Drake yelled and shoved the man backwards. "You idiot, get out of my way."

He covered the rest of the hall to the alcove. The curtain covering the attic door stood pulled back slightly.

You're so bad at hiding. I got you cornered – no place to go.

He flung open the door and lumbered up the steps. No reason for subtlety at this point. Nowhere to run or hide anyway. A smile crept across his face as he imagined which little tramp he caught in his trap. His face dropped at the top of the stairs. An empty cot, total silence. Nothing beneath it or hiding in any of the corners.

Smitty plunged into the room and nearly knocked him down.

"Stupid, they aren't here. Didn't you lock the door?"

"Of course not. This was your trap, remember."

"Then where are the little mice?"

Smitty shrugged, looked down the stairs, and slapped his hand over his mouth as he uttered curse words.

He pointed. "The balcony."

"No. There's no way down from there, except to jump."

"Or climb down the trellis." Smugness, or was it disdain, shadowed Smitty's face.

Drake narrowed his eyes. Heat burned his ears. Uncontrollable jerking overtook him, raced down to his hands and around Smitty's throat, choking as he flung him alternately against both walls. The man's eyes bulged as he fought back, clawing at Drake's hands. Nails dug deep into skin and fueled the anger.

Smitty's eyes rolled upwards; only then did he release the grip. Shoving the man to the floor, he took two steps at a time down into the alcove and crashed through the French doors. Glass shattered as he threw them wide against the balcony railing.

A small band raced across the yard and over the fence. Four of them. In spite of the darkness, he recognized Haniel's form. The confident arrogance of an apparent win taunted him.

The brashness! Sneak into the house again and take my women, not to mention he did it in the dead of night.

So unexpected.

Haniel always operated in the light of day, preferred it as much as he desired the cover of darkness. Almost beaten at his game, he slammed a fist against the trellis. Admirable stealth from his opponent; he underestimated the man. He wouldn't repeat the same mistake. But he wasn't finished.

The floodlights snapped on from the motion detector and covered the expansive yard. From this distance, they did little to clue him in on which women escaped with the rogue. Hatred crept from his belly up to his throat as he yelled across the yard.

"I'll kill all of you before this night ends." Without turning, he yelled louder. "Smitty, bring the dogs—and my shotgun."

As the prisoners moved away from the fence, he seethed, turned back inside and caught his assistant by the shirt.

"Find Edna. Make sure she didn't join them. Then assess the damage. I want to know how many and which of them escaped."

"Yes, boss."

The sniveling coward didn't look so smug. He drank in the smell of terror smoldering from the man. He should have put him in line days ago instead of tolerating the drunken incompetence. Disgusted, he shoved him aside and spat on him.

Thirty seconds passed in silence before he yelled again. "Go. They're getting away."

"Yes, boss." Smitty lumbered down the staircase and through the door into the dungeon.

Drake walked back into Edna's room, checked the closet and bathroom, stepped out onto the balcony in case she retreated there and fell asleep on a lounge chair.

Nothing.

He went back inside. An almost full glass of champagne rested on a table beside the bed, left tousled, the emptiness mocking. Her silk garments remained on the floor where he'd tossed them earlier. He fingered the red lipstick on the glass.

Betrayed.

Loneliness crept over him. He offered her everything, and still she ran with the others. Her scent lingered in the room. They complemented each other so well, much alike in many ways.

He took a deep breath, ran his finger over the glass, grasped and sipped from it, then flung it across the room into a beveled mirror. Glass shards bounced off the hardwood floor. He stroked his beard. Bad luck – but not for him.

He flung off the emotions, suddenly aware of wasted time, and fled to his room. Time to get dressed and go hunting.

Chapter 58

Six dogs pulled against thick chain leashes, their barks spilling into relentless humidity. Two men, massive biceps bulging, held them at bay. Sweat soaked Smitty's shirt and matted his hair. His hand trembled as he held out a shotgun.

Drake snatched it. "How many do we have left?"

Smitty gulped and backed away from Drake. His upper lip twitched.

"Answer me."

"None." He raised fisted hands, and ducked his head, half-ready to fight, eyes pleading for mercy. "They're all gone. Edna too."

A strange calmness fluttered down over Drake as he shook his head. "Too bad for you."

He raised a handgun and squeezed the trigger. The blood drained from Smitty's face. Fear dissipated to shock and then morphed to horror. Hands dropped to his side as a red spot grew on his chest and his knees hit the ground.

Drake tossed the gun toward one of his men, who tucked the weapon into his belt.

"Bring the dogs. Let's go." Drake kicked Smitty over as he walked past.

Chapter 59

Haniel took the lead as the small group moved away from the fence. Charissa stayed behind the other women. No trail, they glided silently through a wooded area. Trees branches slapped at her face, thorn-filled vines grabbed at her legs, stinging. The pace quickened, trees murmuring urgency along the escape route. She sucked in air, burning lungs pleaded for rest. Leg muscles screamed for mercy, but she dared not stop.

A tree root breached the surface, innocent, non-threatening, virtually hidden, yet snagged her step with vengeance. She stumbled, almost went down but regained her balance as the trees broke and revealed a flat rock surface with a descending narrow path. A sudden stop caught her off guard, almost causing a collision with Edna. Haniel held up one hand and peered into the darkness. She heard nothing except wind whispering through the trees and gasping breaths.

Haniel's soft whistle filled the stillness. A similar sound came from beneath them. Motioning for them to follow, he led the way. They'd been here before. The rocks and trickling water…

Thank God. We're safe.

As the small group reached the bottom, three women moved from behind a rock.

Dierdre stepped forward. "We were beginning to get worried. Glad you made it—hope you didn't bring company with you."

Charissa said, "I think we're okay for now, but I'm sure Drake will come after us."

Haniel's eyes met hers. "Get a drink. We have to keep moving."

"Why? We were here before, well hidden."

"Yeah, with only two of us. The rock isn't big enough for everyone."

He turned to the other five women. "Ladies, I know some of you are tired, but we can't stop here. Drink from the water coming off the rock and we'll get going."

Edna scrunched her nose. "Drink that? Don't you know river water carries parasites and who knows what else? I'm not drinking it, and I'm not running any more. I can't. This looks like a perfect place to me."

He answered with a gentle, yet firm voice. "Suit yourself. The rocks purify the water, so it's pure enough. Stay if you want, but the rest of us are moving on to a place of refuge."

Fear covered Valorie's face, but she tentatively moved beneath the stream of water and drank a little. Her chest still moved in rapid rhythm with her breathing. The other women joined her for a cool drink. Edna huffed, waited until they all finished and then took her turn. In the distance, dogs howled. Haniel crossed the stream to another trail, scrambled up and then down again a different way.

"Drake has the dogs out," he said. "We're less trackable walking down the streambed than going back up to the main trail. I went up and down enough to confuse them and maybe buy us a few extra minutes. Let's go."

Edna hung back, but when Charissa waited too, she moved into the stream.

After what we experienced in the dungeon, how could a little water intimidate her?

She offered a hand, but the other woman shrugged and tossed her hair. Even when Edna slipped on a rock and almost went down, she maintained an air of independence.

She's still trapped, isn't she?

The vision of shackles and chains hung over the woman, unreal in the natural realm but thicker and heavier than before when seen through spiritual eyes. No one else seemed to notice, but she couldn't ignore the bonds. The truth about Edna pierced a soft place in her heart. No matter what transpired back in the dungeon, Charissa hurt for this woman as the invisible chains seemed to permeate every inch of her body.

Lord, please set her free somehow.

They picked along the streambed as darkness deepened. The barking of dogs in the distance grew more intense. Surely, they smelled the group of former prisoners; bore down in the task of staying on the scent. If Drake caught them...

No. Think about something else.

The oppressive humidity nagged, making every breath more difficult. Rock walls rose on both sides. A thick row of trees edged up to the side of the cliffs, providing a sense of security from below. A squirrel might nudge between them, but nothing much larger. Little growth stood near the upper edge. With plenty of room for trails and footpaths, an extreme sense of vulnerability drifted downward. She looked up, half-expectant, yet praying nothing appeared at the top of the ridges.

Exhaustion tugged at her body, numbed her thoughts. She moved forward with robotic movements—not thinking or feeling, merely responding mechanically, following those in front of her. A branch snapped, bringing her mind back to reality. No longer trudging along a streambed, the slight trail ascended at a sharp angle. The group weaved through thick brush on the ridge and onto a smooth trail. They walked in silence for about a hundred yards before they stepped onto flat rocks, then descended a steep trail covered with limbs, loose rocks, and decayed leaves.

An eerie quietness flooded the forest floor, except for the gentle movement of water flowing over rocks. She strained her ears, listened for dogs, and heard nothing. Wider than the previous stream, but not quite a full river, the water flowed much stronger, swirling around rocks and splashing against boulders. The dim beam from her flashlight provided little help in the vast darkness. She slipped and almost fell several times. On both sides, trees created a canopy over the water, hiding every turn. They meandered in and out of the water as a tactic to throw off the dogs if they came near.

They rounded a corner where the trees widened as if they entered into a great ballroom, open and airy. A sudden freshness chased away the humidity. A cool breeze brushed her face and, against a thunderous crashing of water, tiny droplets splashed over her. She inhaled deeply as predawn light chased away the darkness and revealed a massive waterfall cascading into a gentle pool at its base. The other women plunged into the pool, moved beneath the water and lifted open mouths upwards, drinking deeply of the precious liquid. Haniel faced the trail with an intent gaze. She tripped on a tree root, stumbled and welcomed his strong arms as he caught her. In the early morning light, the familiar sparkle in his eyes offered strength and courage.

"Is it safe here?" she asked.

He shrugged. "There's a cave behind the waterfall. We can rest there for a while anyway. I hid some food there on my way in, and we have a continuous source of water. We'll be well hidden, but able to see from behind the fall. The water's loud though, so I'm not sure we'll hear the dogs barking if they approach."

"At least we would see him coming and if we stay in the cave he won't see us."

"We can't stay here too long, not with the dogs. Eventually we have to leave and make it back to civilization. When the time comes, I'll sneak out and check the area before bringing everyone into the open." He hesitated. "Drake won't give up easily you know."

"No, I'd expect not."

"We'll rest here for now, move again under the cover of darkness."

He motioned for the other women to join them. Reluctantly they left the refreshing flow. Charissa envied their free abandonment under the fall. She wanted to join them, stand beneath the water and let it wash away this nightmare. She ached for the cleansing waves rushing over the rock ledge above them. But responsibility for the women weighed heavy on her shoulders; it bore down, crushed and created fist sized knots in aching muscles. Overwhelmed by potential danger, she fought back an urge to cry, swallowed the ache in her throat.

Haniel addressed the women. "We'll rest here and move again at dusk. Follow me."

Edna said, "This doesn't look so secure. Drake can find us here. We should keep moving."

"Trust me. The rocks offer the perfect hiding place. We're all too tired to keep going."

She stared him down, but then conceded. "Oh, all right. But you better not be wrong."

Invisible chains clinked.

Why did she come with us?

Haniel nodded at the water. Charissa smiled and mouthed thank you. As he gathered the other women and led them over some rocks, she cupped her hands under the water, caught it and forced it down. Pure, sweet, cold liquid cooled the fire of thirst. By the time she finished, Edna's backside disappeared over the top of the rock. He held out his hands, which she accepted gratefully. Her feet left the ground without any effort on her part. For a moment, he engulfed her and then kissed the top of her head.

"It'll be okay, Baby Girl. Rest, but don't give up now."

His uncanny way of reading her mind once infuriated her. On the rock, in his arms, she welcomed comfort for her weary soul. He released her, jumped down from the rock, and lifted her to the ground.

Several passageways led away from the opening. All of the women hung back. Her pulse quickened, along with short gasps and little quivers of air mimicking those of the others. Valorie visibly shook all over. Haniel grabbed a torch from the wall. A swift stroke of a match against rock and the smell of burning oil filled the tiny entrance.

Five pairs of eyes looked between him and her. The thought of following any man deeper into a cave added tension to shoulders already so tight the tendons might snap at any moment. Rubber replaced the strong muscles in her legs as she steadied herself against a rock wall.

Get a grip, girl.

Haniel—not some man. Cave—not a dungeon or prison. The other women waited, looked for her lead. If she didn't move, neither would they. Even Edna hesitated and moved back toward the rock-lined entrance.

She took a deep breath. "Let's go."

Haniel walked onto one of the paths. She followed and then stepped aside while the others entered in front of her. Edna lingered near the entrance, face full of trepidation. Finally, she too, strolled to the passageway and ducked under the low rocks. Charissa closed ranks, barely able to see the torch's glow against the walls.

About twenty feet into the tunnel, the path ended in a sharp turn and opened into a large room. The torch light shimmered and bounced off colorful formations. Stalactites dripped from the ceiling with the look of tiny icicles in the damp, cool air. Sparkles in the rocks bounced back against the dim glow and brightened the room. Small chambers lined the wall, pure and inviting. The smell of human bondage did not exist in this place. Fresh air held a brush of chill laced with the gentle smell of earth, and wafted into her nostrils bringing a sense of peace.

The women looked at Haniel and the flat rocks scattered around. He smiled and nodded gently. Each woman chose a rock or small chamber, climbed onto it and lay down. Soon, snores of various degrees collided into a symphony of sound and filled the room. Haniel stuck the torch into a cleft and stretched out across the pathway.

Secure, exhausted, Charissa closed her eyes. At first, she fought away drowsiness, determined self-proclaimed protector of the small group. The coolness of the cave, soft sounds of the others, and unrelenting weariness soon lulled her into a senseless state of comfort in spite of the hard surface.

For once, she slept peacefully without dreams.

Chapter 60

"He's coming. He's coming." Edna's voice shattered the stillness of the cave.

Charissa consciously pushed the cobwebs of sleep from her mind. The peacefulness of the cave melted into panicked flurry as the women jumped from their makeshift beds, bumped into one another, fell, got up and ran in circles. For a moment, Charissa imagined a group of clowns at a circus until the soft earth smells of the cave brought her back to reality.

"Shhhh." She commanded.

The cave grew quiet again. In the distance, she heard only the crashing streams of the waterfall. The spot in front of the pathway loomed empty and still. The torch remained in the rocks. The light burned with intensity and bounced off the cave walls with the same shimmer and warm glow as before. She stood, strained for any sound other than the water.

Nothing.

She turned to Edna. "What makes you think Drake is anywhere near here? I don't hear a thing except water."

"I don't know. I sense him maybe. We have to run – get out of here before he finds us."

"No. We wait."

"Yeah? Where is your precious Haniel? I swear he's gone to find Drake and bring him back here. Look at this place. No escape anywhere."

Charissa looked around the large room. Other than the main pathway, she saw rocks and dirt. No other passages, light, or escape route. But she knew Haniel. Betrayal and abandonment ran against his nature. She loved those things about him, and trusted him.

"I'm sure he went to scout the area before we leave. He won't betray us."

Dierdre approached, a familiar glint in her eye. "Are you sure?"

Charissa looked her square in the face. "Dierdre, you broke those chains. Don't pick them up again."

The sound of footsteps against dirt made her whirl toward the entrance. Relief coursed over her, tears welled up in her eyes as Haniel appeared in the doorway. He carried a bundle with him.

"So the sleeping beauties are all awake then. Good." His smile illuminated the little cave.

Charissa crossed over to him. "Yes. Some of them seemed a little anxious about getting out of here."

Edna glared at him. "Well, what was I supposed to think when I woke up and you were gone?"

"Sorry. You all looked so peaceful I didn't want to wake you. I scouted the area and found some food for us."

He opened the bundle, revealing a variety of nuts and berries.

"It isn't much," he said. "But hopefully it will keep us going long enough to get back to the highway and safety."

The women didn't argue. Even Edna rushed to his side and grabbed handfuls. As they ate, the pile never seemed to diminish. Ravishing hunger drew Charissa to the bundle, but she waited as the other women grabbed what they wanted. As they moved back, she reached in and took a handful. No fruit ever tasted so sweet or nuts so crisp and fresh. She cared less about the technical names, but flavor burst with each bite. She refilled her hand several times, careful not to eat too much. With a hike ahead, she knew better than to overfill her stomach. The others took her lead and stopped while a large pile remained.

Haniel led the women to the front of the cave. He stood guard as they let the cleansing flow of the waterfall pour over them. They drank the refreshing water again, without resistance or mention of potential danger. Either they all felt more trust, or simply were too grateful to care. He pulled a couple of canteens from the backpack and filled them.

A faint bark tumbled against the crash of water against rock. Haniel seemed unconcerned. Perhaps she imagined it. After several minutes, the sound came again.

This time, Edna perked up and looked over the ridge. "Did you hear that? I told you he's coming."

Haniel stepped down from a rock. "He's still a long way from here. We're not in immediate danger, but it is time to go. Follow me."

Much to Charissa's surprise, he headed around the fall and back into the cave. Near the entrance, he retrieved two more torches. He lit and handed them to Charissa and Valorie.

Edna said, "We're not going back into the cave. There's no way out."

Haniel smiled. "Trust me, Edna."

He led the way with the women falling in line behind him and Charissa bringing up the rear. Instead of taking the same pathway from before, he chose a different one. They moved deeper into the cave where paths turned and crossed. Her head spun as if they went in circles. Finally, the corridor straightened and narrowed, the walls closing in with a smothering effect. In spite of the coolness, sweat beads graced her forehead. Relief swam over her when another large room loomed in front of them. She saw no way out, but above them, a large hole opened into bright sunlight.

Haniel climbed the rocks to the top and peered through the hole. He pointed at Shamira first. She grabbed Valorie's hand, and tugged her halfway up the rocks. She pushed Valorie past, looked up and planted herself. Haniel nodded in agreement.

Dierdre went next and offered a hand to Ariana. When they reached Shamira, she took Ariana's hand and continued the rest of the way, half pulling the larger woman with her. Edna scaled the rocks like a pro. She nudged past Dierdre and shimmied to the top.

Charissa climbed onto the first rock and slipped, regained her balance and gratefully accepted Dierdre's hand. The two finished the climb together.

Haniel motioned for quiet as they stepped through the top of the cave onto a dense trail. Far below, Charissa caught a faint sound of dogs. They barked, stopped, barked, and stopped. The hair on her arms rose as a chill ran down her back in spite of the hot sun and new wave of humidity. They weren't free yet.

Chapter 61

The small band trudged along, sometimes on a narrow trail, at other times moving off, but always keeping an even pace. Haniel led the way up and down hills, around rocks, under trees. Charissa found keeping up easy, as did most of the others, but not without a thick stickiness from head to foot. Clouds rolled in, but rather than provide relief, they only increased the humidity. She missed the coolness of the cave. From her place at the end of the troop, she moved easily behind the last two stragglers, Shamira and Ariana. The sun rose higher in the sky, as they moved for long periods, then hid, rested for only a minute or two and headed out again.

As the sun topped the middle of the sky and slowly descended, Ariana huffed over the trail with an ironic spring in her step. With rapid, short breaths and dripping sweat, she did her best to maintain the pace. A whispered hum of a praise song escaped occasionally, but between the struggled breathing and quietness around them, the sound dissipated almost as soon as it started.

On occasion, she glanced back. The forced smile from the dungeon no longer existed, and instead a warm joy filled her face. Even when the smile slipped, a twinkle remained in her eyes. A soft glow covered her face, from either the heat and humidity or maybe pure joy. Nevertheless, her poor physical condition impeded progress and annoyed Charissa as they fell behind the group.

Shamira concerned her. The shallow breaths seemed out of place, along with the tentative movements. Even from behind, the avoidance of bending and twisting spoke volumes to a trained nurse. Drake's harsh beating along with the grueling trail, wore on the youngest woman in the group. Possibly cracked ribs, definitely blood loss, both contributed to her weakness. They desperately needed some rest, but the urgency to get out of this place forced them forward.

As if he read her thoughts, Haniel moved behind a large rock and motioned for them to follow. They plopped to the ground or leaned against rocks and shared water. No one spoke. Stillness hung in the air. A gentle breeze swept across her face, licking away the beads of sweat from her forehead. Tension remained in her shoulders and neck in spite of the relative peace, an illusion of hope. At any moment Drake might appear. The thought sent tremors through her body.

A high-pitched howl drifted through the air. Still far away, the unmistakable sound of a hound dog drove her from the ground. Haniel remained calm, but a shadow of concern moved from one side of his face to the other, confirming her assessment.

In a gentle but urgent voice, he said, "Let's get moving."

They both offered hands to the other women, pulled fast and hard. Shamira grimaced when Charissa tugged. She changed tactics, placed her arms around the girl and gently lifted the small frame. The pace quickened as they moved away from the resting place. The trail twisted downward which helped, but the shortness of breath in both Ariana and Shamira slowed them. Charissa pushed gently from behind, praying Ariana didn't suffer a heart attack.

Dog barks grew louder. Haniel went off the trail, through brush, over rocks. At every stream or bit of water, he splashed through it motioning for the women to remain in the water as he ran back and forth, in and out of the stream. At the rear of the group, Charissa did the same. Throw the dogs off their trail if possible and buy them more time, perhaps a few moments of rest.

Her muscles ached and the other women showed signs of weariness. All the while, the continuous barking grew more insistent. As they climbed over rocks and into another hidden alcove, the hills became quiet. Apparently, the dogs lost their scent at least for a moment.

Haniel spoke to her in hushed tones as she climbed into the alcove. "I'm going back a ways – try to lead the dogs as far off our trail as possible. I can at least gain a little time. Rest here with the others."

She whispered, "How much farther, Haniel? I'm not sure some of these women can take much more."

"I know. The river is still about a mile away. Once we reach it, we'll have to cross. If the current isn't too bad, walking in the water may help hide our scent. I'll move in and out of the water on both sides so the dogs won't find it as easy to pick up the trail again. We'll still have almost another mile to reach the highway. If I can get a signal, I'll make a phone call to someone in the area I trust. He'll find us."

He trotted back over their footsteps.

"Haniel."

He turned.

"Please be careful. We need you." She hesitated. "I need you."

He winked, smiled and turned to go. Rays of sun bounced off his hair and then disappeared behind grey clouds.

A slight wind replaced the gentle breeze and shifted directions. She inhaled the scent of fresh water. Thunder growled in the distance. Clouds rolled across the sky as the wind picked up strength. She chose a rock sheltered by a massive oak tree and scrambled to the top.

The trail wound downward into the water. The river snaked around and flowed lazily in and out of rock cliffs, sometimes invisible from this vantage point. She wished for a camera. Something so beautiful, and yet behind them lay the most evil spot she ever experienced. The trail looked easiest to follow, but also the most obvious route. Still, if they moved fast...

In the distance, overlooking the river, a large structure loomed out at her. A house? If they reached it before Drake found them... She dared not hope, but then again, when she lost all hope, Haniel came for her.

Lord, please get us to a resting place where Drake can't reach us.

A loud crack of thunder reverberated against the rocks, close enough to feel the impact. Great. Just what they needed right now. She slid off the rock as Haniel reached them again.

"I spotted a place beside the river—maybe a house. If we can reach it before dark, we might be able to hide there—rest for a little while."

"Maybe. How did you see the river?"

"Hmmmm...hid behind the big oak over there and climbed up on a rock. Incredible view."

He laughed softly. "Charissa, only you could find beauty at a time like this."

"Sorry. The scenery's so awesome—I couldn't help but admire it."

"Don't be sorry. It's one of the things I love about you."

He disappeared behind the tree. His muffled voice assured her that he found a cell phone signal and contacted their rescuer. Relief flooded over her as the wind shifted again. Once again, the dogs' strong barks drifted across the trees, steady and sure. Her neck cracked as she turned her head toward the women.

They all clamored to their feet and fell in line without a word as Haniel rounded the tree. The trail rose and fell beneath her feet as they moved along at a new level of speed.

Thunder clapped again as big drops of rain fell. They moved off the trail where more rock and less dirt lined the path.

In the distance, the dogs sounded confused again. Perhaps the rain washed away their scent. What seemed a curse might save their necks. Slipping over rocks, stumbling along, they kept moving. As one, they all seemed to sense a new urgency. As lightening moved into the area, rain poured down, and if the dogs still barked, the thunder and pelting water drowned out their voices.

The trees grew thick, forced them back onto the trail. A slight rise, sharp bend, and a rock surface greeted her as they reached the river. She resisted the temptation to run into the strong current. Without warning, her feet slid on the wet rocks. Pain crashed over her rear as the icy water rose to her waist, stole her breath. Gasps surrounded her, followed by giggles and outright laughs.

"Shhhh." Edna whispered. "If Drake is anywhere around, he'll hear all the cackling."

But even she placed a hand over her mouth and muffled a laugh.

Haniel reached out a hand. "Are you okay?"

"Nothing broken, except maybe a little pride."

Muscles in her arm tensed as she pulled against his hand, her feet slipped and she fell again. Not sure whether to laugh or cry, she tried again. As Haniel pulled her up, his foot slipped against the rocks at the river bottom and he fell backwards, pulling her down with him. Laughter rose up and spilled out of her throat. They found footing, stood, slipped and fell again, unsure whether to hold onto each other or fend for themselves.

Her heart lightened. Perhaps reaching the river gave her a sense of security, or maybe the playfulness of the moment released stress. Either way, hope coursed over her being. The mood over the entire group seemed lighter even with the steady rain.

Haniel finally found firm footing and pulled her up. She stood for a moment and assessed the situation. The current moved fast as the continued rain fed the river. Walking in the middle looked treacherous, but at some point, they must cross.

Haniel said, "If we move downstream, the river has a low water crossing. Let's stay close to the bank for now, and then cross to the other side."

Valorie shivered. "This looks dangerous."

Edna rolled her eyes. "Stay here then and wait for Drake. I'm sure he is so much safer than the river."

Charissa reached out a hand. "C'mon, Valorie. We can do this together."

As they stepped into the river, the rain lightened and the thunder rolled off into the distance. The skies brightened, but gray clouds remained. The group moved in silence without nature to cover their voices. They held to each other and traveled at the pace of snails. When one slipped, the other stood firm.

Less than one hundred yards away, the bend in the river seemed miles from them. As the river turned, a slight break in the clouds revealed a brilliant sun. Colors melted together in a breathtaking aura of shimmering tones. They bounced off riverbanks and skipped across the water like sparkling diamonds.

Filled with wonder, she froze and watched as the sun slipped behind a cloud and created silver around the edges. Beyond the bend, dark clouds rolled, steadily growing nearer. The deep gray, almost black tint stole her breath. Lightning flashed. Suddenly, the walk in the river became a frightening prospect.

Haniel moved farther into the river. The other women stared in his direction. Charissa's mouth flew open. Impossible. Literally walking on top of the water, he flashed a big smile and motioned for them to follow. One by one, each woman moved into the river and rose above the water.

Chapter 62

Unbelievable.

Charissa followed. What if she couldn't do it? What if she sank like Peter did when Jesus told him to walk on ocean waves? As she moved into the river, large rocks beckoned her. She chuckled. Sink — probably not. Slip — high possibility.

She picked her way across the rocks with great care. As she stepped off the final rock, her foot slipped. Sharp pain shot up her leg. The grumbling of thunder drew her attention to the sky. Dark clouds turned, billowing and growing with a thick gray threat. Not a welcome sight for someone in the middle of a river. The throbs of pain in her leg matched the pound of blood in her head.

Keep moving. Deal with your leg later.

They sloshed through the water near the bank. Haniel motioned for them to move forward as he stepped out of the water, moved up the riverbank, slid back down, moved a few feet in the water and repeated his actions. If Drake got this far and suspected they crossed the river, the dogs would pick up Haniel's scent in multiple places, again giving them another few extra minutes.

The water lapped around Charissa's knees, and rose to her thighs. Her leg stung until the chill of river water numbed the pain. She moved with caution, squashing a compulsion for speed. With the distant thunder and rising water level, she dared not stop.

The women ahead of her struggled against the current, which grew stronger with every step. Some of them stood in water swirling around their waists. Her heartbeat rose with the water. Sudden chills crept up her body in spite of the warm air. The humidity still hung around them, but without the intense heat. The trees on the bank moved in a gentle sway. Valorie clung to Dierdre when they moved into deeper waters.

Anxiety pulsed against Charisa. The current pushed her along with an invitation to lift her feet and swim instead of struggle for strong footing. Her strength wore thin while Haniel jumped into the river ahead of the women and moved out again, this time nodding for them to follow.

She reached the bank, grabbed a tree branch and pulled herself out of the water. No one stopped at the trailhead, as if an unseen force pushed the group along with insistence. She hurt all over, but the same persistent rush moved her forward too, even with weariness bearing down.

Her leg throbbed again. She glanced down and gasped. Without the cold of the river, blood gushed and ran down into her shoe. In the distance, dogs barked. Drake. He still followed them. She had to stop the bleeding or risk leaving a path of drops. She ripped part of her shirt, wrapped it around the wound, and limped with a half jog to catch up.

Trees hung across the trail, whipped in the growing storm. Soon the small band stepped off, moved alongside the narrow path, and avoided footprints in the mud. The trail curved, and a small footpath veered off to the left. A bridge connected the path to a steep incline. The entire group disappeared from sight, urging her to ignore pain and break into a full jog. As she rounded another curve and topped the path, her face met Ariana's back. She skidded to a stop behind the panting woman.

A monstrous structure rose before them. Weathered boards, gray with exposure, creaked and moaned. Not much more than a stilted gazebo, narrow boards formed a stairway to the upper deck. The makeshift roof swayed and several boards in the railing hung down, wedged between the rail and floor of the building. One side overlooked the river. Afraid to walk underneath, she skirted around the perimeter and faced the steps.

Unnatural darkness fell over them as gusts of wind pushed against balance. Without warning, a loud boom echoed against the rocks. Rain beat down, with a harsh sting.

Haniel's voice strained against the wind, barely audible. "Quick. Get inside."

The women alternated looks between each other, the steps, and darkening sky. Valorie shook her head viciously. Charissa didn't blame her. The entire structure groaned as the clouds increased in volume, roiled and took on a green tinge. A rickety structure, which might or might not hold, or a sure bet on hailstones. Not much of a choice.

She pushed Valorie up the stairs. "Go. It's better than getting hit with a baseball of ice."

Valorie looked up at the sky, shrieked and took the first step. The others followed with hesitation. Ariana went last. Three steps up, a board cracked and fell beneath her. She grabbed the rail, steadied herself and moved forward a little more tentatively. Haniel motioned and Charissa moved onto the first step. The board creaked beneath her weight. She lunged upward over the third step and several more, broken long before any of them passed. Were they crazy? If the wind got much stronger, the entire thing could blow over and crash into the river below them.

Pushing aside doubt, she reached the top step. The women huddled in the center far away from broken rails. The motion seemed less noticeable inside than from below.

Perhaps whoever built this place considered the probability of storms. Uncertainty tainted her comfort, but the thought gave her a semblance of hope. At least the rain no longer buffeted her agonizing body.

She moved slowly to the side hanging over the river. Below, the falls rushed between rocks the size of small cars. The water swirled and tumbled for a short distance, and then settled into a large pool surrounded by trees clinging to their last fall leaves. Evergreen dots peaked between hardwoods, creating a picturesque view, ironically surreal with Drake in pursuit. A small beach lay almost hidden on one side. When this all ended, she could come back and rest on the beach beside Haniel.

His voice startled her. "It's quite beautiful down there isn't it?"

Her voice caught in her throat and came out as a whisper. "Yes."

"The water is very deep, even above the fall."

"I sure wouldn't want to jump into it from here."

He smiled. A mischievous look rose in his eyes. "Where's your sense of adventure? Don't tell me you've never cliff dived before?"

"No way. I've seen what happens to fools who dive off rocks into too-shallow water."

He chuckled. "This isn't one of those places. It only looks dangerous."

"Well, let's hope we don't have to find out for sure."

Charissa flinched as an earsplitting boom rolled across the sky. Dark, green-tinged clouds emitted another torrent of rain. Pea sized hailstones bounced against the wood and landed on the ground beneath the structure. Suddenly, the dilapidated old building transformed, becoming a sure friend who protected them from a harsh storm. The wood swayed, creaked and groaned under the strain, but held firm.

She turned and joined the other women as hail beat on the roof.

"You're bleeding." Sympathy laced Shamira's voice.

Charissa looked down. "Yeah. Hazards of slipping in a river."

Haniel bent down. "Let me see."

She sat. He unwrapped the bandage, and with gentle pressure, wiped away the blood with her shirt. He pressed down and checked the bleeding. Tiny clots formed along the gash, as the flow gradually stopped. Perhaps the endorphins suppressed a vicious throb, but for whatever reason, the wound no longer hurt.

Don't even think about all the bacteria in the river. Don't go there.

Haniel grinned. "Not too deep, could use a little attention. I think you'll survive with a very nice battle wound."

"Thank you for your assessment, Dr. Haniel." She shook her head and smiled at him.

"Hey, I'd rather be a savvy trails man than a doctor any day of the year." He winked.

The hail stopped as quickly as it began. Raindrops pattered on the roof in soft contrast to the pelts of ice. A collective sigh rose from the group. Thunder rumbled in the distance, announcing a retreat, while a new line of clouds approached from the other direction. Reprieved from the storms, no one seemed rushed into moving from the dwelling. A hush fell over the area and brought a gentle peace with it. The women lingered in the silence. Haniel stood, crossed back to the railing and looked down the trail. His eyes searched the tree line with a concentrated gaze.

Charissa stood, approached him. She started to ask what he saw, but a faint sound stopped her. From below, the howls and barks of dogs split the air and rose up with fresh fierceness.

Inconceivable. Would Drake ever give up?

Haniel turned and motioned for the women to stay down and quiet. He and Charissa squatted in shadows but close enough to the rail for a good view of the bridge.

The dogs grew louder. Tension gyrated up her back, through her shoulders and neck. She froze, unable to move, breathe or think. Closer, the dogs barked against the air and Drake's gravelly voice mixed with them. The sounds bounced off the rocks, upwards to where they hid. She glanced back over her shoulder where the others huddled, quiet and still, but eyes closed and lips moving softly.

Shadows lengthened as the sun slipped below the clouds and disappeared behind the cliffs. Beauty hung in the sky for one instant before a stormy darkness fell around them. Even if Drake crossed the bridge, the dim light might provide enough cover to keep them invisible. The barks grew louder and closer. Everything in her wanted to run, but her feet gripped the spot, paralyzed. Her legs quivered, numb to any feeling. She dared not stand up for fear of giving away their location. Her breaths came quicker as she scanned the trail below the bridge. Nothing so far, but the dogs sounded so near.

The noise below them grew softer, then moment by moment faded even more. The sounds passed and began to disappear all together. He moved right past them without catching the little footpath.

Thank you, Lord.

Relief poured out, gentle rain following a storm.

Without warning, Edna sprang up and bolted down the stairs, crashing through one of the boards. She sprinted across the bridge and yelled for Drake. Thunder boomed, drowning out her screams.

She kept running.

Chapter 63

Drake stopped in the middle of the trail. "Hush those dogs. I thought I heard something."

His men silenced the dogs. Thunder resounded in the wooded area and wiped out any other sound. Wind whistled through trees as they bent under strong gusts. A whisper cut through the heavy air.

"Drake, wait."

"Edna?"

Anger crashed over him a perfect image of the ominous storm brewing in the air.

Traitor.

Perhaps she found the prospect of capture and a slow torturous death less appealing than groveling before him.

Let her come to me.

He didn't move an inch closer to the sound of her voice.

Feet pounded the trail, branches snapping beneath them. The woman certainly knew little about the stealth required for hunting. Even animals would detect her entrance, not to mention a cunning adversary like Haniel. He breathed heavily in anticipation of her appearance.

She rounded a tree and sloshed along the wet trail. "Drake. I'm so glad I caught you."

"I'll bet you are. I suppose you're gonna tell me they kidnapped you, forced you to go with them. But don't bother. I saw you running with them, going over the fence. You weren't wearing any ropes or chains, traitor."

She stared at him wide-eyed, her chest heaving.

He smelled fear as she gazed up at him.

"I did it for you."

He slapped her face. "Liar. You betrayed me."

"No, no. I didn't. They already had the others, so I pretended to be on their side. I knew you'd follow. I tried to bring them out in the open earlier, but Haniel and Charissa didn't listen to me."

"Why should I believe you? You're a whore who'd sell your newborn child to get what you want."

"Look, I won't deny you have sufficient reason to doubt me. But you're wasting time while Haniel is probably leading the other women away from their hiding place. Which, by the way, you tromped right past."

"Why didn't you stop me then?"

"They were all huddled around me. If I moved or yelled then, they would've stopped me — probably thrown me over a cliff or something. I waited for my chance and then broke away."

Blood rushed from his head, leaving fuzziness in the wake. Recovering quickly, he drew in a deep breath of air. Heat rose to his face. He resisted the urge to grab the woman's throat and squeeze with all his strength. He clenched his teeth and stared down at her until self-control returned.

"Show me their hiding place."

She grabbed his hand. "This way. Hurry."

Chapter 64

Charissa stared in disbelief.

"Oh, crap." Dierdre yelled. "I knew something wasn't right with her."

The other women all started talking at the same time. Haniel held up a hand and silenced them.

Charissa spoke softly. "Now what? She'll bring him back here. I wondered why she followed us so easily, then fought against us."

Haniel looked down into the river. "There's only one way to escape without him catching us, and we don't have much time."

Charissa searched his eyes. "No way."

"It's the only way."

"No."

"He's out for blood. He'll kill all of us, Charissa, and you know it."

"So we stay and definitely die, or jump over the cliff into potentially shallow water and maybe die or worse?"

The other women collectively muttered their opinions, none of which agreed with the plan.

"You won't die if you jump. I promise. But it's now or never."

He turned to the group. "Can you all swim?"

They nodded their heads, except for Valorie, who appeared paralyzed. Her eyes, wide enough to hold a nickel, glazed over with a blank stare. Her lips parted slightly as if she wanted to scream but didn't know how. If they threw her over instead of letting her jump, would she survive? Doubtful. The choice belonged to her alone.

Dierdre finally broke the silence. "Let's do it."

Haniel quickly gave them instructions on the best way to jump and filled them in on where to find the best trail leading from the deep pool only a mile or two to the highway. He handed Dierdre the flashlight.

"It's supposed to be waterproof, so you'll have some light. Wait for the others and then all of you stick together. I'll see you soon."

He braced his knee on one of the boards, waited for lightning and then as the thunder cracked, broke the board beneath his weight. He pulled Dierdre over. Another streak of lightning, and she jumped. The fall took only two or three seconds. Timed perfectly, the thunder rolled over her splash. Ariana swallowed hard and kissed Haniel on the cheek.

"Just in case I don't survive, thank ya for everything."

"You'll be fine," he whispered.

Lightning flashed and she jumped.

Shamira moved to the edge. Charissa looked down into the pool. Dierdre moved close to the beach area, but stayed in the water. A blaze of light moved across the sky again, Shamira jumped. Ariana's head popped above the water far below and moved as she swam toward the beach.

Valorie moved back toward the opposite side. The sound of barking blended with the howling wind and moved closer. They had minutes. Charissa lunged in Valorie's direction, but Haniel grabbed her arm.

"Let me talk to her," he said.

"Okay – hurry."

"You go ahead and jump."

"No. If she won't go on her own, it'll take both of us to get her over the edge."

Valorie joined their conversation. "I'm here you know."

Haniel answered, "Yes. You are. Valorie, I'm not carrying you over this time. It has to be your choice."

"I'm afraid."

"I know. It's scary — a long way down to the pool."

"With lots of rock cliffs between here and there."

"And Drake coming up the trail behind you. Which will it be? Drake or the leap?"

She shook all over. Tears streamed down her face. "I don't want to be afraid."

"You've come so far. We're right here with you, but I'm not letting Drake take Charissa again. If you choose to stay here, you choose existence, not life, with him."

"No." She shouted. "I'm not going back."

"Then jump. And do it now."

"I can't do it on my own. Will you help me?"

"We'll be with you, but you have to overcome your fears and jump. You have to break off those chains around your heart."

She nodded.

"C'mon." He pressed gently on her back.

Valorie moved to the edge, and as she jumped with a loud scream, footsteps pounded on the bridge.

"Go now, Charissa. Go."

"What about you?"

"I'm right behind you."

The steps groaned and creaked as Drake bounded up them and leveled his shotgun.

"Don't even think about jumping over the edge, my dear Charissa. I'll shoot before you clear the rail, and then the next shot will be straight into Haniel's heart."

She looked over her shoulder. Drake lunged for her, but Haniel moved in between them.

"Charissa, jump." Haniel shouted. "Now!"

She stood frozen, as if walking through a nightmare, willing herself to wake up, but unable to do so. Haniel punched Drake. He fell backwards, but leaped back to his feet. The clang of metal rang and a glint of steel flashed as Drake pounced across the structure in her direction.

Haniel stepped between them. A knife blade pierced his chest. Drake drew the blade back. Haniel shoved him and struggled to her.

"Jump." With the single word, he pushed hard.

She fell through the air, parachuting down with nothing on her back to open.

Deep breath in, hold it as feet hit water.

The cold liquid pricked her skin with the tingle of a million thin needles. Dazed and scared, she kept her eyes closed and kicked against the water. Up, moving in the direction of the surface. Her lungs burned, begged for air, but she resisted.

Gotta get up and out of the way. Haniel will be right behind me.

She fought against the urge to breathe, kicked harder and moved her hands. Despair washed over her with the waves and she opened her eyes to darkness. Her lungs burned, begging for oxygen. As the last ounce of will power ended, the water gave way. She gasped and filled her lungs with fresh night air.

Disoriented, she looked around. Eerie darkness settled over the pool. A flash of light broke through the sky and pointed to the beach right in front of her. Her arms stroked across the water, propelled her from the middle. She listened for the splash behind, but none came.

Dierdre reached down and grabbed her hand, pulled her up and wrapped an arm around her.

"Wait. Haniel."

She looked up at the two men fighting in the shelter, the perfect hideaway only a short time ago. Ariana, Shamira and Valorie joined them at the edge of the water. They couldn't see much from their vantage point.

Dierdre spoke first. "We have to go, Charissa."

"Not without Haniel."

"Drake knows we're here. Haniel will meet us at the highway. He'll jump when he can, and then he'll run the trail. He'll catch up."

"Without a light?"

Thunder and lightning collided in answer. Large raindrops pelted all around them. They moved out of the water and onto the beach area.

Ariana soothed Charissa with soft words. "I think God might be big enough to provide a lil' light for someone who loves Him."

No arguing with logic — or childlike faith.

A loud crash reverberated through the night, but this time it wasn't thunder.

Chapter 65

Drake let Edna pull him down the trail as thunder rolled across the sky. Flashes of lightning flickered high above them, brightening the dark clouds and splitting downward toward the land.

Within a few hundred yards, he spotted a half-hidden footpath. Dead leaves and branches lay across the entrance with a huge tree to one side. From the other direction, the giant trunk hid the path completely. No wonder he missed it. He underestimated Haniel's knowledge of this area.

Lightning hurled through the sky accompanied by a sharp clap of thunder. Dirt from the trail whipped across his face, stinging with a razor sharp bite.

More trees hung down shielding the steep incline, which became visible as they moved along the rocky way to the top. He knew this place.

Of course. The old shanty at the top. A perfect place for shelter from the storms, if it didn't fall apart from the gusts. A grave mistake, considering the structure hung on the side of a cliff with no escape.

A streak from sky to ground flashed nearby, sizzling with a pop and deafening crack. Undaunted by the fierceness of the storm, he pushed forward. Perhaps the little entourage escaped back along the trail after Edna bailed. With a point to the dogs and trail, he sent his men back toward the river.

Pushing Edna aside, Drake scaled the rocks with ease, topped the ridge and ran for the bridge. Across and around the curve, he darted beneath the building as another bolt from the sky barely missed him. The stairs groaned and cracked beneath his weight, but didn't dissuade the determination of reaching his enemy. Victory soared along his veins, spurring him forward despite the danger from decaying wood.

A surge of power rewarded him at the top. Haniel stood beside Charissa near the opposite rail. With her back to him, she appeared about to jump. Unthinkable. They risked death against rocks or drowning at the bottom of the waterfall, rather than run back down the trail where his dogs no doubt would have caught them.

Of all the sneaky, underhanded tricks.

He leveled his shotgun.

"Don't even think about jumping over the edge, my dear Charissa. I'll shoot before you clear the rail, and then the next shot will be straight into Haniel's heart."

She looked over her shoulder. The blood drained from her face as she stared into the barrel. Her lips parted but uttered nothing.

He lunged at her, fully intending a horrible, slow death as her hero watched. She could not go over the side. Haniel moved between them, and knocked the shotgun out of his hands.

"Charissa, jump." Haniel shouted. "Now!"

She froze.

Ready to move, Drake never saw Haniel's fist coming at him. Stunned by the blow, years of bitterness against this man climbed from the depths of his soul and fueled his body. He leapt back to his feet. The sweet clang of unsheathing metal rang as he ducked around Haniel, dagger in hand. The glint of steel flashed as he pounced across the structure. Haniel threw himself in front of the woman.

The blade slowed only for a split second before it sunk into flesh. He drew the blade back, purposely twisting so the flesh tore as it released the steel.

Haniel shoved him back and struggled to Charissa. "Jump." With the single word, he pushed.

She screamed and went over the edge, arms and legs flailing through the air.

Drake screamed at his rival. "You'll die for freeing her. And then I'll find your precious Charissa and ravish her multiple times before I finally end her life."

"You will not take her. I'll always protect her from you."

Haniel's eyes flashed with fierce anger. Lightning reflected off the irises. Undaunted, Drake circled him, sizing up his opponent. He gripped the knife, fixed on causing as much damage as possible. The sharp thrust forward missed the mark as Haniel arched his back away from the blade, spun and caught him with a blow to the back. He pitched forward, regained his balance and spun around in time to duck another blow to the face.

A kick to his midsection forced air from his lungs. Still upright, struggling for breath, he landed a blow. Haniel's muscle tightened beneath his knuckles, but distracted him. Drake brought the knife down again and connected. The tip hit the collarbone and sent a quiver through the weapon. Drake yanked it back. In spite of the new injury, Haniel's left arm caught his hand and shook the knife loose. Metal hit wood.

He lunged downward for it, but a foot met his face and drove him into a beam. Pain shot up his back into the base of his skull. He slid down the wood as his weapon sailed over the railing.

He glanced around, looking for his shotgun. It teetered at the edge only a few feet from him. His muscles ached as he moved toward the gun. Haniel pounced with relentless blows to his face. The taste of iron and salt mingled with saliva, while the peripheral vision in his left eye slowly faded. Sticky, wetness ran from his nose, cascading down his lip on one side and from his mouth flowing over his chin on the other.

His mind grew fuzzy, and the blows subsided. Haniel stood above him looking satisfied. The gleam of victory bounced off his face, any sign of pain from wounds hidden beneath the glow.

Drake panted and looked over the horizon. Skirting the clouds, a soft glow appeared for seconds and then dipped below the hills. Sunset. Onset of the wonderful cover of darkness, when he operated best, settled around them. As lightning pierced the sky again, and rain poured from the skies, anger burned into a roaring flame. Adrenaline raced through his veins. He drew from unnatural strength, bounced to his feet, and pushed hard against the man.

Haniel flew backwards and landed with a thud against the wooden flooring. A board cracked and fell to the ground below the structure.

Drake shook his head to clear the fogginess and in a single motion, retrieved the gun, positioned himself over his adversary and pointed the barrel at his head.

"Now who's gonna protect them from me?"

He drew back the hammer and pulled the trigger. The gun's boom collided in the air as the butt kicked his shoulder and Haniel's feet hit his midsection. Wood connected with his rear and gave way. The gun flew from his hand as his backward momentum carried him through the air. He pulled his feet beneath him as best he could before he hit dirt. The shotgun smashed against a rock.

Every fiber of Drake's body begged for mercy. Edna rushed to his side.

"Drake."

Groans escaped from his mouth as he pushed her aside. He willed his body upright, but pain beat against him until he collapsed back and closed his eyes. A heavy foot planted on his chest.

He conceded. "You win. I've got nothing left."

This time anyway. I won't quit.

"You'll skulk away like a wounded animal for now, but I know you, Drake. You'll try again."

He opened his eyes, and met the harsh glare of a flashlight. "Then we'll meet again, and next time I will defeat you. The next time will be our last, and I'll leave you lying on the ground – for good."

"Get behind me, you devil. And leave my daughters alone."

The flurry of wings rushed through the air all around him. A shudder ran over him with the sting of harsh raindrops buffeting his body. He looked at Edna who knelt on the dirt near his head, in the edge of the light's circle.

Haniel spoke to her first. "Come with me, Edna."

She looked back and forth between the two men. For a moment, her eyes softened and she took a step in Haniel's direction. Then, a dark smolder returned, as she looked deep into the enemy's eyes.

Her voice crackled into the night air. "I'd rather stay with Drake then have a million powerless days with you." She moved to Drake's side.

Haniel shook his head. "Last chance. He is not what he seems."

"I'll take the risk. Go away."

The darkness hid Haniel's face, but Drake pictured the sadness in those eyes. He saw the look when he took Zoe, would have seen it with Charissa. For a moment, he pitied the man. What a fool to love someone so deeply who still rejected him. But the moment passed and triumph soothed away physical pain. He drew power from Edna's loyalty.

The light disappeared and brisk footsteps assured him of Haniel's departure. His faithful dogs filled the night with barks, and soon a fresh beam of light from a torch flooded over them.

One of the men handed leashes to another and came to his side. He offered water to Drake, who drank greedily. Edna reached out for some, but his faithful servant slapped her hand away.

"The master drinks first."

When Drake finished, he nodded, and the man tossed the canteen in her general direction. The servant lifted him from the ground, bearing his weight to prevent another fall.

"Boss, can you walk?"

"Yes. I'm fine." He seized a gun from his servant's belt and tucked it into his own. "Where were you five minutes ago? I could've shot Haniel in the back. I should shoot you now, but with the fool Smitty gone, I need you."

He turned to Edna. "My dear, come steady me on our journey home."

Without a word, she moved to him.

"Wait. First, kneel here before me. Kiss my ring and vow your allegiance to me."

She knelt willingly. "I am yours forever, my love."

Rising, she slipped an arm around his waist. They crossed the bridge and limped along the trail slowly back in the direction of his mansion.

As they approached the river, the hum of a motor broke the silence. Two of the men picked up Drake and placed him gently into the small craft. He motioned for Edna, and she approached the boat.

"Are you sure about your decision to follow me?"

She nodded.

"No regrets or hesitation?"

"No, of course not. I am yours forever."

Warmth covered him. He swelled inside, her answer providing immense pleasure, assurance he still controlled her.

"Yesssss. You are, my dear."

He pulled his pistol and fired one shot into her heart. Unlike Smitty, she fell without shock appearing on her face, dead before flesh hit dirt.

He tucked away the gun and closed his eyes to rest.

Chapter 66

Charissa rushed to the pool. "That was a shotgun, wasn't it?"

A strong arm grabbed her from behind. She whirled around ready to fight. Dierdre looked straight into her eyes, and spoke in a loud whisper.

"Charissa. Listen to me. We're all worried about Haniel, but look at Shamira and Ariana. They aren't in great shape."

Dierdre shined the light over the little group, huddled together on the dark trail. Charissa looked at them. Tears spilled out of her eyes and snaked down her cheeks. She didn't want this choice. Her heart tugged, willed her back to the structure where Haniel fought against the most evil man she ever knew. But these women, even Dierdre, needed her. They looked to her with fear and wildness in their eyes, like orphaned little girls waiting for rescue.

She understood what Haniel meant. Her heart for orphans applied to more than children. In the darkness, surrounded by the unknown, these women needed her more than any child in a foreign country did. They wanted direction and leadership out of here. Fear and helplessness overtook her reasoning as she sobbed against the pouring rain and loud claps of thunder.

Trust me, and I will lead you home, Baby Girl.

"God, I hear you. I'm as scared as the rest of these women, and I can't lead them alone. Please help me."

She threw her head back and let the rain wash over her face. The water removed her tears. Self-doubt fused with fear and sorrow, tumbled to the ground into a pool at her feet. The cleansing rain renewed strength and courage. She leveled her gaze at Dierdre who stared at her with wonder and a quizzical look that said plainly "girl you've lost it."

"You're right, Dierdre. Thank you for keeping me focused. Let's go."

She accepted the flashlight and moved to the front of the group.

"Let's stick close together and get out of here as fast as possible."

The women moved into pairs; Dierdre supported Ariana and Valorie placed an arm around Shamira's waist. Charissa nodded approval, turned and trudged along the gravel-lined path. The dim flashlight played over the trail as they moved silently through the night.

After what seemed like hours, they approached a hollowed out rock. The rain beat hard against them. Wind howled with strong gusts pushing against her. Did they dare stop here? She glanced back over her shoulder. Several feet spread between her and the others. As the others caught up to her, a hailstone plopped against her forehead.

"Quick. Get under the rocks. We'll stay here 'til the hail stops."

The women moved beneath the covering and sat against the rocks, uneven breaths spilling into the air. Charissa turned off the light. They needed battery power for as long as possible. No telling how far to the highway, or if Haniel's contact really waited for them there.

Sorrow welled up as she stared into the blackness and the falling ice mixed with rain. Praying crossed her mind, but she didn't know what to say. Filled with questions and no answers, despair settled in spite of her desire to believe Drake had not hurt her friend. The image of blood on his shirt where the knife entered mocked her innocent belief of everything being okay. He bore at least one wound, and the gunshot...

No. I won't let my mind go there. Haniel isn't dead. I won't believe.

Yet, heaviness of heart argued with resolve.

More sudden than the storm began, the rain and hail ceased, and the wind stopped. In the quietness, a soft, sweet voice rose behind her.

"The Lord is my Shepherd. I shall not want."

Silent tears streamed down Ariana's face as she quoted the twenty-third Psalm. The words comforted Charissa's soul, renewed her spirit. In the midst of sorrow and anxiety over whether Haniel survived the fight, peace drifted past like a soft summer breeze.

"...even though I walk through the valley of the shadow of death, I will fear no evil..."

She pulled in a deep breath and exhaled slowly; the peace descended from her head to her heart.

"...and I shall dwell in the house of the Lord forever. Amen."

"Thank you, Ariana."

Charissa turned and faced the women. "Shall we go now?"

The women rose to their feet and fell back into line, ready to follow. She switched on the light and moved from beneath the rock.

They stayed on the gravel-lined trail. The over-grown surface indicated little use. Small pools of water stood in spots, but without mud, the way seemed less treacherous than the trails from earlier. Still, darkness surrounded them, so she stepped lightly and maintained silence.

Sidestepping potholes and sticking to the grassy areas made the most sense. With every inch, the flashlight grew dimmer, until finally it disappeared all together. Someone bumped into her and nearly shoved her down.

"Hang on a second," she whispered.

She blinked against the darkness hoping her eyes might adjust. She closed them, counted to one hundred and opened them again. The faint outline of grass flanked both sides, providing some navigation alone the route. She moved forward a little. Hands grasped her shoulders.

Good idea.

"I can barely see. Everyone line up with a hand on the shoulder in front of you. Whisper up the line when you're ready."

The word "ready" whispered in her ear. She grasped the hand. Thin and cold, Shamira she guessed. With a quick prayer and slow steps, she moved along the road. Twice she tripped on rocks hidden by the night. Both times the hand on her shoulder tightened, supporting balance. At one point, grass rose in front of her, adjusting steps around a slight curve.

Reached out fingertips brushed the top of grass, providing guidance. Slowly, her eyes adjusted to the dark. Still unable to see much more than shadows, her steps continued at the pace of a snail. She almost wished for lightning. At least then, she'd have a clue about their location.

In answer to the thought, a bright moon broke through clouds. For a brief moment, the light lingered, revealing a rather steep hill about six feet in front of them, and then the moon disappeared again behind another set of clouds.

With renewed fervor, she picked up speed so when the ascent came, they had some momentum going. Her heart rate increased even before the hill rose beneath her feet, and tiny drops of sweat broke out across her forehead. She wiped it with a free hand and kept moving. At the top of the hill, she stopped, allowed the rapid, shallow breaths to come. Tired, yet exhilarated and energized by the workout, her muscles felt the strain. The other women surely felt it as well.

The moon broke again. She glanced forward at the road, which remained flat with a sharp turn to the left about ten feet ahead. What idiot designed that? Another minute passed. She waited until the breathing slowed.

"Let's go."

In the stillness, she heard ready whispered up the line four times. Unable to control the urge, she giggled.

"What's so funny?" Shamira asked.

She put her hand over her mouth to muffle the giggles, but it spread until all of them joined. If Drake, or anyone, hid nearby, they gave their location away. But she couldn't help laughing, and the release felt incredibly good. Finally, the sound trailed off; she patted Shamira's hand, and then moved forward.

She counted steps and let the grass brush against her fingertips again. When the blades disappeared, she turned left around the sharp corner. A few steps more and the grass brushed her fingers again. She exhaled. Would this road ever end? This had to be more than a mile.

The grass dropped away. She peered into the darkness. Nothing. The moon didn't break through and she saw only the rise and fall of deep shadows. She wanted to stop. Stand still and wait. Wait for what? Sunrise? It might still be hours from now.

The ride Haniel arranged might have already given up on them. Her stomach knotted at the thought of her friend. Keep going for him. The sooner they got out of here, the better. She'd send the local authorities back for him, even if she didn't know exactly what local meant.

Her feet inched forward. An abrupt change in the road caught her off guard.

Pavement.

She started to bend down and kiss the highway. Not a great idea in the middle of darkness. She scanned both directions. No lights from cars or overhead. Some highway. A long line of reflectors marked the edge of the road, offering some hope.

The women gathered around her all talking at once, trying to determine which way they should go.

Charissa hushed them. "Shhhh. Everyone be quiet. One at a time, and speak softly."

Shamira sounded weak and tired. "I think we came from the right, so we go left away from Drake's lair."

All of the women agreed. She wished one of them offered to take the lead, but none of them wanted it any more than she did.

"Does anyone need to sit down for a minute?" She asked.

"Where we gonna sit, honey child?" Ariana asked.

"On the ground I guess."

"Then we'd have to get back up; easier to keep walkin'."

"Okay. Let's go then."

Within a few steps, the clouds broke, and the moon appeared high in the sky. The light bathed the entire area with brilliant light. The highway reflectors and white lines down the middle and marking the shoulder contrasted visibly from the grassy area where they stood. She moved onto the shoulder and hurried their journey.

A distant motor shattered the silence, coming toward them; at least she thought it came from ahead. As she topped a hill, bright headlights swung up from below and bore down on them. The vehicle moved along slowly, nowhere near a normal highway speed.

She halted. Only seconds to make a critical decision. Their ride, or perhaps a decent stranger, drove straight at them. But what if Drake or one of his cronies passed by earlier and now turned back and headed to his place?

Before she decided, Dierdre moved to the edge of the road and waved wildly. The other women joined her.

God, I hope they're right.

The vehicle dimmed its lights, pulled onto the shoulder and stopped a few feet in front of them. Either way, the nightmare ended, here and now.

Chapter 67

Charissa held her breath. Blood raced through her veins again and pounded against her temples as she waited for the door of the SUV to open.

Out of nowhere, red and blue pulsated against the night. Charissa dropped to her knees, consumed with sobs. The women behind her jumped up and down, yelling and cheering, as a young DPS officer stepped into the headlights.

He spoke with controlled calmness. "Are you ladies okay?"

Charissa wiped away tears and rose on rubber band legs. "We're tired, thirsty and hungry with some minor injuries, but nothing life threatening."

"Were you with Haniel McCrae by any chance?"

"Yes. You know him?"

"Long time friends. I'm John. He called me hours ago. I've been up and down this highway a hundred times looking for you. I about gave up; planned on sending out a search party in the morning. Where is he anyway?"

Tears stung for release, but she fought against them. "We don't know. We jumped into the waterfall, and the last we saw, he fought against a man named Drake Hannibal. I heard what sounded like a gunshot, but I'm not sure."

The other women fell silent, walked to Charissa and wrapped arms around each other.

John covered his chin with a big hand. "Don't worry. Haniel can take care of himself, but we'll comb this area in the morning. I know Drake, and would love to bring the man in. But experience tells me he's long gone by now."

"I hope so." Charissa said.

The others echoed, "Me too."

"Well, let me get you to the station. There's a small ice chest in the back with water, fruit and cheese. Help yourselves."

They gave Ariana the front seat, and the rest of the women climbed into the back. Charissa hesitated. Was this man really Haniel's friend? A faint voice echoed in her mind.

Trust, Charissa. You need to trust.

The voice reminded her of the many times Haniel challenged her. Trust for any man didn't come easy, and even less so after the ordeal with Drake. She pushed the doubts aside and climbed in with the others. If he went the wrong way, even gave the appearance of heading to Drake's place, she'd jump from the moving vehicle.

Valorie leaned over the back seat, retrieved bottles of water and passed them out along with the food. The SUV pulled onto the highway. Charissa gripped the door handle, ready to pull it open. When they reached the gravel road, he swung onto it and maneuvered a perfect u-turn. She exhaled, leaned her head back against the seat and accepted an apple.

Munching ensued as John picked up the radio and notified dispatch of his location and passengers. She bit into the apple and let the juice run down her throat in spite of her stomach churning and knotting at the thought of food. Reflections of Haniel surrounded her and closed off attempts to swallow. She gave up after a few bites.

Ariana's head tilted against the door as she gave into slumber and a soft snore drifted backwards. Soon, the back seat fell silent as the little band of women huddled together and leaned on each other. Shamira's head fell onto Charissa's shoulder. Eyes closed, lips parted, total peace filled their faces in sleep.

Not her. The last time she fell asleep in a stranger's car, she ended up in a dungeon. This time, four ladies depended on her too. But weariness crept up and hit her hard. She nodded off. Her chin dropped, jolting her awake.

No. Stay awake.

She fought hard, afraid to give in to the desire.

As they traveled east, the sky changed and a soft glow ascended in front of them. Light peeked above the hills with various hues of yellow, pink and orange. A big ball of light rose slowly, reflected on the bottom of dark gray clouds and created a silver outline, which bounced back against the trees.

Overwhelmed by the beauty and awe in the moment, Charissa gasped.

John glanced toward her. "Beautiful, huh?"

"Yes." She whispered.

The tears broke free without resistance. Sorrow, fear and sheer exhaustion bore down on her shoulders.

Lord, I'm so tired. I can't stay awake any longer, and I'm afraid for myself and these other women. Please protect us; bring us home safely.

Peace enveloped her. Drowsiness overtook her, and she succumbed to deep sleep.

Chapter 68

A cacophony of birds ushered in early morning outside Charissa's windows, their song an ironic blend of sounds. Doves cooed, blackbirds squawked, and a myriad of other birds joined the chorus with an assortment of inflections. She snuggled down deeper into her bed. Sleep beckoned her to linger, refuse facing the day.

Her mind became fully alert. Was she in the dungeon dreaming of home or safe in her bed waking from a long nightmare of imprisonment? She pressed her eyes tighter, afraid to open them.

The radio came alive with morning traffic and weather. The promise of a beautiful Saturday ahead comforted her.

Her eyes shot open. Saturday? Did he say Saturday? How long was she in the dungeon? She lost all track of time there, but only days passed, not even an entire week. Or did it? She grabbed her cell phone and looked at the date. She stared in disbelief.

The dungeon—all of it—a dream.

Rusty nuzzled her from beside the bed. She buried her face in his fur.

"It seemed so real, boy. I've never had such a vivid dream."

Her muscles rebelled, as if she put them through hours of agonizing workouts during the night. Absently, she rubbed her calf, hitting the lump of a scab covering a large gash.

Funny. I don't remember cutting my leg. Probably happened when I went camping.

She pushed herself out of bed and padded through the apartment. The cards remained on the table where she and Haniel sat and argued over Drake. Rusty panted beside his mistress, waiting patiently for a leash and open door. While he took care of his morning business, sirens went off in her head. She promised Drake a lake date today, but after the dream...

"Well, he may be disappointed, but it ain't gonna happen," she said aloud to herself. "I'm not taking a chance."

Back inside, she double-locked the door, fed Rusty, made coffee, and spotted her Bible. She puttered around a little longer and finally settled in a chair, mug in one hand, Bible and journal spread across her lap.

Absorbed in writing and reading, time passed quickly. She glanced at the clock. Already 8:15? She expected Drake at 9:00. She didn't plan on going with him. Nevertheless, she didn't want him to catch her in pajamas. Reluctantly, she closed the journal and placed it gently with the Bible on an end table, then headed to her bedroom. The inviting promise of a warm shower beckoned. A nightmare never left her with so many pains and popping joints before.

She flipped on the TV for one last weather report before choosing clothes for the day.

"In national news, a prominent New York attorney was found dead this morning, shot with a small caliber handgun."

Charissa froze. No way.

"The name has not yet been released pending notification of family."

Get a grip. Just because Edna went back with Drake doesn't mean he killed her. Listen to yourself. It was a dream!

Nevertheless, her pulse increased with a rapid release of adrenaline. An overwhelming desire to run as fast and far away as possible pounded in rhythm with her heart. Instead, she opted for a long shower with water capable of drowning out the doorbell and any amount of fierce knocking.

She stepped into the bathroom, removed the pajama top and turned to grab a brush for detangling hair before getting into the shower. She seldom looked in the mirror, but a gentle voice whispered in her mind.

"Look up, child."

She looked into the mirror. Nothing special. Then she saw it. A long, red scar crossed her abdomen from one side to the other. She gasped and reached for the counter as her knees buckled beneath her.

Shamira's cut.

The room whirled as her mind grasped for reality. She touched her stomach. Tender, but not painful, the slight ridge convinced her of the certain existence of the dungeon. Her brain fought for comprehension—found none. Impossible, yet real nonetheless. How didn't matter. Great sobs overtook her amidst a barrage of emotions. She survived Drake's dungeon, and the experience changed her, set her free. How much, she didn't know, yet deep within, her spirit glowed with new hope and strength.

She stayed in the bathroom floor for a long time, or so it seemed, unable to move or think, but overwhelmed with a reality she couldn't explain or verbalize.

Finally, she pulled herself up and looked at the clock. Ten. No Drake. He stood her up.

Thank God.

Chapter 69

Charissa walked through the ER door. Nothing new, yet everything changed. A few people milled around the waiting room. No one with major injuries waited for treatment; no agitated family members yelled across the reception desk. Good way to begin the workday. She smiled to herself.

From the corner of her eye, a young woman caught her attention. Familiarity screamed from the slim body, covered with scars and bruises. Impossible.

Shamira crossed the room and stood before her.

"It wasn't a dream, was it? The dungeon—everything—it was all real."

"No, Shamira. I can't explain it, but yes, Drake had us in a dungeon for days, and yet no time passed at all."

"It doesn't make sense."

"Nothing is impossible with God."

"That's what my friend, Selma, always says."

"She's a good friend then."

"Yes." She paused. "She's been telling me to leave Doug for a long time. When I woke up in the same place and time, he beat me again. I went to the diner, but I didn't wait for Drake to show up and rescue me. I got my last paycheck and left town. I ended up here somehow, and I'm not even sure why. I can't go back to him, ever."

"You shouldn't. You deserve so much more."

"I know now, and I actually believe it. I still have some past to deal with, but staying with Doug…"

She trailed off. A tear slipped down her cheek. She brushed it away and continued. "I might as well go back to the dungeon and slap those shackles on my wrist, ankles and neck."

"Haniel saved us for freedom, not to stay chained."

"Exactly. But I have nowhere to go right now. No job. Nothing."

Charissa narrowed her eyes and bit her bottom lip. She gazed into dark eyes, no longer hollow, still somewhat sad, but with a glimmer of hope. For all the differences, the young woman looked so much like one of the orphans, full of hope, yet terrified of another disappointment. She reminded her of a lost puppy someone kicked once too often.

"Yes, you do. Stay with me, at least for a little while. We'll figure the rest out later."

"Are you sure?" The glimmer grew into a genuine sparkle.

"Without a doubt; I always wanted a little sister."

She fished in her bag for a spare key, jotted down directions and sent Shamira home.

∞∞∞∞∞∞∞∞∞∞∞

The morning passed with a welcome respite from any excitement – until Ann met her in the hallway.

Dr. Stone stood outside a patient's room, jotting notes in the chart. Surrounded by a group of aides, Ann barked directions, flashed a coy smile at the doctor and then set her sights on Charissa.

"Well if it isn't our little missionary. Save any orphans today? Perhaps the girl I saw you chatting with minutes after you arrived? Your conversation made you late. I will note it in your file." She sneered, raised her eyebrows and tossed her hair as she turned and swayed her hips all the way back to the nurses' station.

Charissa hung her head in shame, then lifted it and locked eyes with Dr. Stone. Compassion, maybe even a hint of anger flashed across the vivid blue of his irises. He shook his head, jaw tightened, but refrained from saying anything.

She breathed and exhaled hard. "Not this time."

She twirled and followed the supervisor. Stopping directly in front of Ann, she took a deep breath and confronted the woman.

"Ann, I do my best to respect your position, but you were out of line. I am an RN and when you reprimand me in front of the aides, you undermine my authority with them. I admit I've made some mistakes in the past and have not always shown proper respect for you. I have no excuse for my behavior, and I'm truly sorry. I may not be able to take care of orphans right now, but I do a great job of taking care of my patients."

"Hold on..."

Charissa raised her hand against the interruption. "From the day I came, you've ridiculed and belittled me in front of everyone. No more." She swallowed. "I apologize for my attitude in the past. Perhaps my actions caused you to treat me with disrespect. I am a Christian and proud of it. But I am not a doormat, and will no longer stand by and take it—especially not in front of patients and other staff members. If you need to reprimand me, please show enough respect to do it in private."

Ann's eyes grew wide. A pale line formed around tight little lips. Nostrils flared. Charissa braced herself for thunder.

Instead, the supervisor spoke with tight control. "Of all the insubordination; I'll have your job for this."

"Call it what you want, but I will not allow your harassment any longer."

"And neither will I, Nurse Stanford." Dr. Stone stood beside her. "I've watched it and kept my mouth closed far too long. No more, Ann, or I'll have your job."

"Yes, sir."

Charissa turned away from Ann; a little gloat flooded over her. Unexpected turn of events from Dr. Stone, but definitely desired. The faint smell of his aftershave drifted across her face as he called her name. She stopped and turned around.

"Yes?"

"I had to tell you I'm proud of you for finally standing up to Ann. I'm not sure what happened over the weekend, but you have a new sparkle in your eyes."

Heat rushed the full length of her body. Tiny beads of perspiration popped out under her bangs.

"Thank you," she mumbled, full of hope her underarms didn't join her forehead in a race for producing the most sweat.

He smiled and a mischievous twinkle flashed in his eyes. "It looks really good on you."

Now she felt certain her face grew as red as the inside of her mouth, which she realized hung open. Her throat constricted and nothing came out; good, because her mind seemed rather fuzzy at the moment.

The doctor continued. "So are you serious about wanting to help orphans?"

She somehow found her voice. "Yes. It's been my dream since I went on a mission trip at sixteen."

"You know, I do some mission work—go and treat orphans in other countries. I have a hard time not bringing one or two back with me every time I go. I actually have one planned in a few months, and I'm in the process of putting together a team for the trip."

"I didn't know that about you."

"Hmmm. Probably a lot you don't know about me. You wouldn't be interested in being part of my team, would you?"

His tone carried a great deal of teasing, which only served to increase the heat that rushed along with her pulse through her veins and escaped in the form of outright sweat.

"Of course I'm interested."

"Good. Can we discuss it over dinner one night this week? Preferably without the nervous twitch." He smiled.

Now she hesitated. An attractive, single doctor wanted to share dinner and a ministry opportunity with her.

Run! No don't run. Take a chance.

She wiped away the sweat. "Okay, if you promise not to make me blush anymore."

"Well, I'll try." He winked. "Tomorrow night at seven?"

"Yeah – tomorrow night is great."

"Perfect." He turned away, stopped and looked back. "Oh, by the way, you remember the guy who died from a gunshot wound?"

"How could I forget? I pretty much lost it."

"I noticed. The sheriff is taking a closer look at the whole situation – thinks it's suspicious."

"Why?"

"Well, first of all this is dove season and most people hunt deer, maybe wild turkey, around here. Besides a very important fact…the gunshot came from a small caliber pistol at close range, not a rifle or shotgun. Never seen a pistol used to hunt large game. We never got a straight answer from the friend about who shot the man."

"Yeah, he acted strange—not at all like someone who lost a friend."

"Exactly. From everyone's statements, the guy seemed frantic initially, but completely cool afterwards. Plus, the timing doesn't measure up with where he told the sheriff they hunted. He took a long time getting the man here, almost as if he wanted him dead but without an investigation. A lot of questions without clear answers."

"Wow. So I guess they're looking for the man who brought him in?"

"Yeah. My guess—he's long gone, but keep your eyes opened, and expect a visit from the sheriff."

"I'll do what I can to help."

"You always do." He smiled, turned, and walked down the hall emitting a soft whistle.

A song reverberated through her soul, as feet lifted off the floor onto a cloud and she danced down the hallway.

Across from her first patient's room, Haniel leaned against the wall. White teeth gleamed between his broad smile. She broke protocol, sprinted the last few steps, and wrapped her arms around his midsection.

"Haniel. I'm so glad to see you."

Their eyes met and lingered. No words passed between them, yet a deep understanding unfolded. An ocean of thoughts and events coursed through the embrace. He finally ended the silence.

"So, you got something going with Dr. Stone?"

"No teasing."

He laughed. "No. It's great. He's a good man."

She looked up into his face and for the first time, the gray hair at his temples and soft creases around his eyes became real. She never noticed those things before. In one instant, realization tumbled like fall rain. In his face, words, affection—in his very heart—she saw a father's love. The love she ached for from her dad and didn't receive came in the form of her dear friend.

"I love you, you know." She whispered.

"And I love you, Baby Girl. I'm proud of you. You survived the dungeon, and went back in spite of your fears. Nothing is beyond your reach, if you remember one thing. Don't let fear keep you from the very thing God meant for you to accomplish."

"I won't. And if I do, you can always dangle a chain in front of me as a reminder."

"I don't think that'll be necessary. But I'll let the good doctor in on our secret if you want and let him do the job for me."

"Stop it."

He laughed again, and she joined him. The joy released a wealth of endorphins throughout her body, and she smiled up at the man who gave her so much hope and strength.

"It was real then? Not a dream?"

"Very real."

"The attorney found dead in New York—was it Edna?"

"I'm afraid so. She chose Drake, and with her choice, death."

"That saddens me." She reflected for a moment and then brightened. "But Shamira's here. She's staying with me for a while."

"Yeah, I know."

"How do you know everything? You drive me crazy."

He shrugged and grinned.

She tilted her head. "What about the others, Haniel? Ariana, Dierdre and Valorie? I can't get them out of my mind."

"They're home. Different, not quite as bound as before. God isn't finished with them yet. They still have some chains to remove, as do most of us."

"Hmmm. Will I ever see them again?"

"Maybe. But not today. Now get back to work, before Ann comes looking for you."

"Okay. See you later?"

"I'm always here for you, especially when you think you don't need me."

"I know. And I'm so glad you didn't go away when I told you to."

He smiled, winked and sauntered off down the hall, calling back, "Later, Baby Girl."

"It is for freedom that Christ has set us free. Therefore, keep standing firm and do not become subject again to the yoke of slavery."

Galatians 5:1

ABOUT THE AUTHOR

Lisa Bell is a published author of books, articles and devotionals both online and in print. She has a passion for fiction, but also writes non-fiction of all types, including (but not limited to) technical and ghostwriting projects. She loves helping other writers grow and learn new skills, and after years of participating with NTCW now leads one group and serves as a writing coach for three groups.

Lisa spent many years in the corporate world honing technical writing and training skills. In February 2011, she stepped out of that world to write full-time. She now works part-time on special projects for a large corporation as she continues writing, while teaching and encouraging others to pursue writing goals and dreams.

Lisa has a BS in Business Management and is a CLASS graduate and member of NTCW Association. She lives in Texas where she enjoys spending time with four adult daughters and six grandchildren. For more information visit her website: www.bylisabell.com.

www.ingramcontent.com/pod-product-compliance
Lightning Source LLC
Chambersburg PA
CBHW071239170626
46809CB00001B/13